Praise for the Nauti Boy series

"The Nauti series is one that absolutely no one should miss. The characters are brilliant, sexy, and real, while the high-octane action and soul-gripping plots have you on the edge of your seat. I loved it!"
—*Fresh Fiction*

"Steamy, smoking, hot, erotic, risqué. Romantic . . . Intriguing and hard to put down."
—*Night Owl Reviews*

"Completely blown away by this surprising story, I could not put [it] down . . . and before I knew it, I had read this entire novel in one sitting. Lora Leigh has spun a smoldering hot tale of secret passion and erotic deceptions."
—*Romance Junkies*

"Wild and thrilling."
—*The Romance Studio*

"The sex scenes are, as always with Leigh's books, absolutely sizzling."
—*Errant Dreams Reviews*

"Heated romantic suspense."
—*Midwest Book Review*

Nauti
Temptress

Lora Leigh

BERKLEY BOOKS, NEW YORK

THE BERKLEY PUBLISHING GROUP
Published by the Penguin Group
Penguin Group (USA) Inc.
375 Hudson Street, New York, New York 10014, USA

Penguin Group (Canada), 90 Eglinton Avenue East, Suite 700, Toronto, Ontario M4P 2Y3, Canada
(a division of Pearson Penguin Canada Inc.) • Penguin Books Ltd., 80 Strand, London WC2R 0RL,
England • Penguin Ireland, 25 St. Stephen's Green, Dublin 2, Ireland (a division of Penguin
Books Ltd.) • Penguin Group (Australia), 707 Collins Street, Melbourne, Victoria 3008, Australia
(a division of Pearson Australia Group Pty. Ltd.) • Penguin Books India Pvt. Ltd., 11 Community
Centre, Panchsheel Park, New Delhi—110 017, India • Penguin Group (NZ), 67 Apollo Drive,
Rosedale, Auckland 0632, New Zealand (a division of Pearson New Zealand Ltd.) • Penguin Books
Rosebank Office Park, 181 Jan Smuts Avenue, Parktown North 2193, South Africa • Penguin China,
B7 Jaiming Center, 27 East Third Ring Road North, Chaoyang District, Beijing 100020, China

Penguin Books Ltd., Registered Offices: 80 Strand, London WC2R 0RL, England

This book is an original publication of The Berkley Publishing Group.

This is a work of fiction. Names, characters, places, and incidents either are the product of the author's
imagination or are used fictitiously, and any resemblance to actual persons, living or dead, business
establishments, events, or locales is entirely coincidental. The publisher does not have any control over
and does not assume any responsibility for author or third-party websites or their content.

Copyright © 2012 by Christine Simmons.
Cover illustration by Danny O'Leary.
Cover design by Lesley Worrell.

All rights reserved.
No part of this book may be reproduced, scanned, or distributed in any printed or
electronic form without permission. Please do not participate in or encourage piracy of
copyrighted materials in violation of the author's rights. Purchase only authorized editions.
BERKLEY® is a registered trademark of Penguin Group (USA) Inc.
The "B" design is a trademark of Penguin Group (USA) Inc.

PUBLISHING HISTORY
Berkley trade paperback edition / November 2012

Berkley trade paperback ISBN: 978-0-425-24564-4

An application to register this book for cataloging has been submitted to the Library of Congress.

PRINTED IN THE UNITED STATES OF AMERICA

10 9 8 7 6 5 4 3 2 1

ALWAYS LEARNING

PEARSON

For Bret,
because you're the son I never imagined you would be,
and you're turning into a man I find
more pride in each day.
I wish I could take credit
for your compassion, generosity, and strength.
And I hope those qualities always remain
a part of your incredibly giving heart.

PROLOGUE

The fat, evil little leprechaun was interfering in their lives again in a way they would never recover from. Rowdy could feel it.

It was like a chill chasing up his spine. It was a premonition of hell. It was a certainty that perhaps they should have just shot his ass when he interfered the last time.

But that last time hadn't been with one of the Mackays, just a friend, and not an old and dear one at that. The brother of an old and dear friend wasn't exactly the same.

Standing in the marina office and staring out the heavy glass door, he wondered what the little bastard was up to this time. His eyes narrowed against the bright summer sun as the fat little bastard, a.k.a. Timothy Cranston, stood at the open back passenger door of the black Ford Excursion, his attention on the occupants he was obviously speaking to. He was apparently debating something with them, Rowdy thought. The tension in Cranston's shoulders was a sure indication that his frustration level was rising.

There were times Rowdy and his cousins might like the former Homeland Security agent, but other times he was more trouble than he was worth.

Rowdy had a feeling he was about to become more trouble than he was worth again.

"What the fu—hell is he up to?" Natches murmured as he paced to the door to stand beside Rowdy.

Rowdy didn't miss the word his cousin had almost used instead. A grin quirking his lips, he slid Natches an amused, knowing look.

"Bliss said the F-word the other day." Natches sighed in disgust. "Chaya's of course blaming it on me."

"I never hear it slipping past her lips, I have to admit," Dawg drawled from behind them. "Warned you about that, cuz."

Rowdy glanced behind him where his cousin Dawg sat back in the easy chair next to the desk, his long legs stretched out, a newspaper in hand as he read an article on a story he'd been following for a few weeks now.

He seemed unusually interested in the reporter's far-fetched evidence that there was some conspiracy brewing in the mountains of Kentucky, West Virginia, Maryland, and Pennsylvania where homeland militias were concerned. The article was being written by a reporter that had somehow managed to infiltrate one of those militias.

"I'm telling you, it doesn't slip around Bliss. I don't want her to hear me talking like that," Natches bit out in frustration, his arms crossing over his chest as he glared at each of his cousins before turning back to Cranston.

Normally, Rowdy would have agreed, because Natches was normally not one to slip up once he put his mind to something.

"You say it often enough when you think she's not around," Dawg said, glancing around the side of the newspaper.

Natches just shook his head.

As he caught the tight-lipped scowl on Natches's face, Rowdy knew it would do little good to argue with his cousin over it. He was convinced he hadn't said the word around his daughter, therefore, as far as he was concerned, he hadn't said it. Until they actually managed to catch him and point it out, then he'd continue to fight against the idea that he'd let it drop. Rowdy was more inclined to think it had happened out of Bliss's sight, just not out of her hearing. The three of them usually managed to hold back the words they didn't want their daughters to hear, whether the girls were around or not. They were all too aware of the fact that their girls were growing up and prone to be present whether they could be seen or not.

As far as Rowdy knew, he himself hadn't said that word since the last time he'd suspected Cranston was up to something.

It never failed that the F-word slipped out whenever that little bastard was messing in their lives.

Holding his hand up in a "wait" gesture to the driver, Cranston closed the passenger door to the Excursion and began walking quickly to the marina offices.

He wasn't as fat as he was the last time they'd seen him, Rowdy noted to himself. Not that he'd been overly round, but he had been a bit portly.

His brown hair was still a little thin in the front, though, cut short everywhere else and standing on end as the wind whipping off the lake only made it worse.

The tan suit he wore was rumpled and wrinkled, as though

he'd slept in it for more than a few days. Beneath the suit, it appeared he might have been working out just a little.

Frowning, Rowdy glanced to Natches, wondering whether he'd noticed.

Natches wasn't saying anything if he had.

Giving an irritated snort, Natches turned and paced back to the desk and the chairs Rowdy had placed behind it for his cousins. Cranston's chair sat all by its lonesome in front of the desk.

Stepping back from the door and crossing his arms over his chest, Rowdy scowled as Cranston pushed into the office, his hand moving to smooth his hair back rather than running his fingers through the normally disheveled strands.

And he looked more harried than usual.

If Rowdy wasn't mistaken, the former Homeland Security Special Agent in Charge of Investigations looked downright worried and possibly even a little uncertain.

"Rowdy, damned good to see you." Cranston frowned as he stepped into the office and extended his hand. "You ignored my invitation to the party last week, by the way."

Shaking his hand, Rowdy raised his brows in surprise. "That was really from you? I couldn't believe it. I was afraid it was a trick to get us all in one place to kill us all at once."

Cranston's frown turned suspicious, and evidently the innocent smile Rowdy gave him did nothing to alleviate the suspicion.

Cranston's jaw tightened.

Turning to Dawg and Rowdy, he sighed deeply.

Dawg was still engrossed in his newspaper, and now Natches had a part of it—the comics, no less—and appeared just as involved in it.

"So that's how it's going to be?" Cranston muttered, sounding strangely disappointed.

The look he shot Rowdy had a curl of shame rearing its head that only managed to piss Rowdy off. Hell, he had no reason to feel ashamed.

"What did you expect?" Rowdy asked as he walked to the desk and took his seat behind it. "Come on, Cranston; we know you. When you make one of your infamous requests that we all meet you together, it means you're going to pull us into one of your schemes, get us shot at, and piss our wives off. We're not playing this time."

"Yet here you all are." Timothy waved his hands out to encompass the room, that glimmer of somber disappointment still gleaming in his eyes.

"Out of curiosity," Rowdy assured him as both Dawg and Natches lowered their papers with a snap.

The other man sighed—tiredly?— before moving to the desk, though he didn't sit down.

"There's no scheme," he assured them, his voice matching the resignation in his brown eyes.

"Sure there's not," Dawg expressed doubtfully. "You're still breathing; that means there's a scheme."

"The party was thrown, Dawg"—he singled Dawg out, and it wasn't missed by any of them, especially Dawg—"to allow you to meet four young women and their mother."

"We're not bodyguards; nor are we in the market for a woman," Dawg snapped.

At this point, Cranston sat down. Slowly.

His brows lowered, his brown eyes darker and flickering with what Rowdy had always said were the fires of hell. It was actually the green coming out in the dark hazel of his eyes.

They just appeared brown until he was pissed.

He was pissed now.

He watched the three of them silently, his jaw clenched and granite hard.

"At what point have you failed to miss the fact that I am completely besotted by your wives and children? And since you acquired those wives and children, at what time have I asked you to do anything dangerous?" he asked them then, and Rowdy had to admit he hadn't expected to hear that edge of some emotion akin to hurt in the agent's tone.

Dawg and Natches both put their papers aside as Rowdy tensed. They'd seen Cranston in a lot of different moods, but they rarely saw him pissed off at them. And they had certainly never seen him give the impression that his feelings were hurt.

They had seen him pissed at others, often— But he'd never seemed to care enough about anyone that they could actually prick emotions they'd never known he had.

"That doesn't mean you're not trying to draw us into one of your damned operations," Natches growled, clearly missing the fact that Cranston didn't get pissed at them for saying no to a mission.

"Natches." Rowdy said his name softly, warningly, his gaze locked on the former agent. "Let's see what he has to say."

"Why?" Dawg grunted. "He's obviously out to cause trouble."

"Or to alleviate some," Cranston stated softly, the cool smile that crossed his lips sending that chill racing up Rowdy's spine again.

Cranston stood slowly, the expression on his face hinting at not just anger, but also that inner disappointment that had Rowdy confused as hell. "Had I known this would be my reception, I would have just told you over the phone," he stated.

"Rather than believing we had been friends for the past four years."

Rowdy's shoulders tightened as Cranston focused his complete attention on Dawg.

Natches and Dawg had stiffened as well, the undercurrents suddenly whipping through the room finally piercing their suspicious anger.

"Told us what?" Rowdy growled.

He knew Cranston. It was too late to repair whatever insult he'd perceived. Better to just get this meeting over with and find out what the hell was going on.

"Three months ago, Homeland Security received an alert from the Louisville Office of Vital Statistics," he stated coolly. "Someone was requesting information on Chandler Mackay's heirs."

Dawg stiffened further as Rowdy shot him a warning look. They needed to hear what he had to say.

"I thought you resigned from Homeland Security," Natches reminded him mockingly.

Timothy shook his head, his expression pitying. "Son, you never officially retire from Homeland Security. One of these days you'll figure that out."

"I was never part of it," Natches reminded him.

"No, but Dawg was." He nodded to Dawg. "And because you'll stand with him, no matter the danger, that means you'll be there to realize it as well."

"Whatever," Dawg growled. "But DHS and Chandler Mackay are not one and the same. He's dead, and his heir doesn't give a fuck, remember?"

Rowdy's head whipped to Dawg. Hell, Dawg hadn't said the word "fuck" since his daughter was still crawling.

"I remember." Cranston nodded. "But tell me, Dawg, would you turn your back on Janey if she needed you?"

"Janey is family." Dawg came out of his chair, causing Rowdy and Natches both to stand with him, as Timothy had always said they would do.

"So are the four young girls sitting in that vehicle outside," Cranston stated. "They're your younger sisters. Four girls, Dawg, still in their teens with no place to go because DHS found the property your father had bought for them, and because he hadn't changed the title over to the mother, they seized the property as well as the bank accounts their mother was using to help support the girls. They're homeless, without resources, and Mercedes never allowed the girls to work. She wants them to get an education. Now, are you going to turn your back on them as well? Let me know if you are, so I can have DHS drive them to the nearest corner and put them and their few belongings out. There might be some room left under a bridge somewhere."

Dawg sat down slowly, at the same time Rowdy and Natches found themselves sitting as well. Rowdy's knees felt damned weak, and his senses in chaos. God only knew what Natches, and even more so, Dawg, were feeling themselves.

Rowdy stared at Cranston, shock warring with the resurging shame. Hell, they should have known that invitation to dinner that they had ignored a few days before—Cranston never invited a soul to dinner—was more than some ruse.

"Chandler Mackay has been dead for thirteen years." Dawg shook his head, obviously trying to reject the information. "That can't be possible."

"The youngest girl is sixteen." Cranston nodded. "Not one of them is more than one year younger than the sister born before her. When their mother lost the little boy she'd been carrying, the year your father was killed, he never returned to the Texas home he'd bought, though payments on it were sent from a Cayman account until DHS was able to shut the account down and trace the payments. Now, what do I do with them?"

Dawg shook his head.

"Fine." Cranston nodded his head. "I'll tell the driver to take them to Somerset and drop them off."

He turned to leave.

"Wait." Rowdy stepped forward, desperation and surging disbelief making it hard to think. "The *Nauti Buoy* is empty right now. Put them there."

Cranston turned back, his lip curling in a disapproving sneer. "Son, their mother, Mercedes, is as proud as they come. She's not going to just unload her daughters on a bachelor barge and consider herself lucky. If she had been that sort of mother, then I would have handled this far differently. She wants to meet you. She wants to be accepted, not pushed to the side until forced to come begging."

There was something in Cranston's tone that Rowdy had never heard before: an edge of bafflement as well as respect.

There weren't many people Timothy Cranston respected.

From the corner of his eye Rowdy watched a muscle jump in Dawg's jaw.

"How old are the girls?" Dawg finally snapped.

"The eldest girl, Eve, turned nineteen on New Year's Day. Piper turned eighteen in February. Lyrica turned seventeen in March, and little Zoey just turned sixteen this month." Timothy gave them all a hard look. "Hell of an age to live under a bridge, don't you think? Ever been there, Dawg? Ever seen what it was like? What it's going to be like for four teenage girls that I'm betting my pensions are still virgins?"

They all had. They'd had nightmares for weeks.

Timothy sighed heavily. "Their mother, Mercedes, was only fourteen when she gave birth to her first child. She would have had five children if she hadn't lost the boy she conceived only weeks after Zoey was born. Her body was just too weak for another child. She developed an infection that forced the doctors to do a hysterectomy. She's thirty-three years old with four girls to raise, and she's not lazy any day of the week, but neither does she have family and only very few friends. Those friends are not in a position to help her. The only education she's had since she was fourteen was what she's taught herself. How do you go to college with four babies?"

Dawg was slowly shaking his head. "She was a baby herself," he whispered hoarsely, his eyes filled with horror. "She was just a baby. Fuck me. God, she's younger than I am."

She was almost seven years younger than Dawg, and she had four children by his father. It was unthinkable, even knowing the depraved bastard Chandler Mackay had been.

It was all Rowdy could think. All any of them could think, he imagined.

"He raped a baby." Dawg's voice sounded like a wheeze.

"Not much more than." Timothy sighed, the compassion he felt in this moment making his shoulders droop as he watched the three men, wishing he could hide this part from them. "Chandler bought her from her parents in Guatemala. She was pregnant with his child when he slipped her into Texas and procured papers for her. She knew no English, had no way of supporting herself, and she didn't have the option of running. If she ran, he told her the police would find her, and they would then send her back to Guatemala without her babies."

"The babies of a rapist?" Dawg whispered as he stared back at Timothy in shock. "And she stayed?"

"She loves those girls, Dawg," Timothy assured him, the sorrow he felt at this moment more than he wanted to deal with. "She's given everything to her daughters, and survived at less than poverty level with the funds Chandler had arranged for her to receive along with the few jobs she had working under the table. He didn't provide her a car; he didn't provide her a means of supporting herself. And he paid others to ensure she didn't date, have lovers, or dare to marry. If she attempted to have a lover, he promised her, then he would take the children, have them split up and placed in foster homes, and have Mercedes sent back to Guatemala. Then he proceeded to describe to her in graphic detail a horror story of what American foster families did to the little girls given to them." He said the last with a sneer. "You can imagine the nightmares he gave her. The one time she dared to assert her independence and attempt to acquire her GED to enable her to acquire a better job, he had her babies stolen as she slept. She was a month getting them back and they all still have nightmares of those weeks."

"He was a monster," Rowdy whispered, his stomach roiling at the thought of what his uncle had done to another innocent child.

"Exactly," Timothy agreed. "Hell is what she has lived in for quite a while. Then the money that paid the bills was suddenly cut off, the house taken, and with it the vehicle she busted her ass for years to buy because she'd been forced to forge Chandler's name to it to acquire it. She was thrown on the streets and taken in by one of the Texas-based Homeland Security officers there that day. The woman called me immediately. She knew I'd worked the Mackay case here, and that I was still in the area. They were ready to fucking deport her, Dawg, and do just as Chandler warned her, take her children and put them in foster homes. I went after them, had them set up in a safe house until I could verify everything and run DNA tests on the girls." He wouldn't give any of them a chance to deny the girls or their mother. "They're definitely Chandler's daughters," he told them. "And considering the fact that I made damn certain the majority of what Chandler had, that I knew of, was very illegally placed in your name and backdated far enough that it couldn't be taken, I thought perhaps you could help Mercedes and her daughters. Because if you don't, then she doesn't have a chance of remaining in the States with those girls."

The fact that he wasn't so certain that Dawg would help wasn't lost on Rowdy.

"You said she worked." Natches looked as dazed as Timothy had felt as Mercedes told him what her life had been.

"She did, at a restaurant. She worked cleaning homes, or whatever she could do and still take her kids, until Eve was old enough to help with them, allowing her to take on additional house cleaning jobs to provide a little more for her children."

"She couldn't have made much," Rowdy whispered. "Not with four girls to care for."

"She had to have made friends." Dawg seemed more in shock than anything.

"Would you have, if it meant your children would be placed in foster care if your so called friends or employers ever learned the truth of your presence in America, or the life you were being forced to live?" Timothy asked.

"Why keep the kids?" Natches questioned. "She had to have hated Chandler."

"Her daughters are her heart and soul. Never doubt that." Timothy sighed, wondering whether he had been wrong all these years about the honor and integrity of the three men he was facing.

As he opened his lips to say something more, Rowdy's gaze jerked to the door.

Timothy felt his stomach drop as the door was pushed open, and the tiny, delicate little bundle of fire, Zoey Mackay, burst into the office.

"They don't want us, do they?" Pain radiated in her face, her voice.

She could have been Dawg's daughter, so much did the kid look like his own kid, Laken: delicate and fragile, long black hair falling down her back, celadon eyes filled with tears, her face sculpted into lines of such beauty it made a grown man want to weep.

Timothy rushed to her, bending to one knee as he placed his hands lightly on her fragile shoulders and stared into her eyes.

"Zoey, I told you to stay in the vehicle until I finished," Timothy reminded her, his tone gentling.

Hell, he couldn't yell at her; he couldn't get mad at her. She knew the hell her mother and sisters faced if Dawg turned them away.

Dawg rose slowly to his feet, causing her to flinch as she followed the movement.

"If they wanted us, it wouldn't take this long," she accused him, her voice rough, big tears filling her eyes as she turned back to Timothy. "They would have wanted to meet us by now."

"I was just asking some questions." Dawg could feel something inside his soul bleeding.

He hadn't thought Chandler Mackay could do more to make

him hate him. That it was possible for the bastard to make him despise him more than he already did.

Until he stared at the girl glaring back at him.

She looked like an older version of his precious Laken.

His baby was only three, and already, her delicate, too-fragile body was forced to keep up with the fire that burned in her soul.

"What kind of questions can't we answer?" Zoey propped her little fists on her hips angrily, demanding that he take her into consideration, that he make a choice and he make it now.

"Zoey, Mr. Mackay and his cousins might have liked a few minutes to process everything," Timothy chastised her gently as he straightened and stared down at her.

"And what makes you think Momma has time for him to process anything," she cried out, her voice trembling as the tears that filled her eyes suddenly spilled down her cheeks as fear and anger filled her expression. "He'll either help us or he won't. Either way, Momma's sick again—"

Timothy moved.

Rushing past the little girl, aware Dawg, Rowdy, and Natches were moving quickly to follow behind him, Timothy ran for the Excursion at a run.

Racing to the passenger-side door opposite the office he saw the young Homeland Security agent standing next to Mercedes Mackay, his expression concerned.

"Agent Rickers," he snapped. "What's going on?"

"Mr. Cranston." Agent Rickers straightened quickly and moved back, his young face pale. "She's weak again, sir. I was trying to make her more comfortable."

The other girls had moved farther back to the third row of

seats, watching their mother fearfully as she breathed heavily, her pale face reddened, perspiration pouring from it.

"Timothy, I'll be fine," Mercedes promised weakly. "You know how frightened they get."

But she wouldn't be fine, and Timothy knew it. Not if she didn't get the help she needed.

"My dear, you should have sent one of the girls for me before you became so ill," he chastised her as he took the damp cloth the other agent had been using to wipe the perspiration from her. It did little to cool her skin. Few things did when such attacks occurred. They came with a suddenness that couldn't be predicted, and often left just as quickly.

"Timothy, get her in the office; we'll call for Doc," Rowdy ordered from the other side of the vehicle.

"Come on, Mercedes." The gentleness in the leprechaun's voice shocked not just Rowdy, but his cousins as well, though the young women in the vehicle didn't seem surprised at all.

Cranston picked her up as though she weighed nothing, and she had to be three inches taller, at least, than the former agent.

Pick her up he did, though, and carried her quickly into the office, all the girls at his heels.

"What's wrong with her?" Rowdy questioned the older man as he laid her on the office couch, the girls hovering around her.

Cranston sighed heavily. "The doctors aren't certain, but she's refused to see the specialists she's been referred to."

"Why?"

Cranston's jaw tightened, a muscle ticking at the side furiously. "No insurance and no money, Rowdy. I told you, once Homeland Security found that Cayman account two years ago, they've had to live on what she had saved and the money she made working three jobs. She refused to let the girls work. The girls weren't even aware Mercedes was no longer receiving the money until DHS showed up at the house and threw them out."

Rowdy started to say more, but the sight of three concerned women moving quickly across the parking lot had a grimace pulling at his lips before he turned to his cousins. "Shopping trip's over," he announced, nodding toward their wives as they moved purposefully for the office.

"Where the hell were they?" Natches rubbed his jaw in confusion.

"My guess, close enough to see why the hell we tried to push them into going shopping this morning." Rowdy sighed. "We're getting out of practice, boys."

"I thought someone was calling a doctor." The little powerhouse who had interrupted the meeting earlier stood from where she had been kneeling next to her mother.

"Zoey, enough," Mercedes chastised her. "Where are your manners?"

"They promised, Momma." Pleading with her eyes, clearly afraid for her mother's health.

"I sent the text," Rowdy promised her. "His nurse just texted back."

He handed the girl the phone.

"Half an hour." She murmured the nurse's reply before handing the phone back to him and staring up at him with eyes the same pale, intense green of Dawg's, yet in this child's eyes lurked a deep, haunting fear he knew he'd see in his nightmares.

Her celadon eyes were surrounded by a wealth of long, heavy black lashes, he noticed. She was a beauty already, and keeping the wild hearts and even wilder men away from her for the rest of her life wouldn't be easy, Rowdy thought in resignation.

And there was no doubt she was a Mackay.

If he had seen any of the four girls on the street at any time, he would have known he was looking at the daughter of a Mackay. The dark looks were simply unmistakable.

As Rowdy pushed the phone back into the holster at his side, the door to the office was pushed inward and three concerned, though borderline furious Mackay wives were moving into the room.

Kelly, whose gentle features had matured in the past five years since her daughter's birth, though she still looked far too young for her husband Rowdy's experienced features.

Chaya, Natches's wife, whose brows were drawn into a frown, her brown eyes going between Eve, Piper, Lyrica, and Zoey in suspicion before dropping to Mercedes Mackay.

But Dawg's wife, Christa, was stark pale, so white-faced Dawg moved for her instantly.

"No, no, no, no." He shook his head desperately as her eyes began to fill with tears. "Oh, hell, no, baby. Sisters. They're my sisters, not my kids. I swear. Sisters, Christa."

Her gaze moved to him slowly, reluctantly. She frowned deeply, though her face was still stark white as she slowly shook her head.

"This is all Timothy's fault." He glared at Timothy before pointing his finger at the not-so-fat little bastard as Timothy stared back at him in confusion.

"What's my fault?" Timothy glared back at him, obviously offended by the accusation.

The four girls and their mother were staring at him as though he had dropped into the room from outer space, while Rowdy and Natches simply watched him warily.

Christa swallowed tightly. "I don't think they're your daughters," she whispered.

"Then what's wrong?" he demanded. "You're as white as a damned sheet."

She shook her head and turned back to the four girls again. "Oh, my God, Dawg, what did Chandler Mackay do? They could be, your twins," she whispered. "As though they were cloned from you."

"Oh, God, just shoot me now," Zoey spat in disgust.

"Momma, I don't think I can ever forgive you." Eve sighed.

"At least it's him we looked cloned from and not one of the other two," Lyrica said with a grunt. "That would have sucked."

"It still sucks," Piper assured her younger sister.

"Brats," Rowdy murmured, though there was no heat in his tone; he actually seemed rather amused.

"Brats? Try bitches." Natches grunted, his gaze carefully shuttered, though Dawg could detect the amusement. "And that little one works at it, too."

"But not very hard." Zoey slid him an arch, cool look. "If I had, trust me, you'd know it."

The girl's comment had Kelly's, Christa's, and Chaya's gazes moving then to Timothy. Then they shifted instantly to the woman stretched out on the couch.

Hell, Dawg thought, this woman didn't look old enough to be the mother of the four obvious hellions staring back at the Mackay wives.

"Natches, sweetheart, what's Cranston doing here?" Chaya, one of Cranston's former agents, stepped to her husband and let him pull her close to his side.

As she did so, Kelly stepped to Rowdy, while Christa moved to Dawg's side and gave him a gentle kiss on the cheek. It was the look on his face, Rowdy thought, that look of blank devastation in his gaze that had Christa bestowing a kiss to assure him there was nothing for him to worry about.

"It would appear we've added to the family," Natches told his wife softly. "Meet Dawg's sisters. I'm certain they'll introduce themselves as soon as Doc gets here to check out their mother."

Timothy wiped Mercedes's face again. Rowdy could have sworn the leprechaun's hand was shaking.

"What did you do, Mercedes?" he asked her gently. "Didn't you rest last night?"

Mercedes's lush lips almost tilted into a smile. "What do you think, Tim?" she asked, forcing her eyes open.

Tim?

No one, but no one, had ever been allowed to call Timothy Cranston "Tim."

"I think you were up all night pacing and worrying." He sighed. "I told you there was nothing to worry about."

"Is there not?" she asked him sorrowfully. "Chandler's son is suddenly besieged by four young females he knew nothing of, and a sick mother to boot? Ah, Tim, do you not know human nature far better than this?"

"I know the Mackays far better than this," he assured her, praying he was right. "And the Mackays do not turn their backs on family."

The look he slid them assured the Mackays that they'd better not start now.

"Is Doc on his way, then?" Christa asked Dawg as his hand tightened on her hip, his need to draw her closer evident.

"Half hour, his nurse said."

"Twenty minutes then." She nodded.

Dawg watched the young woman; hell, she had four grown daughters and she was younger than he was. He watched her, watched her daughters, and in their eyes he saw pure, raw fear.

"Cranston, what do the doctors who have suggested a specialist say could be wrong with her?" Dawg asked; the low rasp of the tone wasn't lost on the former agent.

Cranston swallowed tightly, the action at first almost unnoticed. But the slight flinch of his facial muscles wasn't missed by Dawg.

"They think she could have an advanced form of chemical poisoning that's slowly weakening her lungs. One of the jobs she had was at an industrial chemical processing plant that's since been shut down for its unsafe working conditions." Clearing his throat of obvious emotion, he lifted his gaze to Dawg's, and no one missed the plea in his eyes. "The treatments she needs are expensive—"

"Timothy, no." Pride was evident in Mercedes's weak voice as she laid her hand on his arm. "Let's not talk of this. Let the girls and their brother talk."

"Mercedes, I won't let you lie here and suffer," he snarled, his voice hoarse and filled with emotion. "Not anymore."

Timothy Cranston was in love.

Dawg lifted his gaze from Cranston, only to realize the four girls were watching him suspiciously, fearfully. There wasn't one of them who didn't expect him to turn them away.

"Doc's here," Christa stated as a vehicle pulled up in front of the door. "He's early. He must have already left the office."

Dawg nodded. "Let's get your mother taken care of," he told the girls. "Once we have her checked out, we'll talk." His gaze dropped to Cranston's again before lifting back to the girls. "But have no doubt: You're family. And we stick by family."

"One of you killed your cousin," the eldest stated. "I heard one of the agents talking about it after we arrived at Tim's. Is that how you take care of family?"

She might have resembled Dawg enough to be his kid, but it was Natches's emerald eyes she stared at him from.

"Eve." Her mother gasped, obviously shocked by her daughter's rudeness.

Dawg just gave Eve a mocking smile as his hand tightened at Christa's hip once again. "Only those who betray us and have a gun trained on the someone we love," he assured her. "Then, Eve, trust me, it didn't matter who he was then; Johnny was dead."

Eve's nostrils flared before she finally relaxed enough to simply nod her head.

"Mackays don't betray one another." Cranston tore his gaze from their mother long enough to stare back at each girl with a glint of steel in his eyes. "Remember that, girls. You stand for who you are, what you are, and for family. That's what your mother's taught you, and that's what you live by."

"Only if you stand for us first," Lyrica spoke up warily.

Dawg nodded. "Understandable. And we'll show you our good faith." He glanced to Natches and Rowdy. Each of his cousins nodded in turn. "We'll take care of you and your mother, because you're family, and that's what families do. Whatever treatments your mother needs, whatever care, she'll have it. Just as you'll return to school and do your part."

"In return for what?" the other girl asked suspiciously.

"In return for being part of the family," Dawg growled back at her. "I just told you that. Loyalty begins somewhere, and I'll make that first step. From here on out it's up to you. But betray us or yourselves, hurt us, yourselves, or another of the family, and you'll risk all of it. Come to us, talk to us, and we'll help you the best way we can. But you don't lie to us, you don't cheat us, and you don't dare betray one of us."

What the hell was he supposed to do with four sisters?

Each girl nodded before the door opened, heralding the doctor and his nurse. Within an hour an ambulance arrived and, with Cranston riding with her, whisked Mercedes Mackay to the hospital and left four clearly suspicious, frightened, and exhausted young women in his keeping.

And Dawg would soon learn, along with Rowdy and Natches, just what they might have to face in another decade or so.

With their own daughters.

ONE

It was after two in the morning before Eve Mackay stepped into her bedroom and closed the door behind her quietly. Staring around the small suite, it was damned hard to believe how her life had changed in five short years. From destitution to security. From paralyzing fear of what the future would bring, to looking forward to each day as it arrived.

From losing the meager roof over their heads to partial ownership in the business her mother now owned.

Luckily, her room was on the more private side of the large house her mother had turned into Mackay's Bed-and-breakfast Inn. The two-story sprawling farmhouse had been completely renovated and redecorated with the private residence on the second floor, the eight guest suites, large chef's kitchen, and open television and game room on the main floor.

A wide porch wrapped around the house, allowing guests

easy access to the balcony doors into their rooms when the main entrance was locked after midnight.

Eve had taken the smallest guest room at the back of the house for herself, rather than one of the bedrooms in the up-stairs residence, as her sisters had done. She'd needed the privacy, whereas her sisters had still needed the closeness the upstairs rooms provided to their mother.

Now she was thankful for it. Arriving home after two in the morning and going through the main residence would be guar-anteed to alert her mother, and her mother's lover, that she'd arrived home.

Living upstairs would have enabled her mother to keep tabs on her, too, and as much as she loved her mother, she had no wish for that.

Opening her eyes and drawing in a deep breath, Eve reached back and rubbed the tense muscles of her neck before moving to the bathroom and a hot shower.

Releasing the heavy weight of her long, straight black hair and massaging at her scalp with her fingertips, she wondered why she had gotten none of the curls that her younger sisters had in abundance. Zoey's hair fell to her waist in soft corkscrew curls that Eve used to threaten to cut off out of pure jealousy.

No matter how hard she'd tried, Eve had rarely been able to get her hair to take curl for more than a few hours. A few days at the most only after a trip to the salon when she had a chemical wave put in it.

It hadn't been worth it.

She'd learned to live without the curl her other sisters had in varying amounts. Piper's hair was wavy. It fell to her shoulders, thick and heavy as it framed her aristocratic features and gave her exotic sea green eyes a lush shimmer.

Lyrica kept her hair to a length that fell just below her shoulder blades. The deeper waves in her hair bounced and gleamed with a blue-black sheen that went perfectly with her summer green gaze.

Zoey's hair fell below her waist, clear to her hips in those long, corkscrew curls that were impossibly soft and silky and made other women want to kill for them. Her hair was just as exotic as her eyes, which were the same celadon as their brother Dawg's, that pale, ethereal color that always drew second and third looks.

Eve's hair was more like Natches's: straight and thick. It was impossible for her to do much in the way of styling it. She pinned it up, put it in a ponytail as she had tonight, or just left it long to the middle of her shoulders.

Her eyes were the same emerald green as Natches's, but her looks, like her sisters', were closer to Dawg's.

Big, bold, and as familiar in Pulaski County, Kentucky, as the mountains themselves, Dawg and his cousins—her cousins—Rowdy and Natches had been all that had saved her and her family at a time when they'd been certain life as they'd known it was over.

It had been, she guessed, but Dawg, Rowdy, and Natches had made it better. They'd taken her, her sisters, and her mother under their wings and gave them a life.

Her mother was given the house that had once been taken away from Dawg by the cousin that had betrayed his country and his family and had nearly killed Dawg's wife, Christa. The same cousin Eve had heard agents accusing Natches of having killed. After Johnny Grace's death the property had reverted back to Dawg, and had been sitting empty for nearly three years before Eve and her family showed up.

He'd had the renovations done under her mother's direction, agreeing to allow her to sign a promissory loan for the amount it had taken to renovate it. Mercedes Mackay had then opened the bed-and-breakfast she'd always dreamed of having.

Her sisters were in college, and Eve had graduated from the local technical college with a bachelor's degree in business administration.

As she stepped from the shower, wrapped her hair in a towel, and quickly dried off, she grimaced at the paleness of her skin.

It was June; by now she usually had a nice golden tan over her body, and instead of coming in at two in the morning from a job, she'd been sneaking in after a night of carousing herself.

When had the fun and good times started leaving a bad taste in her mouth? she wondered as she brushed her teeth.

She'd been in Somerset for five years now, and the past three years the nightlife she had once sworn by had quickly become boring, with a heavy air of immaturity.

Quickly applying a moisturizing facial cream, she then lotioned her body and spritzed a toasted-vanilla body spray over herself.

It was a lot of work to go through just to go to bed, but after eight hours at the bar where she worked, Walker's Run, and waiting on tables in the outside smokers' patio, she smelled of old tobacco smoke, the sweaty bodies that had brushed against her, sawdust, and the greasy food she'd served.

She couldn't bear the thought of going to bed smelling like the bar.

Mackay's Fine Dining, previously Mackay's Restaurant and Cafe, the restaurant Natches's sister Janey owned, wasn't as bad, but it still called for a shower. Maybe she'd go work for Dawg at the lumber store for a while. Natches would readily let her work at the garage as well, but Eve wasn't ready for the oil baths she had experienced the few times she'd worked there. His redneck mechanics thought it was funny to find ways to upend the pails of old oil in ways that left her covered in the nasty sludge. And though Natches always fired the responsible party when they could be identified, after the first firing, Eve was always careful to ensure no one was identified.

She had just been there temporarily because she liked working on cars. It wasn't a job she needed to feed her family and she wasn't going to be responsible for having a man with a family fired because he was offended by a "girl," as they called her, doing their job.

Pulling on one of the summer-thin camisole-and-shorts pajamas she preferred, Eve moved to the balcony doors she'd slipped through earlier and opened one side quietly. The bed-and-breakfast had a full house for the next few weeks, though several of the rooms had been rented for more than two years now by three guests who often gave their free time to Mercedes to do odd jobs around the inn. Her mother greatly reduced the amount of their stay in return, and one to two days a week the three men took care of repairs needed in and outside the inn as well as yard work.

The one beside her was one of them.

Stepping outside, she moved to the oval wicker chair hanging from beneath the second floor wraparound balcony, with its thick, fluffy cushions and curled into it with a weary sigh.

She was exhausted, but she'd never go to sleep easily if she went to bed now.

Why couldn't she be one of those people that dropped right off to sleep? Instead, she spent far too long staring up at the ceiling or with her eyes closed, fighting for peace. Or far too many sensations raced through her body, demanding satisfaction, as they were tonight.

As they had been since the first hour on the job that night, when Brogan Campbell had walked into the bar.

It was that arrogant swagger that made him so tempting. Or maybe it was that slightly tilted curve to his lips. As though he saw beneath the facades of those he talked to and was amused by the deceptions they practiced.

It sure couldn't be that red-gold hair with all the sunlit and burnished brown highlights it held that framed his hard-hewn face and tempted her to touch it to see if it was as warm as it looked. And it couldn't be the arrogance in those icy gray-blue eyes, or the subtle darkening that always affected them whenever she caught his gaze.

Whatever it was, the second he'd entered the bar that night she'd known it.

She'd known it and responded to him.

Her breasts had swelled, her nipples becoming hard and peaked as her skin seemed to sensitize. She became so aware of the sensitive folds between her thighs that she felt them dampening, felt the slick juices as they made their way along the tender tissue of her vagina to ease out along the lips beyond.

She had become so horny so fast she'd almost dropped the tray of drinks she'd been carrying.

That was the effect Brogan had on her. And knowing he was sleeping in the suite next to hers didn't help matters, because she knew—knew beyond a shadow of a doubt—that he wanted her as well.

That was the reason she was working the job that would bring her home at the latest possible hour and work her the hardest. Unfortunately it wasn't working her hard enough, evidently.

"Eve. Hey, Eve, you there?"

Eve glanced up at the bottom of the balcony at the sound of her sister Lyrica's voice hissing from above.

"You're supposed to be asleep, Lyrica." She grinned, keeping her voice soft as she answered her.

"Oh, great, that was you I heard drive up." Her sister's loud whisper was followed by the sight of a slender foot bracing on the outside of the balcony railing.

A second later the other foot joined it; then her sister was reaching for the thick post next to her and shimmying down it like a pro. Hell, she was a pro. All three of Eve's sisters were. They'd learned early how to slip from the house and make the most of a perfectly good summer night.

They hadn't fooled their mother, though. It never failed that their brother, Dawg, or one of their cousins, Rowdy or Natches, or one of their friends would find them after an hour or so and escort them home. They were never out long enough to get into trouble, but always long enough to satisfy the thrill of escaping for a while.

Lyrica dropped from the lower balcony railing, barefoot, dressed as Eve was in a pair of shorty pajama bottoms and a snug camisole.

Her long black hair was twisted into a braid behind her as she leaned back against the rail she had just jumped from, her hands gripping the vinyl-covered railing.

"Aren't you supposed to be helping Mom with breakfast in the morning?" she asked her sister.

"Well, that's kind of what I wanted to talk to you about." Lyrica tucked a stray strand of black hair behind her ear as she shifted on her feet and smiled back at Eve brightly. "I was hoping I could get you to cover for me."

Eve's brow lifted in doubtful surprise. "Did you even notice what time I came in tonight, or what time it is now?"

"Yeah, you came in at two thirty and it's now ten after three." She waved the time away. "Come on, Eve; it's really important. I know you won't get much sleep—"

"Try no sleep," Eve reminded her. "What would be the point of going to sleep if I just have to get up again in less than two hours?"

"I know; that will so suck." Lyrica pouted as she brushed another strand of hair back and shifted on her bare feet again. "So you'll do it for me?"

"I didn't say that." Eve laughed. "I said what would be the point of going to sleep if I were to do that? And I have to be back at the bar at six tomorrow evening. I'm closing with Matteo, so I'll be even later getting home. I'll need some sleep."

"Come on, Eve; you can get to bed before noon, and that will easily give you five hours' sleep."

"And I easily need eight," Eve pointed out. "What's so important on a Saturday that you can't help Mom and Piper with breakfast?"

Lyrica blew out a heavy breath, her head tilting to the side as she gazed down at the boards of the porch. A second later, her gaze lifted as she stared back at Eve. And Eve knew that look. Her younger sister was considering the best way to work her oldest sister to get what she wanted.

"Tell me why," Eve bargained. "Otherwise I'm going to bed. Like I said, I have to help Matteo close the bar, and I need my sleep if this isn't important."

"Maybe it's just important to me." Lyrica shrugged. "I was invited to go with some friends to Louisville for a spa day."

Her expression became animated, her voice filling with excitement. "Massages, a mani and a pedi, and being spoiled and rubbed and oiled for hours and hours." Lyrica was all but jumping in anticipation. "Please, Eve, pretty please cover for me. I can't just slip off and leave Momma a hand short. Piper would kill me if I did that."

Because then Piper would have the majority of the work in the kitchen as their mother fixed coffee, set the long dining room table, and made fresh-squeezed orange juice and the fruit bowls for the guests who came down early to catch the news, read the paper, or just socialize as they checked e-mail before breakfast.

Piper would get together the individual orders that were turned in the night before, prepare all the ingredients as well as the plates and silverware. She would have to do all the cooking and carry all the food out as well if her mother didn't finish early to help her. And normally it was impossible to finish one job early to help someone else with another when all the rooms were rented out. Lyrica wasn't even lucky enough that most of the rooms only held a single guest. With the exception of the three long term guests, it was couples.

Eve's suite didn't count. It was a smaller suite. The other side was a pantry connected to the kitchen and the large laundry room with two heavy-duty stacking washers and dryers that were used by guests as well as their mother to wash the bedcoverings in.

"So I'm supposed to give up eight hours of sleep so you can go have a girls' day?" she asked.

"Come on, Eve. The invitation came from Kyleene Brock. I've been trying to make friends with her for months now."

Eve rolled her eyes. "No, you've been trying to get close to her brother for months now," she retorted.

"Same thing." Lyrica waved the protest away. "If I have

to back out because of breakfast, then it's going to be just horrible."

"Just horrible, huh?" Eve tucked her feet up in the chair and knew she was just making her sister wait before giving in to her. Because she knew she was going to do it.

Lyrica had had a crush on Graham Brock for years. She'd been plotting just as long to get into that inner circle of friends Kyleene was so careful before making.

As one of the larger land owners in the area, and one of the few influential bachelors since the Mackay cousins' marriages, Graham was well sought after. Because of his popularity, Kyleene was extremely careful of the friends she made.

"Come on, Eve, please," her sister asked again, this time quietly, and with much more restraint. "Kyleene has invited all of us back to the house for a late lunch after we're finished at the spa, and Graham is home on leave."

Graham was serving his second tour in the Middle East, and Eve knew her sister had been watching for him to come home for months.

"Fine," Eve agreed impatiently. "I'll do it. But you owe me big-time, Lyrica."

"Oh, my God, Eve, thank you so much." Lyrica jumped across the short distance, reached into the chair, and wrapped her arms around Eve's neck tightly. "Thank you, thank you, thank you."

Drawing back, Lyrica threw her fist into the air in a silent victory shout before gripping the porch post and pulling herself up the railing again.

"You can use my door to get to the stairs, Lyrica." Eve laughed quietly. "You don't have to risk life and limb climbing like a damned monkey."

"Where's the fun in that? Love you, Eve." Her sister blew her a swift kiss before her gaze swung to the side of Eve's patio door. "Morning, Mr. Campbell, I hope we didn't wake you."

Eve tensed with a silent groan of frustration.

"Not hardly, Ms. Mackay," he drawled. The spicy sweet scent of his cigar reached her nostrils and had her body reacting to the sensual smell.

She pretended to hate the scent of it, but during those times when she forced herself to be honest, Eve admitted, to herself anyway, that the evocative scent would always be associated with wanting this man.

"Night, sis," Lyrica whispered again before gripping the post and hauling herself up as she used her feet to push herself the short distance to allow her to grab hold of the railing overhead and pull herself up.

"That girl's related to apes, or she's missing a hell of a career in the circus." Brogan chuckled as she disappeared over the upper balcony railing.

"Probably a little of both," Eve agreed, swallowing nervously as he moved to the railing in front of her, where Lyrica had stood moments before.

"She knew you'd agree," he drawled, clenching the slim cigar between his teeth for a moment before removing it and holding it negligently between his thumb and forefinger as he tapped the ash from the tip.

"She probably did."

"Graham Brock's too old for her." He frowned at the sound of the door closing above. "If he even deigned to notice her, he'd break her heart and grind it in the dust without realizing it."

Eve sighed heavily. "You can't convince her of that."

For a moment, she thought he'd say something more before

he brought the cigar to his lips and muttered something that sounded strangely like, "Someone needs to talk to him 'bout that."

"Let it alone," Eve warned him. "If everyone keeps padding her falls she'll never learn how to handle the bruises."

Eve watched him carefully, as if he were a wild animal that could attack at any moment.

Or maybe one she wished would attack?

She kept that amusing thought to herself as she crossed her arms over her breasts and prayed he couldn't see her hardened nipples beneath the thin camisole.

He made her ache so badly. Just looking at him, seeing the danger and the steel hardness inside him, all she wanted to do was touch him and feel it for herself.

With Brogan standing across from her, his six-foot-four frame wasn't overly wide or muscle-bound. He had that natural muscled look, iron hard and powerful without being overblown.

The dark shirt he wore was unbuttoned several inches past the collar. The long sleeves were rolled to his elbows, the hem tucked into jeans that fit his thighs perfectly. A leather belt cinched his tight hips, the fit of the shirt hinting at the powerful abs beneath.

A male animal.

That was the thought that drifted through her mind every time she saw him.

"I tried to catch up with you while you were on break at the bar earlier," he stated, his voice quiet, the early morning silence of the land around them lending itself to discreet whispers rather than a normal tone of voice that would carry through the night.

"Why?" Tucking the damp strands of hair falling over her face behind her ear, Eve stared up at him curiously. "Did you need something?"

"A dance." His lips quirked into a smile as he lifted the cigar and drew in the fragrant smoke before exhaling, all the while watching her between narrowed, red-gold lashes.

"Oh, I can't dance with customers." She stood abruptly. "It's getting late now; I have to go."

She turned to rush back into her room, then froze, completely still, like prey suddenly aware of the predator lounging lazily just behind it.

His fingers were curved around her lower arm, not really gripping or holding her in place, but the knowledge that he could was clear.

Eve turned her head, glanced at the hand on her arm, then lifted her gaze to his.

He was once again amused. His lips were tilted to the side just a bit. That knowing look on his face had her wondering exactly what it was he knew, and was amused by.

"Why do you keep running from me, Eve?" He moved closer, his head bent, his lips settling at her ear as he asked the question. "Every time I think I can get close enough to touch, you jump and run like a scared little rabbit."

Her skin was tingling where he was touching her. Sensitivity radiated from his touch, spreading through her body and making her nipples, her clit, throb in protest. Why should he be touching her arm, when the rest of her body hurt to be touched?

"Maybe I have the same instincts for when danger is near," she suggested with attempted lightness. "I don't have time for dangerous men."

He chuckled at that, and the sound sent a rush of sensation washing down her spine.

She couldn't calm her breathing. It was deep and heavy, rougher than before as her breasts lifted and fell with a quicker rhythm. And no doubt from his position he could see her nipples pressing—

His hand caressed up her arm, the calloused palm and fingertips making direct contact and stimulating already too-sensitive nerve endings.

"I have to go," she whispered breathlessly.

Something warm and incredibly soft rasped against the top of her shoulder then.

Eve trembled at the realization that it was his beard. He was stroking the skin of her upper shoulder with nothing but the closely cropped growth of his facial hair.

The sensation was incredible. It was lashing heat and a cold storm. It was laying a banquet in front of a starving woman and daring her to eat.

Eventually, she was going to take a bite.

His lips brushed against her shoulder then as he curved his arm around her waist, holding her close to him, warming her back as his lips against the bare skin of her shoulder sent flames chasing over her body.

Nothing should feel this good. Nothing should destroy her defenses and her self-control this quickly.

"Why are you doing this, Brogan?" Her hands gripped his arm; her head fell back against his chest. "Why this and why now?"

"Because I'm damned tired of chasing after you, Eve Mackay," he growled before delivering a heated little nip against her shoulder. "I'm tired of watching you avoid me, of always being one step behind you and never close enough to touch. Maybe you should have stood still for a second at some point so I could have prepared you."

Prepared her for that electrical current that zigzagged through her body and struck at areas so sensitive that the heightened sensations were bordering on pain.

"Maybe I've been avoiding you for a reason," she suggested breathlessly.

"Avoiding me while you stare at me with all that heat and need for my touch in your eyes?" he asked, his lips moving against the side of her neck as she tilted her head to allow him access to the oversensitive nerve endings she possessed there.

And there seemed to be a lot of them.

His arm tightened around her waist, pulling her closer against him. She felt his hips at her lower back, the heavy wedge of his erection unmistakable.

What the hell was she doing?

Lifting her arm and curving it around the back of his neck to hold his lips at that supersensitive spot his beard was brushing against, Eve's lashes fluttered in pleasure.

"Like oil and fire," he said in a groan. "That's what it's going to be like, Eve. Once it starts, we're going to burn down the night."

"I don't have fire insurance on my heart, Brogan," she whispered, forcing herself to protest what she knew would happen. "This is a really bad idea. Burning down the night can't be good."

"Oh, sweetheart, burning down the night is the best." His hand flattened against her waist as he pushed beneath the camisole, his calloused palm rasping over the rapidly rising area of her upper stomach as she fought to breathe.

She quivered at the feel of his broad palm, long, strong fingers. They stroked up, lifted, then cupped the underside of one swollen breast.

"For over two years I've watched those little nipples harden every time I've come around you," he revealed. "I've tortured myself wondering if the honey was dripping along your pussy. Every time I see you leave that spa in town I wondered if you had your pussy waxed. If it was all bare, or if you left just a few curls for me to play with. I've wondered, Eve, how the hell I was going to keep my head when I finally got close enough to touch you."

She was shaking.

Eve could feel herself trembling like a schoolgirl finally getting that first kiss from the guy she'd daydreamed about all year. But it wasn't the captain of the basketball team or the football team, or the most popular guy.

It was that guy from the wrong side of the tracks, and she had fantasized that she was the pampered princess who had no idea how to handle him, how to tame him, but was desperate to try.

The problem was, she was, in reality, also the one from the wrong side of the tracks, as well as the wrong side of the blanket. She wasn't pampered or spoiled, and he was far too dangerous.

His thumb raked over her nipple, suddenly shocking her with the burning pleasure that lanced from the sensitive peak to the swollen, saturated bud of her clitoris.

Her vagina clenched.

Her juices were spilling along the sensitive channel, slicking the bare lips, because yes, she did wax. The dampness gathered and built, preparing her for his touch, for his possession.

And she couldn't stop it.

She couldn't stop him.

He began turning her in his arms, eroticism filling the night, the scent of dark cherry and spice from the cigar he had been smoking wrapping around her senses. One hand slid into her hair, clenched in the damp strands, while the other wrapped around her back and dragged her to him.

She stared up at him, watching the usually icy gray-blue gaze darken and flame and swirl with heat as her lips parted.

In that second, just as she was certain she was going to feel his lips against hers, feel the kiss she'd ached for, dreamed of, fantasized about, the harsh, strident buzz of his cell phone suddenly shocked her back into awareness.

Eve jerked away from him, her breathing harsh, staring at him in disbelief as something dangerous, something dark and sensual flashed across his expression a second before that tilted smile curled one side of his lips.

"Run, little lamb," he whispered. "Hurry and escape before the big, bad wolf gobbles you up."

She turned and did just that.

Rushing into her room and quickly closing and locking the door, she glimpsed the light of his cell phone suddenly flaring on as he answered the call, casting his expression in sharp relief.

A chill raced over her body.

As he stared at her, as the glare of the phone's light revealed the shadows and contours of his expression, a flash of pure trepidation rushed through her senses. In his face, in his eyes, she saw hard, certain determination.

He had let her get away this time.

He had let her get away each time he'd been close in the past two and a half years.

The next time . . .

She wouldn't be nearly so lucky—the next time.

TWO

It was so hot in the room, she was dying.

Or was she so hot she was dying?

Eve tried turning the AC down, hoping the additional cold air would help cool her body, but she wasn't quite lucky enough for that to help.

This was killing her.

What the hell had she done to deserve this? To want a man, to ache for him until it felt like her body was on fire, and to know—know to the tips of her toenails—that allowing herself to have him would only end badly.

There were some men a woman just knew weren't good for her. Brogan Campbell had the potential to be just such a man.

It was there in that cynicism that wasn't quite hidden. The mockery that lingered at the edge of every smile she'd ever seen on his lips.

He watched the world as though he knew all its cruel, bitter secrets and merciless games. He knew them, practiced them, used them.

Not that he was a deliberately cruel person, she didn't think.

Oh, hell, no, she was taking that damned thought back. Only a cruel, merciless, coldhearted, soulless man could have done to a woman what he had done to her outside.

Fists clenched in the blankets, she fought the need to relieve a little of the tension. Just marginally. Just enough that she could survive the aching burn in the depths of her pussy.

She'd never wanted a man like this. What the hell was up with it?

All he had to do was be in the room to make her crazy to have him touch her, and now it was just going to be a hundred times worse. As far as she was concerned, she simply didn't deserve the torture.

She was aware of her fingers loosening, releasing the blankets beneath her and moving to her lower stomach. Aware of it, but helpless to stop it.

She had to get up in less than an hour, dress, and fix breakfast for a dozen guests who took the "breakfast" part of "bed-and-breakfast" very damned seriously. And that didn't count the occasional friend of her mother's who stopped by. When she entered the kitchen there could be more orders waiting than the ones Piper and her mother collected from the guests' doors each morning.

Mercedes Mackay didn't run the typical bed-and-breakfast. Along with the regular breakfast fare, guests could choose how their eggs were prepared or if they wanted no eggs at all. They could request toast over biscuits, grits over gravy. Each plate was prepared individually and brought out rather than all the food laid out on the table or a buffet set up.

Breathing out roughly, she let her fingers push beneath the thin camisole top she wore. Her other hand pushed beneath her shorts.

Her nipples were swollen tight, so sensitive she had to bite her lip to hold back a moan as she gripped one between her thumb and the side of her forefinger. Rolling it slowly, exerting enough pressure to make the little tip burn with sensation, she fought to breathe through the pleasure.

The fingers of her other hand pushed beneath the elastic of her panties, sliding over the small area of curls that covered just the top of her mound before pushing further between her thighs to find the saturated folds of her pussy.

She was so wet, so sensitive and swollen that her own touch sent a rush of tingling sensation sizzling through her womb. Capturing her swollen, throbbing clit between her thumb and forefinger, careful to keep the hood covering her clitoris between it and her fingers, she began to work the swollen bud slowly, gently.

A whimper slipped past her lips as her hips lifted involuntarily, jerking beneath her own touch as she imagined Brogan's fingers there.

His touch would be firmer.

Tightening her grip on the tender bundle of nerves, feeling her pussy clench and weep in need, she caressed it slowly.

She wanted to push her fingers lower.

Simply stimulating her clit didn't satisfy her anymore. Once she found her release, her inner flesh still pulsed and ached, demanding penetration. Demanding something she'd never allowed herself. Because the clitoral stimulation had been enough—

Until Brogan.

Arching her head back, she rolled her hips beneath her touch, sparks of heated pleasure rushing through the swollen knot of nerves as the stimulation worked her clit closer to release.

"Oh, yes," she whispered.

She closed her eyes, keeping in her mind the image of Brogan bending over her, his hand between her thighs, his fingers working her clit, stroking her ever closer as his lips surrounded her nipple. He would suck it firmly, she decided. Hungrily. He would draw it in with a demand that refused to allow a protest.

Not that she would want to protest. She wouldn't.

She would hold him to her, feel his tongue lashing at her nipple as his fingers worked her ever closer to release. He'd have no mercy. He'd push her hard, then hold her back, make her beg for ecstasy.

A moan slipped past her lips before she could catch it. She was rife with desperation and ever-increasing need, and the sound reminded her that the burning demand was only growing.

"Yes," she whimpered again. "Oh, yes."

She was close. So close she could feel the burning flames beginning to pulse and rage, the whipping sensations surging through her clit, building.

She was only seconds away.

A heartbeat—

The harsh blasting ring of her cell phone had her jerking, shock pulling her fingers from between her thighs before she could stop herself, cutting her release off as it had just begun to build.

Gritting her teeth, a strangled cry of frustration escaping her lips, she jerked the phone from the table next to her bed without checking the caller and connected it with a frustrated flick of her finger.

"Do you know what time it is?" she snapped at the intruder. It was too damned early for anyone important.

"If I hear one more of those little moans"—Brogan's low growl shocked her into disbelief—"then I swear I'm going to pick the lock on your door, come in, and fuck you until you can't move. Until it's all either of us can do to breathe, let alone mowing the grass as I'm supposed to later, or to help your sister cook breakfast for a houseful of guests. Are we clear here?"

"You can't hear—"

"I know," he snarled. "I fucking know what you're doing, dammit; I can feel it. Just like I always know what you're doing over there. Every fucking time you masturbate, I swear I can hear those breathy little moans you make, and if I hear it one more time, Eve—"

She disconnected the call.

Jumping from the bed, she grabbed her clothes and rushed into the bathroom, dressed, and hastily applied the necessary makeup before pulling her hair into a ponytail. Moving quickly back to her bedroom, she pulled on her sneakers, tied them jerkily, then rushed to the door.

She peeked out the door to the hall, saw no one, then hurried from the room before closing her door carefully behind her.

She was certain she had managed to escape.

She knew she had.

As she moved to pass Brogan's door, it opened with a snap and his arm jerked out, gripping hers with fingers of iron and pulling her into his arms as he turned and lifted her, pressing her against the wall inside his room as he pushed the door closed, trapping her there with his more powerful body.

Before she had time to do more than gasp, his lips covered hers, bold, heated, hungry, and demanding. He took the kiss she'd been dreaming of and instilled an urgency she'd never imagined in the erotic daydreams she'd had.

She couldn't help but wrap her arms around his neck, her fingers pushing into the strands of hair that grew long over his nape and clenching to hold him to her.

Her lips parted, feeling his tongue lick over them before he took a quick, hungry taste. Tilting his head, he slanted his lips over hers as the kiss became deeper, harder. Dazed desperation filled her, the need for more of him growing in her, clawing at her senses until she was shaking with the surging force of it.

"Fuck!" His head jerked back.

The gray-blue color of his eyes was more blue now, gleaming with hunger, with lust as he glared down at her, his expression accusing as they both fought to just breathe.

"What the fuck are you doing to me?" His head lowered, his lips brushing against hers again, then immediately returning to the deep, hungry kisses of moments before.

That was fine with her, because she couldn't get enough of them.

The simple act of lips meeting should never explode through the senses and render self-control a thing of the past, she thought hazily. There should be some measure of control, right?

A hard knock at her bedroom door beside his had them jerking apart again.

The world was conspiring against her.

First his cell phone, now some moron at her bedroom door.

"Eve, are you there?"

Her eyes widened. Swallowing tightly, she jerked her gaze to

Brogan's, certain disaster whipping through her senses at the sound of her brother Dawg's deep voice.

Brogan laid his finger against his lips, then, catching her hand, pulled her to his patio doors.

Opening one side, he stuck out his head, looked around, then pulled back.

"Go," he ordered, the softly voiced command harsh as he stared down at her with naked lust. "Get the hell out of here before it's too late."

She could hear Dawg knock again. His calling out her name a second time, his voice impatient, spurred her to do just as Brogan ordered.

Glancing back at him one last time, she rushed to the porch before turning away from her room and heading quickly to the front entrance. If Dawg was there, then her mother had opened the front doors.

Turning the corner to the main porch area, she saw she was right. The front doors were thrown open, the glass storm door revealing the hardwood entryway and the wide, curving staircase that led upstairs.

Stepping inside, she glanced to the entrance to the back rooms on the side of the foyer and watched as Dawg strode from the entryway.

"There you are," he growled as he turned and moved quickly toward her. "I need to talk to you a minute."

"Anyone dying, dead, or in need of emergency care? For God's sake, Dawg, it's five o'clock in the morning. What could you possibly need?" she asked.

He stopped, his light green eyes narrowing on her between thick, lush lashes.

"No, no one needs emergency care. Not yet." There was a warning in his voice that she didn't have time to decipher.

"Then I have to run," she told him. "I'm covering for Lyrica with Piper in the kitchen and I'm running late."

She was actually running early, but she was so not about to tell him that.

"I'm staying for breakfast," he informed her as he followed her through the large dining room, the small tables already dressed with spotlessly white cloths and the colorful top cloths her mother used.

"Did you put your order in yet?" she asked as she pushed through the swinging doors that led to the large chef's-style kitchen.

Dawg followed. She had really hoped he wouldn't.

"Mercedes has already taken care of it," he told her, pausing just inside the door, obviously finally remembering Mercedes's protests that only the cooks needed to be in the kitchen.

Grabbing the small stack of orders the guests had put in the night before, chosen from the small, select list of choices they were given, Eve quickly clipped them to the magnetic order clips along the wide hood of the combination gas stove and grill.

"I went to your room to talk to you," he told her as she moved to the walk-in fridge on the other side of the room. "Where were you?"

"I came in the front entrance," she told him, stepping inside the cool confines of the shelved refrigerator and pulling together the items they would need to prepare breakfast.

Returning to the kitchen, she was really hoping Dawg would be gone.

He wasn't.

He was standing where she had left him, a frown on his face, his arms crossed over his broad chest.

"Where's Christa?" she asked as she emptied the large tray she'd used to carry everything on.

"Home," he answered shortly. "She and Janey are going shopping or something today. The girls are swearing they need shoes." Bafflement crossed his face. "You'd think a closetful is enough."

The girls were only six, but already Erin and Laken were shoe connoisseurs and purse divas. Eve loved it. She especially loved how her brother and cousins just couldn't seem to understand it.

"So what did you need?" she finally dared to ask as she began preparing the homemade biscuits Mackay's Bed-and-breakfast Inn was well-known for.

Dawg shook his head. "I'll try to catch you after breakfast. I just need to discuss something with you for a minute, and I know what breakfast is like here."

As he spoke, the door was pushed forward firmly, slapping him against his powerful biceps as Mercedes rushed into the kitchen.

At thirty-eight, with four daughters and no gray hair or wrinkles, her mother looked ten years younger. Her long, dark brown hair was pulled back into a thick rope of a braid, revealing the high cheekbones and delicate features her daughters had inherited.

Five feet, seven inches of energy, Mercedes could outwork all four of her daughters most days and still have the energy to go out dancing that night.

Since coming to Somerset, her mother had bloomed. She was

a social butterfly who loved meeting new people, learning where they'd come from and where they were going, and even laughing at their bad jokes.

"Dawg Mackay, you are in the way," Mercedes informed him brusquely as she continued walking quickly to the large pantry across from the refrigerator.

Dawg pushed his fingers through his hair in frustration.

"I'll be in the living room," he growled. "Maybe I can keep a door from smacking me there."

"Only if you don't stand in front of it," Mercedes informed him as she strode from the pantry, her arms full of white china plates and silverware. "Grab those tea lights from the counter and come help me," she ordered him.

Eve almost laughed at his expression of male disgruntlement, but he did as he was told. Not before he glanced back at her, though, his expression warning her that whatever he wanted to talk to her about, he wasn't about to forget.

Breakfast for the inn's guests was usually something Eve enjoyed. She took pleasure in the preparation and in sharing the meal, and though cleaning up wasn't a joy, it could be fun.

Sitting down to breakfast a little after eight, at one of the busier tables after the guests had been served, she honestly thought she'd be safer. Instead, she found herself facing Brogan across the circular table as her brother placed himself to the side.

Each table seated six. There were four tables in the room, and her mother often took reservations for breakfast as well as dinner if she knew the customers well. Normally the extras here were her daughters. This morning it was Dawg and a couple leaving after vacation who hadn't been able to get a room at the inn but had managed to convince Mercedes to allow them to join the meals instead.

Eve found it highly uncomfortable, though, sharing a meal with both Brogan and Dawg. Only hours before she had been in Brogan's arms, dying for more than the kisses and light touches he had been giving her.

It was almost impossible to keep her eyes off him now.

She kept glancing across the table, catching him watching her, then, as she looked away, catching Dawg glowering at both of them.

Her brother ate silently, though, and when he finished he drank his coffee, speaking only when necessary but keeping his eyes on her and Brogan.

Of course, Brogan acted as though her brother weren't even there. He still watched her, though Eve tried to keep her gaze elsewhere.

She tried, but it was impossible.

No one was happier to see the end of the meal than Eve when the guests finally began drifting away. Jumping to her feet, she began to clear tables and carry the dishes to the kitchen as Piper loaded the dishwasher.

Her mother joined her and Piper in cleaning up: first the dining area, then the kitchen. Sharing gossip and plans, they cleaned the two rooms down to the floors. The hardwood in the dining room and the ceramic tile in the kitchen gleamed with cleanliness when they finished and stepped into the foyer, a sense of satisfaction filling them.

Glancing at the clock, Eve sighed wearily, the lack of sleep finally catching up with her as she yawned slowly.

"Lyrica's going to have to give up on this Graham thing," Piper remarked as she caught Eve's yawn. "She has breakfast duty the rest of this week, and you're not going to cover for her every morning."

"Where's Zoey, anyway?" She looked around, realizing she hadn't seen her baby sister all morning.

"She's painting," her mother answered as she took a dust cloth to the aged wood of the sideboard that held the house phone, phone book, and tourist pamphlets just inside the door. "She'll be here to help with dinner."

"So will Lyrica," Piper decided. "If she can make Eve cover for her morning shift, then she can cover my evening shift and let me go out for a change. I've worked a week straight now."

Eve frowned and turned back to her mother. "Zoey hasn't been helping?"

Mercedes turned away again, running the dust cloth over another antique table sitting next to the stairs.

"No, Zoey has not been helping," Piper answered for her mother. "She's been acting like a brokenhearted diva. And I could understand it if she were *seeing* anyone."

"Piper, come on now." Mercedes turned back to her disapprovingly. "I know plenty of times Zoey has worked two or three weeks straight so you and your sister could do whatever you were doing at the time. You and Lyrica can cover things for a while."

"I don't mind covering at all, Momma." Piper sighed. "And if Zoey were actually doing anything then I could understand it. But it's like she's just hiding in her room or disappearing all day and half the night."

"She's painting," her mother repeated. "You know how she gets when she's wrapped up in her paints. You get the same way when you're designing, just as Lyrica does when she's writing. Zoey's covered for both of you when you were wrapped up in that, too. Give her a break now."

"I would if I actually saw a single canvas with some color on it," Piper protested. "But I've yet to see anything."

"Hasn't she been working a lot out of that empty warehouse on the other side of town?" Eve asked. "I thought I saw her taking some canvases in there last week."

"The owner let her use it since it was just sitting there empty," Mercedes agreed. "You know how she is; she'll show up."

And she would, Eve thought.

"I'd help, but I promised Sierra I'd work at Walker's this week and next," she told them. "They've had two waitresses quit on them in the last month and they've not replaced them yet."

Piper groaned and turned to her mother. "I can handle breakfast alone, Momma, but not dinner. You're going to have to talk to Lyrica."

Eve grinned at the familiar refrain. In one form or another, from one sister or another, it was the same argument and had been since they were children.

"You'll have help, Piper," Mercedes promised her with a laugh. "Now let Eve go to bed."

"I need to talk to Eve first." Dawg stepped from the television and game room, leaning against the doorframe as he tucked his hands in the pockets of his jeans and watched them quietly.

There was the barest hint of gray in his hair, Eve realized. Right there at the side, when he turned his head just a certain way, she could see the few strands gleaming in the devil's black.

How old was he now? Forty-four? Forty-five, she believed.

He didn't look it.

His shoulders were still broad, his arms powerful, his abs lean. He was still in his prime, and Eve knew his wife very much appreciated that fact.

He'd waited to talk to her, and his impatience was apparent.

"Is there a problem?" She frowned back at him, surprised he was still there.

It was rare that Dawg became this stubborn over anything, despite his name and the rumor that he'd acquired it because of his steely determination.

"There could be," he growled.

"In what way?" Mercedes moved to them, her maternal instincts instantly rousing.

Dawg looked up to the ceiling as though searching for patience.

When his gaze returned to them there was an edge of amusement in his light green eyes. "Mercedes, it's nothing for you to get worked up over," he promised her. "I just need to talk to Eve about something, that's all."

"Let's get it over with," Eve suggested. "I really need to go to bed."

She entered the television/game room and, turning, watched as Dawg closed the door before turning back to her.

Her brows lifted at the move to keep the conversation private.

"Are you sure everything's okay?" she asked.

"You tell me." His gaze was intent as he crossed his arms over his chest and braced his feet apart as though steeling himself for a fight.

"Dawg, I'm not in the mood for games," she told him, confused by the question. "I haven't slept since yesterday morning sometime, and I have to be at the bar by six this evening." She glanced at the clock. "If I hurry, I might get five hours in before rushing back over there."

His jaw clenched. "Then I'll get straight to the point."

"That's the thing to do," she agreed with a sharp nod as she propped herself on the heavily padded arm of the chair beside her.

"Brogan Campbell," he stated.

Eve stilled. Dawg rarely had much to say about the men she and her sisters dated or seemed interested in. He watched, waited, and was always there if they needed to talk. But he never played the heavy-handed brother. This was the first time he'd ever approached her about anyone she was interested in.

She didn't say anything; she waited.

"There's a lot of talk, Eve," he finally said. "A lot of people are seeing your interest in him."

"So?" She crossed one knee over the other before crossing her arms over her breasts and frowning back at him.

"Are you? Interested?" he asked gruffly.

"I don't know." She shrugged as though it didn't matter. "Come on, Dawg; we practically live in the same house, and see each other often. He's cute as hell, and damned interesting—"

"He's also a suspected traitor who was dishonorably discharged from the Marines four years ago." He shocked her, his tone heavy with disapproval. "You're family, Eve. I'm not going to let you walk into something that's going to end up hurting or endangering you. Brogan Campbell will do both."

Eve forced herself to bite back the sharp retort that would have slipped free if he were anyone else.

"If he's a suspected traitor, then why isn't he in prison?" she asked carefully.

"He was discharged for striking a commanding officer while on duty. After returning to the States he migrated here. Within six months of his arrival high-ranking officers from Fort Knox began experiencing home and vehicle thefts. Those thefts were of top-secret military documents that were under review, or in the process of being transferred to locations where the information was needed. Campbell was seen in or near the area with almost each incidence. He'll be caught, Eve, and when he is, I don't want your name coming up in this. I do not want my sister suspected of being a traitor. That's a stigma that never goes away."

She didn't say a word. She couldn't.

Staring back at Dawg, she racked her brain, trying to make sense of what he was saying.

"There has to be a misunderstanding." She finally forced the words past her lips. "He's an arrogant son of a bitch, Dawg, but Brogan Campbell's no traitor."

He wiped one hand over his face, behind his neck, then turned away from her and paced to the wide window across the room. Standing there for long seconds, he finally drew in a deep breath before turning back to her. The look on his face wasn't comforting.

"When he's caught—and he will be caught," Dawg stated quietly, "everyone he's associated with will be stained by his guilt, Eve. Business associates, employers, friends." He paused, his jaw tightening again. "Lovers."

"We're not lovers, Dawg." Eve rose to her feet, anger and nervous energy refusing to allow her to sit in one place now.

The only reason they weren't lovers was the fact that she feared that first broken heart. It hadn't happened yet, and she didn't want it to happen with Brogan.

"Not yet." He sighed, rubbing at the back of his neck again. "But it's in the air, Eve. I didn't believe it when I heard the talk that he was interested in you. I figured you'd send him packing like you do every other man whose reputation is less than perfect. Instead, what I saw this morning was a man and a woman who couldn't wait to find a bed."

Eve felt heat fill her face as the words passing his lips sent embarrassment racing through her. She didn't drop her gaze, though. She had nothing to be ashamed of, and she wasn't going to act as though she did. If he was waiting for the shame, then he was going to be waiting a damned long time.

His jaw flexed; the fact that he was grinding his teeth was more than obvious.

"Are you waiting for an apology?" she asked as she cocked her hip and faced him curiously. "Because if you are, you're going to be waiting awhile, Dawg."

"I don't want a damned apology," he bit out. "I want you to find someone else to mesmerize you; that's what I want."

Her brow lifted. "He's no traitor."

"You don't know that, Eve."

"I can feel it, Dawg," she argued fiercely, her desperation to prove he wasn't tightening inside her. "You told me once that you've lived by your instincts most of your life; well, I have, too. I've had no other choice, any more than you did. And my instincts tell me he's no traitor."

"Those aren't your instincts, Eve. They're your hormones. And trust me, your hormones will lie to you and have a hell of a time doing it. And when your hormones have betrayed you, you'll find yourself sleeping with a traitor, under investigation for collusion, and your mother and sisters suspects as well." His shoulders flexed, shifting beneath the well-pressed shirt he wore. "Listen to me, Eve; I wouldn't lie to you, honey. And God knows it would kill me to watch you have to go through that."

Eve could only shake her head as her chest tightened with fear, regret, and an aching need she couldn't deny.

"Eve, he will be caught," he warned her again as he moved to her, reaching out to grip her shoulders gently, staring down at her, understanding and anger filling his gaze. "I've never asked anything of you. I've done all I could to protect you, your mother, and your sisters. But I'm begging you now: Don't let him destroy you. Don't let him do what I can see him getting ready to do to you."

This was truly the only thing he had ever asked of her, Eve realized as she felt her heart cracking with the pain of the choice he was giving her.

How could she ignore him? He'd never ignored her, her mother, or her sisters. He'd taken care of them. He'd seen that they were fed, educated, and their futures provided for, and all he asked was that she stay away from one man.

A man she was so hungry for it was eating her alive.

She nodded slowly. "I'll try, Dawg."

He pulled her to him, hugging her fiercely as she returned the embrace weakly.

"That's all I ask, Eve," he said, kissing the top of her head gently. "That's all I ask."

THREE

Brogan glared at Timothy Cranston as he watched the monitor. The television and game room had a small warning plaque just inside the door. Notice: This room could be monitored by both video and audio surveillance. A small smile played at the agent's lips, but his brown eyes were narrowed, his expression thoughtful as he watched Dawg Mackay hug his sister fondly.

Of course it was fondly. The son of a bitch had just played the brother card and forced her to promise to stay away from the big, bad Brogan.

Bastard!

Hell, the ironic part was that he actually liked Dawg.

The Mackay cousins weren't known for their polite society ways, or their ability to soothe ruffled feathers. They were known for quite the opposite, actually.

When they'd first met, Dawg had laughingly told Brogan that he reminded him far too much of his cousins and asked whether he was a Mackay, despite the red hair. Six months later, Dawg had flat-out asked him whether the underground rumors he was hearing that Brogan was involved in the military thefts were true.

Brogan's boss had an agenda, unfortunately. Part of that agenda was pulling the Mackays in without officially asking them for help. Brogan had just stared back at him for long seconds before telling Dawg he was going to have to answer that question himself.

He'd evidently done just that. Since that day, Dawg had been as cold as Lake Cumberland in winter.

"You told me Dawg and his cousins would keep their noses out of my business," he reminded Timothy as he leaned forward in his chair, frowning at the stark pain that filled Eve's expression.

She'd tried to convince her brother that her instincts about Brogan were right. That, like him, she'd had to learn how to depend on them, how to trust them, just to survive. And still, the brother who was known as not just protective and sheltering, but also respectful and tolerant, had demanded she stay away from the man it was clear his sister was unable to stay away from.

"He is keeping out of your business," Timothy murmured. "It's your sex life he's screwing with."

Brogan could feel his jaw aching from the clenched tightness of it. It was all he could do to restrain the urge to stomp downstairs and push his way into that room to confront the other man. To ensure that nothing and no one could pull Eve's attention from him.

His fists clenched, his short, clipped nails biting into his palm as he forced himself to remain sitting.

The last thing he wanted, needed, was for anyone to guess that he and Timothy were more than friendly enemies. Timothy had taken the same public stance on Brogan as Dawg had: a cool reception and a refusal to warm. It was required. Cranston was known as a former Homeland Security agent. Even the Mackays were unaware he was still an Agent in Charge for the Department of Homeland Security.

Unfortunately, he wasn't in charge of this operation. He was only overseeing it. If he had been in charge, maybe, just maybe he could have convinced Timothy to keep Eve out of the operation they were conducting in Pulaski County.

Because the Agent in Charge of this operation had deemed Eve necessary. Even before Brogan had looked into those mesmerizing emerald eyes and knew he wouldn't rest until he'd taken her to his bed, his boss had decided that Eve Mackay's participation was required.

"I have things to do." Straightening from the chair he'd taken in Timothy's small upstairs office, he turned and glared at the agent as Timothy sat back comfortably in his chair. Mercedes had designated the area as Timothy's and no one but no one, she'd declared, entered without his permission. Even her.

"Go on." Timothy waved him away. "You'll be here for dinner?"

"No, I won't be," he growled.

"Ahh, you'll be at the bar." Timothy nodded with a smile. "Eve's not a puppy you can convince to heel with treats, Brogan. I'd remember that if I were you."

"Damned good thing I don't see her as one, isn't it?" he said with a grunt.

Striding to the door, he opened it enough to ensure no one

was in the hall before slipping from the room and taking the back stairs to the kitchen.

Mercedes Mackay left the kitchen open through the day, and plates of sandwiches and snacks in the stainless-steel refrigerator that sat next to the back door. If anyone caught him there, he'd have a reason for it.

He'd used a lot of bed-and-breakfasts over the years, and he had to admit, hers was one of the most unique.

Fortunately there was no one in the kitchen, and no one entered as he strode across it and slipped out the back door.

This was a fucking mess.

He'd come to Pulaski County to find thieves; instead he'd ended up playing the traitor and stealing top-secret files that were never meant to be seen by anyone other than those who were carrying the files.

The files were stolen from four high-level couriers traveling through Fort Knox, Somerset, Harlan County, and Pikeville. Others were stolen from the homes of the high-ranking military officers they'd been delivered to. Each file had contained information unrelated to the files stolen before them.

Brogan had seen the reports of the files they had contained, and he could see nothing to tie them together.

Striding from the porch along the walk to the parking lot, he moved to the Harley and mounted it smoothly. Unlocking the helmet from between the handlebars and sliding it over his head, he activated the Bluetooth headset, then, with a quick flick of his wrist, turned the key and let the powerful motor throb for long seconds before pulling from the parking lot and turning onto the main road.

"Dial Doogan," he said into the headset, activating the hands-free feature built into it.

"Doogan," his boss answered before the first ring finished, his voice a dark, slow drawl that did nothing to indicate the man's impatience.

"Dawg's interfering," he told the other man. "He just pulled the brother card on his sister and made her promise to stay away from the big, bad Brogan," he said with a grunt.

Doogan laughed at the reference. "Do you think she'll listen?"

"Mackays are known to keep their word, and she promised. What do you think?"

Pulling into the light flow of traffic along the main drag, Brogan headed away from Somerset and the temptation to follow Eve to her bed. He wanted nothing more than to make damned certain she didn't obey her brother.

"Fuck," Doogan growled. "Think you can convince her to break her word?"

That was Doogan, always going for the jugular.

Bastard.

"Why should I?" Brogan bit out. "Come on, Doogan; she's one woman with no military connections at all. How can she possibly be of any importance to this operation?"

"Because I said she was." The other man's voice lowered, his tone becoming darker, harder.

"Doogan. I'm the wrong man to keep in the dark," Brogan warned him. "I'm the one man who could jack this operation all to hell just by letting folks know exactly who I am. Don't force me to take that route."

"You'd do that because of one woman?" There was a fine edge of surprise in his boss's voice.

"I'd do that if you risked her, and I'm starting to wonder if that isn't your intention."

There were times he wished he knew the Agent in Charge better. Doogan was a man who had refused to climb the ladder of DHS success. He remained in his position of Agent in Charge far longer than he should have. He could have risen, taken a directorship or even a position as team commander.

"That's not my intention, Brogan," the other man finally assured him. "I'll tell you this much: Eve Mackay is pivotal to this mission. There's one person in Pulaski County who I suspect knows a hell of a lot more than we, or our thieves, want them to know. My contact has spent the better part of eight years watching everything that goes on in that county. He's one of our spotters, and a damned good one at that. But even he doesn't know who this person is. All he's heard where these thefts are concerned is that they are tied together, and that there's one person who could answer a hell of a lot of questions if they would. The only thing, though, that's going to bring them out of the woodwork is if one of those Mackay girls needs them. And they'd trust only whoever they trust. And despite appearances, there're very few people any Mackay trusts. If they see she's in your bed, and in your life, then you could possibly be considered in a position of trust and the situation deemed important enough to come out of the woodwork and reveal his secrets."

"Because if he knows as much as you think he does, then he'll know who I am and what I am." Brogan grimaced.

He didn't like the thought of that at all. The very thought of it had a chill of warning lifting the hairs at the back of his neck. "There should be another way to ensure that this person makes contact," Brogan snapped. "Bringing her into my life might not be the best way to do that, Doogan."

"It's the only way, Brogan," Doogan stated, his tone chilling at the indication that Brogan was second-guessing his orders.

"And how do you know it's the only fucking way?" he bit out furiously. "You're asking me to endanger an innocent woman's life."

"Or save it," Doogan countered. "And don't deny you're interested, Brogan. There's more than one report that's come in mentioning the suspected thief and Dawg Mackay's sister."

Oh, he'd just bet there was. He could practically feel the rumor mill heating up every time they were in the same place at the same time.

"It might not be as easy as you thought it would be," he informed the other man. "She's made a promise now. She won't break it."

"The only way this will work is if it appears Eve is aligned with you, Agent Campbell," Doogan drawled lazily. "So align with Eve Mackay and stop trying to convince me I'm wrong. When you're the one reading the reports and listening to the director tear a strip off your ass because of military secrets falling into the wrong hands, then you can countermand orders. Until then, if it wouldn't bother you too much, try sticking with the plan we agreed on before you went out there."

Brogan could feel frustration and livid anger brewing inside him.

Without another word he broke the link before giving the cycle a surge of gas as he headed into the mountains.

He might not be the one reading the reports or getting his ass torn over the thefts, but he was the one taking the risks and fighting his own lust for a woman he was seriously afraid could end up owning his soul.

His father had once told him that a man knew when he'd met his mate. That if he waited, kept his dick under control, and didn't fuck up, then he'd find that mate.

He was thirty-four. A little old to be finding his mate, he thought.

Not that he believed in the whole mate-finding business. He didn't. But if it actually existed, then there was no doubt he'd found his in Eve Mackay.

The hunger he felt for her was like a white-hot flame burning his senses and his common sense to cinders. He'd waited two and a half years. Waited and watched, flirted with subtle demand, and teased until he finally managed to snag her interest.

Not that it hadn't been there before; it had been. But there were things that had to be done first, plans that had to be placed into motion.

Everything was in place now.

Brogan and his partner, his brother, Brody, now held the better part of the files that had been marked to be stolen. The inside source who had first contacted DHS gave them the information on each file targeted, and Brogan made damned sure he got to them before the real thieves could.

If the thieves wanted to acquire the missing files, then they were going to have to come to him.

According to Doogan, there was only one piece to the puzzle left to acquire: Eve's loyalty and the perception that she was Brogan's lover.

What would make a source contact him if he knew Eve trusted him enough to be his lover? What the fuck was going on in this damned place, and just how screwed up were the criminals operating here?

Pulling the cycle to a wide clearing at the side of the road, he turned around and headed back to town. Like Eve, he'd had no sleep the night before, and if he was going to seduce his wild little Mackay, then he was going to need all his wits about him.

Because seducing her wasn't going to be nearly as hard, he feared, as keeping the independent, unfettered state of his heart intact.

He had a feeling Eve was invading it, and that could only spell trouble for both of them.

Besides, his long-term agreement with Mercedes Mackay included two days per week that he pitched in on the upkeep of the inn and grounds. And it was time to cut the grass.

FOUR

Eve could feel a headache coming on.

Right there in her left temple. It was that heaviness that assured her the discomfort had no intention of going away.

And she should have expected it from the lack of sleep, the upsetting meeting with her brother, and the knowledge that no matter how badly she wanted him, Brogan was out of her reach.

To make matters worse, some of the less desirable members of the small Cumberland Touring and Motorcycle Club had taken a table right beside the step that led from the main floor to the bar area. Two of those members were determined that night to push her headache from irritating to migraine status: Donny Sutherby and his lover, Sandi Mikels.

Donny, nicknamed "Bowie" by the club, was barrel-chested with a bearlike body, thick armed and heavy thighed. His straight, conservatively cut dark brown hair was thinning on top, while his pale blue eyes always looked suspicious and mocking.

Dressed in baggy jeans and a dark T-shirt that did nothing to hide his too-thick thighs and biceps, he swaggered when he walked, and even when he was sober one would swear he was drunk.

Sandi, a part-time stripper in Boston, followed him each summer, taking her place on the back of his motorcycle for the summer road "tours" the group took.

How a part-time stripper could afford to take the summer off, Eve hadn't figured out.

Her overblown figure was poured into snug jeans and the typical summer camisole that was at least one size too small as it stretched across the boob job she was so proud of. Personally, if she were Sandi and she was going to get a boob job, Eve thought, she would have gone with one that more suited her diminutive frame rather than a set of double Ds that made her look as though she were going to topple over forward at any second.

Donny and Sandi were sitting with Poppa Bear. Grady "Poppa Bear" Aarons and his wife, Mary, nicknamed "Momma Bear," were one of the older couples. Poppa Bear had been a commanding officer in the army, discharged at retirement, and as jovial as they came.

He had a Santa Claus look about him, though his beard was shorter, his eyes dark brown, his laughter booming. Momma Bear was only a few years younger, slim and still a handsome woman for being in her late fifties.

Scattered around the large table with them was Poppa and Momma Bear's daughter, Baby Bear, a.k.a. Shanna. Also "Hondo" Grael—Eve had no idea of his real name—"Pooh" Yonkers and his sister, "Marbles," and another brother and sister, Boo and Homer Kennedy.

The table wasn't overly loud, but Bowie and Sandi were ensuring that each time Eve passed their table, some snide remark was directed toward her.

Returning to the bar, she tried to avoid the table, but it was the most direct path to collect the drink orders she had, and she would be damned if she would let the couple know they were bothering her.

"Hey, Evie, is Brogan avoiding you tonight?" Sandi laughed as Eve passed. "He's been here for a while now, ya know?"

Yeah, she knew.

Every tall, hard inch of him was there, dressed in jeans, a wide leather belt cinched at his lean hips, a white shirt tucked into the denim, several buttons undone and tempting her fingers to play with those red-gold curls across his chest. A pair of scuffed leather motorcycle boots completed the picture of hard-core sex appeal and danger.

"Come on, Boogie, be nice," Poppa Bear chastised her, using the nickname he had given her. "Scots might be on the other side of the bar, but he don't take his eyes off her." He laughed boisterously.

Edging up to the bar, Eve sneaked a look in Brogan's direction and saw that Poppa Bear wasn't lying. Brogan might be talking to John Walker, but he was staring straight at her.

Loading the circular tray with ordered drinks and lifting it until she could balance it with one hand, with the other she gripped the handle of the pitcher and made her way back to the bachelorette party she was serving.

"Scots likes all the girls, though," Sandi remarked as Eve passed. "He's not a one-woman man, Poppa Bear."

Eve didn't hear Poppa Bear's answer as she made her way to the bachelorette party.

The eight women had arrived two hours before, and at the rate they were drinking, Eve had a feeling she was going to be calling cabs for the eight. She had yet to see their designated driver, and if she wasn't mistaken, the bride wasn't going to make it until the witching hour, as she had sworn she would.

"Hey, here're our drinks," the bride called out, the bridal nerves reflecting in her eyes belying the goofy smile on her face.

Setting the beer on the table, Eve put their drinks out in front of them, then turned and headed back to the bar for another order.

The bar, newly named Walker's Run, was hopping. The band was incredible, the singers capable of crooning or belting out the latest country hits. With both a male and female singer, the band was able to give the crowd the songs they wanted, the way they wanted them.

Drinks were flowing, the dance floor was full, and the managers, John Walker and his wife, Sierra, were out and about ensuring everything was running smoothly.

It always amused Eve that the owner of the bar, Rogue, had more or less given the bar to her brother and sister-in-law, John and Sierra, while Rogue managed the upscale restaurant, Mackay's Fine Dining, for Eve's cousin Janey Mackay Jansen.

The restaurant was just as popular as the bar, though, and no doubt a line was starting to form at the doors there, just as it would be here soon.

Moving back to the bar, she almost changed direction and skirted the dance floor.

John Walker had disappeared, and Brogan had moved to Poppa Bear's table. He was standing between Donny and Poppa

Bear. Sandi was sitting on Donny's lap, her hand stroking down Brogan's arm where it lay on the table, a sly smile curling her lips as she spoke to him.

The sight of the blond-haired witch touching him had Eve's fingers curling tighter around the tray she was carrying and her teeth clenching in anger.

Oh, she did not like that. Donny and Sandi weren't exactly faithful to each other. They each took other lovers often, and it appeared Sandi had every intention of getting Brogan into her bed.

Serving drinks and gathering payments and tips kept her moving quickly. John had more waitresses coming in the next few weeks, but preferred not to train them on the weekends. That left Eve to fill in for the two girls who had left at the beginning of the summer.

She wished she could get out of it now. Each trip she made past the table, the other woman was touching him, and he wasn't exactly making her stop.

As Eve approached the table again she avoided Brogan's gaze. From the corner of her eye she watched Sandi stand and excuse herself.

Eve was almost past the group when she was suddenly thrown off balance and pushed hard into the wood railing that separated the bar area from the tables.

Reacting quickly, she grabbed the railing, righting herself before swinging to face Sandi.

"Oh, my God, aren't I just so sorry." Sandi breathed out, her eyes widening in innocence.

"Not a problem," Eve gritted in irritation, picking up the tray and stepping up to the bar.

"That witch is out for trouble," the bartender, Dakota

Wayne—or Kota, as everyone called him—warned her as he took the orders she'd brought back. "Watch yourself."

"No kidding," she muttered.

"Hey, while I'm putting your drinks together, could you run to the back and pull me some Jack and Johnnie Walker?" Kota called out.

"Got it, Kota." Shoving her tips into the front pocket of her jeans, she moved quickly to the end of the bar, lifted the hinged top, and entered the "Employees Only" section.

"Keys." Kota tossed her a key ring before turning back to the drinks he and the other bartender were quickly putting together.

Pushing through the swinging doors, she strode down the short hall before turning and heading for the liquor room.

As she entered the dimly lit, cool confines of the storage room and moved to the back shelves where the whiskey was, she was aware of voices in the office next door.

She lifted the large bottles of liquor and placed them in one arm, and was turning around as the sound of a familiar voice had her pausing.

"I don't like it," John protested from outside the storage room. "There are too many variables that could go wrong."

"And if they go wrong, then we're going to watch good friends suffer," an unfamiliar voice argued. "We don't want that."

She didn't want to hear this.

Deliberately bumping into a heavy shelf and causing it to smack against the wall, Eve cursed loud enough that she was sure to be heard.

The conversation abruptly stopped, and within seconds John was standing at the door of the storage room and staring into the dimly lit confines.

"Eve?" Narrowing his gaze on her, he watched her, not suspiciously, but curiously. "Everything okay?"

"Yeah, it's just been a long evening." She moved more fully into the light, knowing he would be able to detect the signs of the headache she was fighting. There were few men, or even women, perceptive enough to pay attention to facial expressions or changes in them; however, there were too many men in her life who did just that: her boss, her brother, her cousins. The men who had saved her and her sisters five years before, and their very small circle of friends, almost seemed to have a second sense for it.

"Need to take off?" he asked, compassion lighting his pale blue eyes as he watched her intently.

"Who's going to cover me?" She smiled back at him, appreciating the offer. "You'll have Sierra out there serving drinks if you lose any more waitresses tonight."

He grimaced at the thought. "She'll start a riot."

"She does every time," Eve agreed with a little nod as she moved to the door and he backed up.

Closing the door behind her, she let him have the keys when he reached for them, and waited while he locked the door before handing them back to her.

"Tell Kota that if he needs liquor to call back and I'll bring it out to him," he offered quietly. "That way you don't have to lug those bottles." He nodded to the two in her arms.

"Got it, boss," she promised, smiling back at him before heading back up the corridor quietly and moving back into the bar area.

Wow, whatever those two were talking about, he didn't want to risk anyone hearing it again.

She doubted it was anything illegal. She knew John Walker and his wife too well, just as she knew her brother and cousins too well, to ever believe they would work on the wrong side of the law.

John and his friend were up to something, though, and that was scary. Because whatever John got into, then her brother and cousins were sure to follow. It was just the way it was when it came to Mackays and their family or friends. And John, his sister Rogue, and the Mackays, were definitely friends. And then—and she knew this well from the stories she had heard—then Timothy Cranston would get involved. . . .

Damn, she didn't even want to consider the consequences there.

As she dropped the bottles off with Kota, he was placing the last of the drinks she had ordered on the tray.

Handing over the keys, she gave him John's message and started to turn away.

"Everything okay, Evie?" he asked her as she paused. "You're looking tired."

"Headache coming on." She sighed. "And I don't think John liked me being in the back rooms, Kota, so I'd feel better if I didn't have to do any more runs."

"What makes you think that?" He tilted his head to the side curiously.

Eve gave a little shrug. "It was just a feeling."

"Hell, the waitresses always go back there." Kota frowned.

She gave a negligent shrug. "I just know what he said, Kota, and I don't want to step on any toes, ya know?"

"Got it, sweet pea." He gave a quick smile and nod, his expression clearing. "I'll make sure you stay on the floor."

Yippee.

Breathing out wearily at the thought, she grabbed the tray of drinks the other bartender, Matteo, pushed to her, and moved back into the throng. Though this time she carefully skirted the table where Brogan and Sandi sat.

She would have loved to know what the hell was going on with John— No, she didn't want to know, she told herself quickly. She knew his type far too well. He was too much like Brogan, her brother Dawg, and her cousins Natches and Rowdy.

Brogan, John, Kota, and Matteo were cut from the same cloth, and to poke into their business was to invite trouble.

No, it was to beg for trouble.

She'd had enough trouble in her life before coming to Somerset to dare invite more. And she had no doubt in her mind that John was up to something. The group of men her brother was close to was always up to something.

She wasn't so certain about Brogan yet, though she had hoped to find out. That aura of danger that surrounded him assured her that not knowing was probably for the best, though. This was as dangerous as she wanted her life to get, she assured herself as she evaded male hands attempting to pat her rear, cup a breast, or convince her to dance.

Her head was beginning to throb like gremlins were attempting to dig out her brains. And the gremlins were beginning to grow.

Glancing back to the table Brogan sat at, Eve saw Sandi running her fingers through his hair as she leaned toward his ear and said something. Eve's temples began to pound even more. Anger was rushing through her, crashing through her system and making her headache worse as she delivered the drinks to the proper table.

"Hey, Eve, that party in the corner is talking about rolling, and I don't see a designated." One of the bouncers stopped her as she delivered drinks to another table. "Should I call a cab?"

"Let me check," she suggested. "Someone came in earlier whom I haven't seen drinking yet."

Moving to the women laughing and gathering their things together, Eve stepped to the table and caught the attention of the newcomer who had arrived late.

Tall, dressed in a pair of knee-length baggy shorts and a T-shirt, the other woman sat back in her chair watching the group with a smile. Her hair was pulled back in a low ponytail, the long excess pulled through the back of the ball cap she wore.

"Hey, Samantha," Eve greeted the detective who had just been hired to work with the Somerset police force. "You designated tonight?"

An amused smile crossed the other woman's strong features as she adjusted the low-profile cap she wore.

"I have them. A friend is waiting outside with another car so we could get them all." Samantha laughed. "Though I'm wondering if I shouldn't just arrest the lot of them."

The women groaned, then laughed as though the detective had just told some incredible joke.

"I'll leave them to you, then." Eve nodded.

"Hey, Evie." One of the partygoers waved at her enthusiastically. "Where's your sister?"

Eve laughed back. "Which one?"

"The one Samantha was asking Mellie about," she replied suggestively, her drunken demeanor more insulting than curious. "Samantha is—"

"Fed up with the drunkards." Samantha rose to her feet, adjusted her cap, and glared back at the others. "Let's go if you're going, or your asses can sit here."

Firm and reminding Eve far too much of the Mackays' tones when they'd gotten tired of the bullshit, Samantha Bryce had the women moving within seconds.

Eve shook her head at the tottering group. She stood aside and watched them make their way to the exit as Samantha herded them along like children.

Poor Samantha and whoever her friend was. Getting those women to their respective homes wasn't going to be done easily.

"You really should give it up and stop casting him those puppy-dog looks."

Turning around slowly, Eve stared back at Sandi, wondering what she had done for karma to want to kick her ass tonight.

"Go away, Sandi," she retorted wearily. She was really getting tired of this crap.

"If he wanted you, he wouldn't be there with us," Sandi stated then.

"Or he could just be waiting for me to get off work." Eve turned back to the other woman, her smile deliberately challenging. "Now, if you'll excuse me . . ."

She didn't wait for Sandi to excuse her or not. Picking up her tray, she moved toward the bar.

"Brogan's not white trash, Eve," Sandi continued behind her.

"You should know, Sandi." What the hell was it going to take to get rid of this woman?

"At least I didn't sell myself to some rich pervert, like your mother did," Sandi stated, disgust heavy in her voice as Eve started to step up from the main floor to the bar area.

Oh, that was it.

Eve swung around so fast, so furiously that Sandi nearly ran into her. The other woman had to back up quickly, nearly tipping and falling on the stilts she called shoes.

"What did you just say to me?" Eve demanded, the anger she had been fighting to keep a rein on all night breaking free.

"Oh, you heard me." Sandi sneered as Eve glimpsed Brogan rising to his feet, his expression suspicious as his gaze locked on her and Sandi. "I might be white trash, but you and your family are nothing but low-class whores."

"Like your opinion matters," Eve mocked.

She wasn't going to resort to violence. There were other ways to finish this, later. Clenching her teeth, she moved to turn away, determined to wait, to bide her time.

This wasn't the place for a confrontation, even for her mother's sake.

Sandi suddenly reached out, gripping her arm as Eve tried to walk away. Eve felt the other woman's nails dig into her arm, breaking skin. A haze of fury rose in her mind, obliterating common sense. The dull ache throbbing at both temples was forgotten as the blood began to rush to her head, fueling the fury rising inside her.

"You might carry the Mackay name, but you're still a no-name little bastard with a tramp for a mother. Brogan doesn't need the likes of you, bitch. You're not part of his world, and he has no desire to be part of yours."

Eve jerked her arm back, feeling the raking talons of the other woman's nails in a distant, hazy part of her consciousness.

Others were watching. She could feel their eyes, their judgment.

She wasn't going to do this here. She hadn't fought in years. She had promised her momma she wouldn't fight unless she had no other choice.

"Get out of my way," she rasped, the need to fight throbbing in her voice. "Or I promise you'll regret it."

"Gonna sic Dawg on me, are you?" Sandi laughed insultingly. "He's so pussy-whipped now he can't find his ass from a hole in the ground, let alone drag his fist out of his wife's snatch. He can't help you."

Oh, God, the other woman was asking for it. She was begging for it.

Why, oh, why had she made that promise to her momma that she wouldn't fight unless she had to? Was she crazy?

She thought she'd try one more time. "Dawg taught me to swat overblown barflies all by my lonesome. If you don't stop fucking buzzing at me, then you're going to find out exactly how he taught me to do it."

As she saw Brogan and Dawg, followed by John, converging on them, she turned to move away again. God, when had Dawg gotten there?

Eve started to turn, Sandi's arm went back, then flew forward, and she backhanded Eve with enough force to throw her into a customer's back and nearly slam his head to the table.

Eve felt her lip split, but not with a sense of pain.

A haze of red descended over her vision as adrenaline crashed through her with a force she had never felt before. Before she could consider her actions, Eve turned, her fist jabbing into Sandi's face.

Right between the eyes.

As the other woman went backward, Eve was on her. She followed her to the floor, her knee slamming into the other woman's chest, holding her in place as she wrapped one hand around her throat and squeezed.

"Stay still, bitch!" she snarled when Sandi went to claw at her face.

To reinforce the order, Eve tightened her hold on the other

woman's neck, her fingers digging into Sandi's windpipe and not letting up until she dropped her hands.

"Insult my mother, my sisters, my brother, or my cousins again—touch me again, bitch, and I'll break your fucking nose. Then I'll damned well ensure those lovely dentures you have screwed into your head require major surgery to repair. Are we clear?"

She could feel the crowd around them.

She could hear them.

Distantly.

She could hear Dawg and Brogan yelling at her. They were cursing, trying to get through the crowd to her, just as the bouncers were.

She was finished with the little piece of trash, though.

Jumping back in a smooth, well-practiced move she still worked at often, Eve landed on her feet just as Dawg and Brogan broke through the crowd across from her.

Her gaze met her brother's—was that disappointment she saw in his eyes? No doubt it was. This was no way to ensure her reputation, her sisters' and her mother's, or his.

Adrenaline was still coursing through her veins, the urge, the hunger to fight flooding her system in such excess that when her gaze locked with Brogan's, it was all she could do not to grab him and stake her claim immediately.

Yet she couldn't.

Tremors were shaking her from the inside out. It wasn't right. She had waited all her life for this, for the knowledge that there was a man out there who could ignite these fires inside her, and now she couldn't have him.

"I'm sorry," she whispered, looking between the two men.

She didn't even know which of them she was apologizing to: Dawg, for wanting the one man he couldn't tolerate knowing she was with, or Brogan, the only man her blood raced for, her clit throbbed for.

Or perhaps it was for herself, because she knew it wasn't the promise she had made Dawg that she was going to end up breaking.

It was the promise she had made to herself.

The promise that at no time would she ever show her brother—the man who had given to her and her family so unselfishly—the least amount of disrespect.

Because she knew the chance of her finding herself in Brogan's bed was growing by the day.

What was he doing to his sister?

The agony burning in her eyes, the color of Natches's and similar to the emotions reflected in their cousin's gaze during those horrendous years he and Rowdy had been certain he would turn up dead, radiated in her gaze. Her face was stark white, blood staining her lip and cheek, the upper curve of one breast, and across her arm.

As she turned and raced from the crowd staring at her in shock, she made the turn around the bar and disappeared into the back rooms, Dawg blew out a hard breath.

Then he turned on Brogan, stopping the other man when he would have followed her by stepping in front of him.

"You've done enough," he rasped, seeing in Brogan's gaze the same swirling emotions, needs, and hungers that he had seen in Eve's. Like Eve's emerald green, the blue-gray color shifted with emotion and fury and a need Dawg knew went soul-deep. He knew because it was the same lashing emotions that had burned in his eyes when he'd thought he would lose his Christa.

"She needs me." The certainty in the other man's voice only sent rage crashing through him.

"She doesn't need you," Dawg retorted furiously. "She doesn't need a traitor, Campbell. She needs a man with honor. Not one willing to trade his soul and his country for a dollar."

It had taken Dawg months to accept that Brogan Campbell was the man described in the reports he'd had pulled up on him. Months of investigation and reaching out to contacts in the highest and lowest levels of the covert world.

Because he'd actually liked him.

Because he remembered the boy Brogan had been when he'd lived in Somerset so many years before, before he joined the Marines, and hadn't wanted to believe the fires that burned in him had turned so dark.

"You don't know me, Mackay." Brogan was all but nose-to-nose with him. "You don't know who I am, what I am, or where my honor lies, and don't fucking pretend to."

He pushed past Dawg, stalking toward the bar before one of the other two men staying at the Mackay Inn stepped in front of him. Jedediah Booker spoke hurriedly, his voice too low for Dawg to catch the words.

Brogan tensed, a curse slipping from his lips before he turned back toward Dawg, then strode past him and headed for the bar's exit.

Now, what the hell was that all about?

When Dawg would have left himself, Donny along with Eve's tormentor, Sandi, began to move past him as well.

Dawg stepped into their path.

He knew these two. Donny and Sandi were usually not much trouble. The girl had always had a mouth on her, but never one so vicious as to cause anyone to attack her. And never had he seen Sandi deliberately go after another woman as she had Eve.

"You looking to make enemies, Donny?" he asked the other man carefully as he glanced at Sandi, disgust welling inside him at the memory of what this woman had pushed his sister into.

"You know I'm not, Dawg." Donny sighed, shaking his head in regret. "This was just a misunderstanding, man."

"I see her around my sister again and you'll pay for it," Dawg informed him. "And you know I can do it, Donny. That is, if I can beat Natches to it."

Donny definitely looked worried now, while Sandi paled fearfully.

Natches's name was synonymous with the bogeyman since the day he had been forced to kill his own cousin Johnny Grace nearly eight years before.

"I told you, I don't want Mackays for enemies," Donny repeated as he pulled at the loose neckline of his T-shirt as though it were choking him.

Sneering at the two in disgust, Dawg pushed past them and moved to the bar, intending on following Eve. Instead, he was brought to a stop as John stepped from behind the bar before he could reach it.

"Sierra's talking to her," John told him, his voice low. "I'll make sure she gets home tonight. Sometimes, as my wife says, a woman just needs another woman to talk to."

There was no loosening the muscles at the back of his neck, but Dawg tried. Reaching around to rub at his nape in frustration, he blew out a hard breath.

"Call me if she needs me," he finally said in irritation before shaking his head helplessly. "Hell, John. How do you survive hurting a sister?"

Because he had hurt her, and he knew it. By making her swear to go against her own instincts and stay away from Brogan, he had a feeling he'd hurt her more than he suspected.

"You let them forgive you and you go on." John finally smiled back at him in compassion. "That's all you really can do."

Clapping him on the shoulder, John turned and went back behind the bar to give the bartenders a hand.

Let her forgive him?

He turned and headed to the exit. He would love to let her forgive him. Unfortunately, he wasn't so certain he deserved it.

FIVE

John's wife, Sierra, was striding furiously through the hall leading to the bar as Eve pushed through it, intent on collecting her purse and leaving. Sierra must have left the bar while she was at the table with the bachelorettes.

Before Sandi had made a fool of her.

Eve didn't want to cry. She hated crying. But as Sierra stopped several feet ahead of her and stared back at her in disbelief, she could feel her throat tightening with the hated dampness.

"I'm sorry, Sierra," she whispered, pushing her hands into the pockets of her jeans as she blinked quickly to hold the moisture back. "I'm just getting my purse. I promise not to try to return."

She knew the rules.

As she had stared into Dawg's eyes after jumping back from where she'd held Sandi to the floor, shame had surged through her.

She hadn't thought about the rules on fighting then. Not until she'd seen Sierra and the fury glittering in her brown eyes.

Shame burned like a cinder in her chest.

When there was a fight anywhere on bar property, then both fighters were banned. The rule made sense. She really could have walked away, but once Sandi had dared to not just insult her mother, but to also use that sissy-bitch move and backhand her, it had been over with.

Besides, jealousy had been eating her alive.

Sandi had been able to sit next to Brogan. To laugh with him. To talk to him without censure, while Eve was restrained by a promise she couldn't break.

"Don't you dare apologize to me, Eve Mackay," Sierra demanded furiously.

The tears fell.

Sierra was a friend, and now she wasn't going to forgive her.

"The fighting rule only applies when I say it does," Sierra continued, moving to her quickly, surprising—actually shocking—Eve as she wrapped her arms around her. "And that rule does not apply to employees whom little bitches like that decide to torment all night."

"What?" Eve shook her head as Sierra drew back, her hands still gripping Eve's shoulders and staring into her face in concern. "I don't have to leave?"

"As if," Sierra said gently, shaking her head. "Eve, that rule rarely applies to employees anyway. Once you get a couple of hundred bodies in one place, drinking and deciding they're more deserving than others, the first person customers take their attitude out on is the waitresses. That's why we have bouncers, and that's why we provide the girls with self-defense classes if they ask for them. Besides, I saw that bitch and her boyfriend watching you, obviously plotting each jibe before it was made."

Eve sniffed, blinking again as she finally forced back the tears.

"I should have ignored her. Or just gone home."

"Come on; we need a glass of wine," Sierra decided as she turned and headed back up the hall. "And you need an ice pack for your cheek. The bitch must have been wearing a ring, because you have a hell of a scratch across it."

Eve lifted the back of her hand to her cheek, then pulled it back to see the smear of blood across it. She couldn't even feel it.

Following Sierra to the office in the back of the building, she sat down on the comfortable leather couch as Sierra went to the refrigerator and pulled out a bottle of wine.

It took her a moment to pull the cork and pour two glasses. Once she did she handed Eve one before taking a seat in the chair across from her, her expression worried as she stared at Eve's face.

"Are you sure you don't want some ice?" she asked, sitting forward in the chair and crossing a leg over the opposite knee to prop her arm on it.

"No." Eve shook her head before sipping at the cold wine. "I'll be fine."

"You surprised me." Sierra grinned. "When I saw how they were taunting you I told Kota to send you back here before I left the bar. I didn't think you'd do anything about it, and I didn't want you having to deal with that viperous bitch while you were helping me and John out of a hard spot. She attacked before Kota could tell you. I cheered when I saw you go after her on the security monitor."

"I should have just escaped back here." Eve sighed. "I promised Momma when we moved here that I would stop fighting. All of us did. We were wild as hell before moving here. At least one of us managed to get into a fistfight just about every day."

Life hadn't been easy before Dawg had taken them in.

"There's only so much you can take." Sierra shrugged. "Besides, she was too jealous to let it go. You've managed to snag a man just about every woman in four counties has been after for years. Congratulations, by the way."

"I haven't captured anyone," Eve denied.

Only in her dreams, in her deepest fantasies.

"The hell you haven't," Sierra said in disbelief. "Eve, that man can't take his eyes off you. Surely you can see that?"

"I didn't say I didn't want him." Eve set her glass on the table before covering her face with her hands for long moments.

Her cheek throbbed. She could feel her busted lip now, the bruise where the inner flesh had been knocked into her teeth.

Her heart was still racing, the adrenaline that had pumped into her system still searching for release.

"God, this situation is going to give me a migraine." She sighed, lowering her hands and staring back at Sierra miserably. "It's impossible, Sierra. For whatever reason, Brogan is the one man Dawg can't abide, and I understand why he feels the way he feels. I just can't believe Brogan would betray anyone, though, let alone his country."

Sierra frowned back at her. "Brogan? A traitor?" She shook her head slowly. "I've heard the rumors, of course, but that's just not Brogan."

"Exactly." Eve flipped her hand out, palm up, before using both hands to rub at her face in frustration. Lowering them again, she picked up the glass of wine, then set it back down. She had to drive home, and the wine would go straight to her head.

"So how do you intend to fight the fact that both of you want each other like crazy?" Sierra asked. "He watches you like a starving man watches dinner."

"I promised Dawg I would stay away from him," she told Sierra miserably, her throat tightening with emotion again. "He's never asked me for anything, Sierra, until now. And he asked me to stay away from Brogan."

"I'm sorry, Eve," she whispered sympathetically. "But really, Dawg had no right to ask that of you."

Eve shook her head. "He told us when we first came here that all he asked was that we never betray ourselves or our family. As far as he's concerned, Brogan has betrayed his country, and to believe in him, to be with him, means I'm tarred with the same brush. To Dawg, that's betraying not just myself, but my family, my friends, and the nation. And to Dawg, that's the worst thing I could do."

It had all been said lovingly, of course. And Dawg had hated saying it to her; she had seen that. But that was how he felt.

"But you don't believe he betrayed his country," Sierra stated.

Eve shook her head. "No, I don't. I can't believe he would do anything so vile, Sierra. He's arrogant, proud as hell, and so damned stubborn he probably makes people want to shoot him. But I can't see him betraying his country."

"And you're in love with him," Sierra said softly. "Aren't you?"

Eve sighed wearily. "I don't know. I know I can't stand the thought of denying myself something I want this badly. But I also know that if that's the problem, then he'll break my heart. There's no doubt in my mind he will. And in turn, I'll break my brother's heart."

Brogan might not mean to. He may hate it, but it wouldn't stop it from happening.

"Do you think you can keep that promise, then?" Sierra asked her.

Eve gave a bitter laugh. "Dawg saved us, Sierra. And I hate myself. I hate myself until I'm sick to my stomach with the fact that the one thing he asked of me seems to be the very thing I can't give him. And he deserves so much more."

Dawg hadn't meant to eavesdrop.

He'd been in the parking lot when Timothy had come around the side of the bar and called him back, bringing him through the side entrance to meet with him and John. What the hell Timothy was doing there, he hadn't yet figured out.

He'd heard Eve's voice as they passed the partially closed door, and stopped just to make sure she was okay.

Now, as he heard the pain in her voice, aching regret filled his chest, he felt like a traitor himself. Hell, he hadn't meant to hurt her, or to make her feel as though she had disappointed him.

He rubbed at the back of his neck again as he turned and followed Timothy up the hall to John Walker's office. Once Timothy closed the door behind him, Dawg leaned against it, crossed his arms over his chest, and glared at the former—he was doubting the resignation story now—Homeland Security special agent and the supposedly unassuming bar manager.

There was too much going on here, he thought.

Suddenly Timothy was lurking in the back offices of Walker's

Run, no doubt because that was one of the only two rooms in the lower levels where the security cameras could be viewed.

When Timothy had texted earlier to meet him there, Dawg had assumed they were meeting in the actual bar, not hiding in the back. And that made sense only if Timothy was conducting an operation.

"What are you up to, you little fucker?" Dawg growled.

Timothy grinned at the insult as though it were a compliment. *Little bastard.*

At least he didn't look like a reject from the CIA anymore. His clothes were actually pressed, his hair combed. And he did smile more now than he had before Mercedes and the girls came into his life. Though Dawg admitted that the thought of Timothy Cranston with then svelte, model-beautiful Mercedes Mackay was just freaky.

"Why do I always have to be up to something?" Timothy asked.

"The last time I asked you that question you called me a suspicious little bastard who needed to go home and get fucked so I wouldn't be so paranoid," Dawg pointed out thoughtfully.

Timothy grimaced good-naturedly.

"Do I have to ask again, or send you home to your girlfriend minus some very important equipment?"

Timothy chuckled at that. "You are too paranoid, Dawg. Even your cousins tell you that."

They did.

"That doesn't mean you're not up to something," he pointed out. "Now, tell me what Brogan Campbell has to do with whatever the hell you're up to, and how do I keep him away from my sister?"

Timothy sighed, then leaned forward, clasping his hands on the desk in front of him.

"Dawg, do you really think it's possible for your sister to be interested in a traitor? Doesn't that go against the Mackay DNA or something?"

"Are you saying he's not a traitor?"

Timothy's eyes widened innocently.

"Innocent" and "Timothy" in the same sentence was damned terrifying.

"How the hell would I know," Timothy protested. "I just thought that, knowing Eve's intuition about people is pretty damned good, it seems funny she could be fooled by a man betraying his country, that's all."

"That's all, huh?"

Timothy nodded with apparent honesty. "That's all." He held his hands out in a gesture of sincerity.

Sincerity and Timothy?

Had he just entered the fucking Twilight Zone?

"You're pulling an op again and you're allowing Eve to be dragged straight into the middle of it. Now tell me what the fuck is going on," Dawg demanded.

"You're asking the same questions I am, Dawg," Timothy admitted. "Who Brogan Campbell really is, and what the hell is going on. What I am fairly certain of, based on the fact that he's lived in the same house I do for the past two and a half years, is that he's no traitor. And I'm fairly certain he's not going to wait much longer before Eve's little heart is torn in two between you and the only man I've seen her interested in since she came here."

Dawg straightened from his position against the door, stalked to the desk, and flattened his hands on the top of it as he leaned forward. "He will get her killed, Timothy. How do you think your lover, her mother, will feel when she finds out you let her walk smack into the middle of this and didn't tell me what the hell is going on?"

Timothy shrugged. "If I knew what was going on, I would of course tell her first. That's her daughter, and Mercedes has an amazing capacity to not just love her children, but also to accept the choices they make."

"Even if one of those choices gets them killed?" Dawg growled.

"That's what we're for." Timothy sighed then. "To keep that from happening." His smile was tinged with acceptance and resignation. "Isn't that what loving them is all about, Dawg? Letting them find out who they are, and doing all we can to protect them as they do?"

"Fuck me." Dawg growled in resignation as he moved back and let himself fall into the chair behind him. "Just let me kill Campbell myself. That would be so much easier."

"Can your conscience handle it, then?" Timothy asked.

"Natches's can," Dawg suggested. And he was certain it could.

"No doubt," Timothy agreed. "But we'll be the ones who will know the truth as she cries. As she haunts the house and wonders what could have been. Is that what we want?"

"She'll be alive," Dawg pointed out logically.

"Will she? Are you sure about that?"

Dawg's lips thinned.

"Would you have been, if something had happened to Christa in that first week after she returned to Somerset?"

No, he wouldn't have been, Dawg admitted. He would have been a dead man walking.

Rising from the chair, he stared down at the Homeland Security agent. "You know what the hell is going on." Dawg was damned certain of it. "If anything happens to her, I'll know whom to discuss it with."

"All we can do is pray, Dawg," Timothy said heavily, the fact that he was worried about her clear in his voice as well as his expression.

Dawg would definitely pray.

His uncle Ray used to tell him, Rowdy, and Natches that praying was good, but God liked to help those who helped themselves.

It was time to back up those prayers with a little old-fashioned action.

Mackay style.

Turning, he stomped from the office without waiting for a reply or an argument. Neither would do any good.

She was his sister.

He hadn't been able to protect her as she was growing up, and he hadn't been able to ensure that her life was lived with at least a measure of security.

He was making up for lost time, and he'd be damned if he would let Brogan Campbell or Timothy Cranston fuck that up.

She should have known he would show up at some point.

On second thought, she *had* known he would show up. She'd actually expected to see him when she'd arrived home.

Stepping from the bathroom, wearing nothing but a towel, she closed the door slowly and stared across the room to where he was sprawled in the easy chair sitting next to the patio door.

As she leaned back against the door, he rose slowly to his feet, the blue-gray of his gaze gleaming in the low light burning next to the chair.

He'd obviously had a shower himself. The jeans he'd worn earlier that night had been exchanged for a lighter pair, the white shirt for a short-sleeved lightweight denim, though the boots were absent entirely, his feet bare. And he still looked far too sexy and far too dressed.

And she was far too underdressed in the large towel she'd wrapped around her body. A body that was becoming far too sensitive as the adrenaline still simmering in her system began to come to a rapid boil.

"Why are you here?" she whispered, fighting the pulsing arousal she had yet to cool.

"I wanted to make certain you were okay." Rising to his feet—her heart began to race furiously—he stalked slowly toward her.

"I'm fine; you can leave now." She really needed him to leave now. Now, before she made the ultimate mistake of jumping his bones.

His lips tilted in a beginning curve of a smile.

"Are you scared, little rabbit?" The amused rasp of his voice sent heat racing through her lower stomach to clench deep inside her womb.

As he came closer, Eve found her grip tightening the towel where it was tucked above her breasts, gripping it with desperate fingers. The heat afflicting her womb flushed her face before racing through her body as the velvet slide of her juices eased from her pussy.

Hell, this wasn't fair—to want him like this, to ache for a man so much, and to have his touch denied her.

He paused in front of her, his hand lifted, the back of his fingers glancing across the tenderness of her cheek.

"It makes me sick, knowing your pretty face has been bruised because of me. Sandi would have never targeted you if she hadn't been aware of my interest." His eyes moved over her face, intent, filled with purpose and regret. "I promise you, though, I'll make sure you never have to worry about Sandi or anyone she knows, ever again."

Shrugging nervously, her breasts rising and falling as she fought to breathe, Eve shook her head slightly. "She just thought she could clear the playing field," she whispered.

"Bullshit," he growled, anger licking at his gaze. "She belongs to Donny, and no matter the rumors about their relationship, there are some rules in the touring club, just because so many couples are so often in such close quarters. One of those rules makes her off-limits to any member of the club as long as she and Donny are together, and she knows it. The rumors of her and Donny taking lovers outside their relationship has never been true that I'm aware of anyway. Besides, she's not the type of woman who draws me, Eve."

Nervous energy had her mouth drying out, her lips aching for moisture—for his kiss—her tongue peeking out to moisten them. Her breasts felt too tight and swollen, her breath catching as Brogan's gaze latched onto the parting of her lips as she fought to draw in air.

"So what type woman does draw you?" she found the breath to ask.

"You draw me, Eve," he answered immediately, his voice low, deep, as dark as sin and sex itself. "More than you know. More than I should have ever allowed."

His hand turned, cupped her cheek, then pushed his fingers

into the hair at her temple, easing back until he could clench the heavy thick strands at the back of her head. The other hand gripped her hip, holding her still as Eve's fingers clenched at the towel with a death grip.

Because she knew what was coming.

Staring up at him, she had plenty of time to say no.

"I promised," she breathed out on a sob instead, torn between this man and a hunger she couldn't deny, and the brother who had saved her and her family's lives. "I promised, Brogan."

Her breathing stalled.

Icy fingers of sensation, internal ghostly caresses feathered over her body, preparing her for his touch.

"What did you promise?" The cropped length of his beard brushed against her cheek, the feel of the closely clipped growth of his mustache rasping against the lobe of her ear as his lips caressed the upper curve. "Did you promise not to be a woman? Not to be hungry for my touch, Eve?"

He brushed a kiss against her ear, moved lower until his lips caressed beneath her jaw, smoothing against skin so sensitive that the feel of his kiss sent tiny explosions of heightened pleasure rushing through her body.

"Brogan . . . please . . ." But what she was begging for even she couldn't say for certain.

Was she begging for release?

Was she begging for more of his touch?

At this point—

His head lifted, his nose rubbing against hers in a gesture that smacked so heavily of affection that Eve was lost.

It wasn't love, but no one . . . no one had ever stared down at her with such hunger in his eyes, such gentleness in his smile, and touched her with such easy affection.

The woman she was couldn't help but reach out for him as the sensualist, normally so well hidden inside her, came out to play, to luxuriate in the added warmth of affection.

When his head tilted, his lips slanting over hers, she had no choice but to accept the deep, stinging kisses and hungry licks. The hunger that raged inside her wasn't for sex. It wasn't just to relieve the lust that burned inside her.

Burning need raged through her body. Equal parts sexual and emotional: the need for touch, for warmth, for that hidden quality that couldn't be faked or practiced overwhelmed her control.

Emotion.

If not love, then affection.

If not forever, then the hope that forever might happen.

Loosening her grip on the towel, Eve slid her hands to his shoulders then behind his neck. One hand slid into the warmth of his hair while the other held tight to his shoulders.

Weakness assailed her, stealing the strength from her knees, sapping the memory of her promise and the will to deny him.

"Eve. Ah, baby," he growled against her lips a second before he lifted her to him.

His hips jerked into hers, the heavy ridge of his erection pressing firmly against the intimate mound between her thighs. The feel of the towel loosening from between her breasts brought only a second's thought before it was pushed away.

She would remember why she wasn't supposed to let him touch her when the cold light of day burned away the sensual illusions he was weaving around her.

For now—for this moment and this man—she needed just a little time, just a night to prove to herself that when morning did come, she would still be the woman she was now.

Brogan's kisses became deeper, more drugging, filling her with such a sense of overriding hunger that nothing mattered but his touch and touching him.

Her hands slid to his broad chest, her fingers shaking, clenching in the material of his shirt. Sensual, sexual intoxication dragged her deeper into the chaotic needs rising inside her, refusing to allow her to think or to control the hunger raging through her.

The feel of Brogan's hand sliding along the naked skin of her hip, caressing its way higher until it rested just beneath her breast, was like pouring an accelerant on the fires already raging out of control inside her.

Her fingers unclenched, trembling; she was desperate to touch him. Struggling with the buttons of his shirt, her hips shifted against his, the ache between her thighs building.

The heavy erection pressing against her had her body reacting with feminine demand, with a need to feel him hot and naked against her, taking her, driving into her with the power and fierce heat she could feel throbbing beneath his jeans.

As the last button slipped free, she pushed at the material, forcing it over his shoulders and whimpering beneath his kiss when the garment would go no farther.

A second later his hands cupped her rear and then turned and strode the few feet to the bed. His kiss never paused; the hunger raging through it never dimmed. When her back met the mattress his head lifted, forcing her eyes to open, her hands to tighten around his neck to bring him back to her.

He wasn't leaving her, as she had feared.

His lips traveled instead to her jawline, then beneath it, moving down the column of her neck as it arched back, an agony of pleasure attacking her senses as his teeth raked against her flesh. His tongue licked and stroked, playing with her nerve endings and sending sensations racing through them. His lips kissed, took fiery tastes of her skin at intervals, and moved lower with each kiss as she arched to him.

Chaos clashed with the pleasure rising through her system as need burned through her senses. Lying naked beneath him, Eve was aware of every point of contact as the material of his jeans brushed against her thighs and hips. The rasp of chest hair brushed across her nipples, sensitizing them further.

His hand was at her hip, holding her still as she tried to move beneath him; she was desperate for some point of contact against the swollen, aching bud of her clit.

A whimper escaped her as her nails bit into his shoulders, the feel of his knee suddenly pressing between hers and driving the hard muscle of his thigh against her pussy dragged a startled cry from her lips.

Her juices trickled from her vagina, saturating the folds beyond and spilling a heated layer of slick warmth along her clitoris as she rubbed herself against his thigh. The stimulation against the bundle of nerves sent shards of sharpened sensation exploding to her womb. The driving need for more—more touch, more sensation—rose inside her with a burning force.

Heat brushed against the curves of her breasts; the rasp of his beard rubbing against the tender skin sent her hands searching between their bodies and finding his belt.

She wanted him naked. She wanted bare skin meeting bare skin from breast to ankle.

His lips brushed against the outer curve of her breast, kissed it in passing, then eased higher, his tongue probing, licking, searching—

"Oh, God. Oh, God. Brogan." She gasped, arching to him as

his lips surrounded the tight, violently sensitive peak and sucked it into the heated depths of his mouth.

Liquid flames surrounded it.

The heated stroke of his tongue against the nerve endings gathered there sent pure ecstasy racing to her womb, her clit, exploding inside them and driving the need tearing through her higher.

Eve tore his belt loose. Her fingers tugged at the metal buttons of his jeans. Pulling and tugging, she struggled with them until they were free, pushing aside the material before freezing in shock. A harsh moan escaped her as her hands found the long, broad length of his cock as it rose between his thighs. The flared crest was slightly damp, the shaft throbbing, pounding with the blood racing through the heavy veins just beneath the silken flesh that stretched tight over the iron strength.

There were too many sensations.

She felt a roughened heat against her nipple as he sucked at first one delicate tip, then the other. With thumb and forefinger he gripped the other peak, tugging and milking it with his fingers as electric forks of sensation slapped at her clit with each stroke.

She fought to breathe. She fought to understand the force of the sensations whipping out of control and blazing through her senses, and couldn't seem to do it.

As his hand moved from her breast and slid down her waist, over her abdomen, then tucked between her thighs as his knee eased back, Eve knew she was doomed.

Right here in this bed on this sultry summer night, she lost herself.

And she wasn't entirely certain she would be able to find herself once the pleasure was over.

SIX

Eve never imagined pleasure could be this extreme.

She'd never before had her control stripped by a kiss or a little heavy petting.

She'd never lost herself to the point that a man had actually managed to get his hands between her thighs, or to the point that she was so wet, so wild, that nothing mattered but Brogan's touch. She'd been waiting for this. For a pleasure so extreme she couldn't deny it or the man giving it to her. Until Brogan, that hadn't happened.

His fingers slipped through the thick layer of juices that gathered between the folds of her pussy. As they slid through the narrow slit, he parted the inner lips, his thumb pressing against her clitoris as he rubbed the clenched entrance with his fingers.

Lifting closer, desperate for his touch, aching for more, Eve whimpered at the heat flooding her senses and the driving hunger spurring it. She parted her thighs further, her hips shifting, arching to him, the feel of his mouth devouring her nipple as his thumb pressed against her aching clit dragging a low, harsh cry from her throat.

Suckling, licking, rasping the hardened peak of her breast, Brogan began to ease the tips of two fingers inside her. The feel of the entrance parting, stretching, her juices flowing to meet his touch suspended her breath for precious seconds.

Her fingers clenched in his hair as a gasp burst from her lips. It was all she could do to keep from screaming with the pleasure.

Sinking, falling deeper into the rapture surrounding her, Eve gave herself to the drowning sensations. So much so that when the sharp knock against her patio door exploded through the room, she wasn't entirely certain what it was, or where it was coming from at first.

Brogan's head jerked up and turned to the doors as Eve stared back at him, dazed.

The knock came again.

"Eve, are you awake?" Dawg called out. "I know you are; the light's on, sweetie. Come on; I just want to talk to you for a minute."

The sound of her brother's voice was like cold water suddenly surrounding her body.

Oh, God, what had she done?

Staring up at Brogan, she was suddenly horrified. The thought that she was betraying Dawg, betraying every belief he had in loyalty to one's country and defending their freedom, rushed through her.

If he found Brogan here he would never forgive her.

If he had been disappointed in her before, how much more would he be now?

"Come on, Eve; just talk to me for a minute," he called out again as Brogan moved back from her, his jaw clenching, his blue-gray eyes flickering with frustration.

Jerking his shirt from the floor, he tossed the towel to her bed and hurriedly moved to the door connecting the bedroom to the sitting area.

Jumping from the bed, Eve grabbed her robe from the tall dressing screen on the other side of her bed and quickly pulled it on, tying it as she rushed to the patio door.

She opened the door just enough to face him, glaring at him, uncertain whether it was Dawg or herself she was suddenly angry with.

"Don't you ever sleep, Dawg?" she questioned him, hearing the roughness in her voice, feeling the heat that still flushed her body, and terrified he'd realize what she had been doing.

The look in his eyes sent guilt tearing through her.

He looked as miserable as she had felt at the bar. His celadon eyes were a shade darker, still such a light color it was hard to tell whether they were green or a very light blue or gray in the dim light of the room.

A heavy frown pulled at his brow as he reached back, rubbed at his neck, and sighed wearily.

"I couldn't go home without checking on you," he admitted. "I had to make sure you were okay."

"I'm fine, Dawg," she said with a sigh, her chest tightening with such regret and pain that the ache actually tugged at her heart. "But isn't it a little late for a married man such as yourself to be running the roads?"

A heavy expulsion of breath met her question. "Some things can only be done at night, it seems." He grinned back at her. "But this couldn't wait."

"Well, as you can see, I'm fine."

He shook his head, ran the fingers of one hand through his hair, then propped both hands at his hips before sliding them into the back pockets of his jeans.

Damn, her brother was nervous. She had never seen Dawg nervous.

"You know," he finally said roughly, "I was damned proud of you tonight at the bar. You kept your head and didn't let Sandi goad you with her insults. But once she struck, you took care of things damned well, Eve. I worry, you know."

He looked away from her for a second, clearly not finished.

"Why?" she asked anyway.

"I worry about you and your sisters," he admitted. "That somehow you'll get hurt, seriously hurt, because I might not be where you need me. Or because someone decided to go on a rampage wherever you are. Knowing you have the ability to defend yourself makes me breathe a little easier. I'll sleep a little better."

God, he was serious.

The surge of thankfulness that he even thought about her while she wasn't in his sight rushed through her. It was almost as strong as the guilt tearing her apart now that Brogan was no longer touching her.

"Dawg, I try to be careful," she promised him. "And I know Piper, Lyrica, and Zoey do as well. You, Rowdy, and Natches have taught us to fight and how to use our heads. The rest of it is up to us. You can't watch us twenty-four/seven."

He nodded slowly, looked away again for long moments, then turned back to her.

He cleared his throat. "About Brogan—"

"No." Eve gave her head a hard shake as her hand clenched on the side of the door. "I can't talk about Brogan, Dawg. Please."

This was tearing her apart. It was destroying her as nothing ever had. As nothing ever could. Guilt at her deception, at the knowledge that Brogan was standing just on the other side of the door between her bedroom and the sitting room, dug into her heart. It was like a lance piercing her soul, the knowledge that she was breaking her word to the only person who had ever given a damn about her besides her mother and sisters.

Dawg knew guilt when he saw it. Just as he knew the agony of thinking, believing something that should have been his never would be.

The day Christa had told him she had lost their baby when she had been little more than a teenager, that summer she had run from Somerset. He'd felt it then. Felt his soul being sliced in two with a jagged blade.

That was the pain he saw in Eve's eyes now as nervous guilt darkened them.

How could he tell her he hadn't meant for her to believe she was betraying him with Brogan without effectively giving her permission or the go-ahead to have a man he knew would endanger her?

She would become a weakness to Brogan as well. A man doing what Dawg suspected Brogan was doing couldn't afford such a thing. A woman like Eve could break a man's soul when she was harmed because of his job or something he was doing. But even more, it would destroy Dawg and ensure that he killed Brogan himself.

"You know, Eve," he finally said, "I've always been proud of you, and I've always been proud to call you my sister."

She stared back at him, the pain in her expression only intensifying as she looked away from him, blinking.

"You'll always be my sister, Eve," he tried again, knowing he was failing.

"Thank you, Dawg," she whispered, nodding as she stared back at him. "That means more to me than you know."

He pushed his hands deeper into his pockets. Maybe he should have brought Christa with him.

"I'm really tired, Dawg." Those were tears in her voice.

He sharpened his gaze on her face, catching the glitter of moisture in her eyes, and cursed himself. He could kick himself if he could reach his own ass, he thought. Son of a bitch, what was he doing to her? Was this the kind of father he was going to be?

His sisters were practice, he'd always said. Lately, all he'd done was make them cry.

"I don't want to see you hurt, Eve," he tried again. Pulling his hands from his pockets, he laid them on her shoulders, forcing her to stare back at him. "Sometimes, just because our instincts might be right about the person, they're not always right about whether or not we can trust our hearts to them, you know?"

"Please, Dawg." She stepped back from him slowly. "Go home to your wife and daughter. Get some sleep. I'm all tucked into bed, safe and sound. No one's going to hurt me tonight."

No, she didn't understand.

He breathed out in irritation and self-disgust.

Yeah, this was a job for Christa.

"I'll do that." He sighed. "Get some sleep, Eve."

"Good night, Dawg."

Stepping back, she closed the door, and a second later the sliver of light at the side of the heavy curtains covering the glass blinked out.

Dawg shook his head, paused, then turned on his heel and forced himself to walk to the main porch entrance where he'd parked.

Once he reached the steps, he paused.

Eyes narrowed, he looked around slowly.

Something wasn't right. . . .

Brogan stepped back into the room, finding Eve as she stood by the patio doors. Her head was lowered, the midnight black silk of her hair falling around her face as he watched her shoulders tremble for a second.

He could shoot Dawg.

The son of a bitch just didn't know when to leave well enough alone.

"I can't keep doing this." Eve shook her head as she lifted it before moving across the room to where he stood.

Walking past him, she jerked the door open and stalked into the other room of her suite before turning to face him.

"Afraid he'll be watching for me?" he asked, unable to keep the mockery out of his voice.

"He's suspicious." She lifted her shoulders in a shrug. "I don't want him to know I broke my promise to him, Brogan. Until I decide what's more important, how my brother feels or what you want from me, then I can't keep doing this."

Crossing his arms over his chest, he frowned down at her. "Have you asked me what I want from you, Eve?" Hell, no, she hadn't. But she didn't have a problem making decisions about what he wanted from her without his input, it seemed.

"I'm not ready to know," she admitted, and that only pissed him off further. "But I do know that Dawg has never asked me or my sisters and mother for anything. Not a damned thing, Brogan, for taking us in and securing our lives and our futures. Everything we have and everything we are, we owe to him. And all he's ever asked is that I stay away from you until you can prove you're not the man his contacts say you are."

There, it was all out in the open now.

His jaw clenched in anger as he glared back at her, wondering whether she believed the rumors or believed in herself and her instincts.

"And what kind of man do his contacts report I am?" he asked carefully.

"That you've betrayed your country," she whispered, her expression so filled with hunger, need, and pain that she tempted him to paddle her ass and show her what she could believe in.

"Do you think I betrayed my country?"

It wouldn't matter about the reports or what she believed. He was going to have her. Tonight had proven to him that without his protection right now, certain people would consider her fair game simply because it was known he was interested. Donny and Sandi had made the first strike, but Brogan knew his interest in her was well known. If the men he was searching for suspected he was a government agent, then it could be much worse.

Even more important, he had to get this operation behind them so he could find the time and the space he needed to figure out what she was to him as well.

"It doesn't matter what I think, Brogan," she whispered. "It's what Dawg thinks he knows."

"And you always obey your brother?" He knew he wasn't being fair to her, but by God, she was his. She was going to have to make a choice, and she was going to have to make it soon.

"It's not that simple."

"I'm making it that simple," he growled as she turned and jerked the bedroom door open.

"That doesn't mean I'll follow along," she retorted, the emerald of her eyes lighting with an inner flame that only made his dick harder. Only made him want her beneath him more.

He wasn't going to argue this with her five minutes after her brother had left. No doubt Dawg had already suspected he was there, and he'd said just what he'd known he needed to. His object was to keep Eve from sleeping with Brogan, and tonight he'd achieved his objective.

"We'll discuss this. Soon," he warned her, stomping to the patio door.

Eve stared up at him, seeing the promise in his eyes and almost shivering at the latent dominance and pure demand in his look.

Her lips parted to argue, to inform him that they'd discuss it when she was ready, when a sudden, horrified scream pierced the house.

The layout of the house put the kitchen directly across from her and Brogan, on the other side of the house. There were two halls leading from the kitchen to each wing. The shortest distance to the kitchen was the narrow hall just outside Brogan's room that opened directly into the kitchen.

Before the scream was silenced, she and Brogan both were running.

He made damned sure she didn't get ahead of him as they turned into the hall, knowing there would be no room for her to do so once they reached the narrow passageway, she noticed.

They had no more turned into the hall than another scream shattered the silence of the night, and the sounds of her sisters yelling through the house could be heard.

Terror pierced Eve's mind as they shot into the kitchen and raced for the open back door. She was terrified of what they would find, knowing her mother was not a woman who frightened easily.

As they pushed out the door to the back porch, Eve came to a hard, sudden stop.

Her eyes widened, horror filling her as she felt her stomach pitch at the sight.

The back part of the wooden porch that surrounded the house was covered in blood, entrails, and body parts of the dozen or more fat rabbits her mother bred and used for the dinner table.

As with the chickens in the chicken house that provided eggs and meat, the turkeys and occasional duck her mother raised, and the deer she convinced Dawg to take her hunting for each year, Mercedes Mackay was known for her fresh meats, like venison during holidays and special occasions.

The rabbits represented five years' work with only a few of the plump animals actually making it to the dinner table.

Mercedes and Eve had raised the four babies she'd bought, and from there began breeding them. Now they were gone in the most horrific manner that Eve could have imagined.

She didn't always agree with her mother's entirely pragmatic approach to food. Mercedes had learned to appreciate more than store-bought meats as a child. And growing up, Eve and her sisters had often been more than grateful for her mother's ability to prepare wild game. Though Eve herself found she much preferred buying her meat from the grocer rather than raising it herself.

Now, staring at the porch, seeing the blood and mutilated carcasses of the animals that had been penned close to the house to ensure that no predators attacked them, Eve well understood why her mother was screaming.

Mercedes had been screaming for Timothy and her daughters, terrified that if someone had been brazen enough to come onto her porch and do something so horrific, then her family could be in danger as well.

Timothy and, surprisingly, Dawg had made it to the back porch ahead of Brogan and Eve. Behind her, she could hear her sisters' gasps, then the silence that filled the room.

"Why would anyone do this?" Her mother was furious.

Turning on Timothy as he held her to him, his gaze hard, cold as he stared at the carnage, Mercedes demanded an answer. "Timothy, why would they do this?"

Timothy could only shake his head before his gaze turned to Dawg, then Brogan.

Brogan had separated himself from the other two men. Enough distance was left between them that Eve had the feeling that he was ensuring that no one could ever mistake him and the other two men for friends.

Who would care?

"Are they pets?" Brogan asked her, his voice low.

Eve shook her head. "We get a lot of hunters as guests. She breeds them for when they stay."

The hunters often swore they came more for Mercedes's preparation of the wild meat than they did for the hunting.

The look in Brogan's eyes was so hard, so frigid, Eve actually shivered.

Casually, Brogan leaned against the side of the house, pulled a pack of the slim cigars he smoked from his shirt pocket, and lit one up.

"I guess you don't know anything about this, right, Brogan?" Dawg snarled as his head swung around.

Several other guests had moved out to the porch, following Mercedes's screams.

It was almost dawn, and most people were asleep, but the guests on Eve's side of the house had obviously been awake.

The two single men, Jed Booker and Eli Grant, stood at the other end of the porch, their eyes on the bloody destruction spread out before them.

"I want everyone to stay as far back as possible," Timothy ordered as he led Mercedes into the house.

Eve slid to the other side of the door as he did so, turning to go in.

Her mother was immediately surrounded by Piper, Lyrica, and Zoey as they led her to the other side of the kitchen and began preparing coffee. Their move allowed her to ensure that she heard whatever the men decided to discuss.

Eve could feel the tension in the air.

Unless they were standing exactly where Eve was, no one could have seen the looks that passed between Timothy, Dawg, and Brogan. But Eve saw them.

Brogan might be giving the impression of distance, but the look they shared assured Eve that they were all three on the same wavelength at the moment.

"Campbell, you and the other guests should return to your rooms," Timothy ordered.

"Looks like a fox ignored the henhouse and went for the rabbits instead," Jed commented as he scratched at his chest through the jersey jacket he wore.

Jeans and a jersey jacket wasn't exactly summer attire, she thought.

He'd pushed the sleeves to his elbows and put his hands in the pockets as he leaned against the corner of the house and stifled a yawn.

Eli didn't say a word, just continued to watch out of hazel eyes that seemed darker in the low light. Finally he gave a slow nod toward the three men before turning and heading back down the hall.

A moment later, Jed yawned again. "I'm going to get ready for work," he finally stated. "By the time I get back to bed it's going to be time for breakfast." He paused, his sharp gaze turning on Eve. "We still having breakfast?"

She almost grinned. She would have, if her imagination and her fear weren't in overdrive.

"Knowing Mom, I'll say yes." She nodded.

"See you then." He turned and disappeared, leaving Eve alone with Timothy, Dawg, and Brogan.

"This wasn't a fox," Eve stated, keeping her voice low as she stared at each man in turn before pausing as she caught Brogan's eye. "Was it?"

Brogan shrugged, but she could see a warning in his eyes, in his expression, as he watched her.

"Whatever it was, it won't be back tonight," Dawg growled. "I'll get Natches later today and get some security cameras up out here. That way we catch the fox doing this and put it out of its misery." His voice hardened.

"You're not calling Alex?" Eve demanded, speaking of Somerset's chief of police and one of Dawg, Rowdy, and Natches's best friends.

"Killing a rabbit isn't a crime, Eve." Dawg sighed. "And if it was a fox—and they are prone to indiscriminately kill—then how is Alex going to help?"

This was no fox kill. Eve had seen a fox go after chickens and kill them, and she had never seen carnage like this. There was that warning in Brogan's gaze, though, as well as Dawg's. A warning to watch what she said.

"Go inside, Eve." Brogan's voice was so low, the tone so dark, that she found herself doing just that.

Casting them all a look filled with irritation, she stepped into the kitchen with her mother and sisters, gritting her teeth as she closed the door carefully behind her.

"Why are you still here?" Dawg demanded, not bothering to lower his tone or attempt to hide what he was saying as he looked up from where he was crouched on bent knees to study the porch.

"I'm nosy." Brogan didn't bother to lower his voice either. "It's not every day I get to see a fox's kill, you know."

Dawg snorted at the comment.

"They're watching you." This time Dawg's voice carried no farther than Brogan's and Timothy's ears.

Lifting the cigar to his lips to hide his reply from anyone watching now, Brogan stated, "Yeah, they are."

"Retaliation?" Dawg questioned.

Would Donny and Sandi go to these lengths?

"I'll find out," Brogan promised.

And he would.

If Donny and Sandi were behind this—and he didn't doubt in the least that they could be—then it wouldn't happen again.

He'd show the two and anyone else what would happen if Eve was struck at again.

They were testing him; he could feel it.

Doogan had warned him when Eve's name had first come up that there could initially be problems. There were those who would do anything to keep her brother from getting involved in their business. That was one of the things that made Eve so important to the operation at this point. The second and even more important reason was the report that someone had information that could clear this case up, and only Eve could convince them to come out of hiding.

The minute the rumors had started that Brogan was interested in her, the report had hit Doogan's desk. A confidential informant had contacted Doogan claiming that the thefts of military files were linked to something far bigger than DHS realized, and there was information that someone had answers besides the thieves. Someone that might be convinced to come forward if he thought Eve Mackay was in danger.

A year of investigation and still they hadn't figured out which of Eve's friends could possibly know about the thefts, let alone know why the files were being stolen.

"What are you going to do?" Dawg murmured, as he seemed to still be studying the death spread across the porch.

Timothy was still silent, but the calculating rage that burned in his eyes assured Brogan that his silence didn't bode well for whoever was behind the bloody mess Mercedes had walked out to.

"Go hunting," Brogan answered just as quietly. "For fox."

SEVEN

Brogan and his partners, Jedediah and Eli, entered the house Donny and Sandi shared in the mountains. There was no proof that the two were behind the destruction of the animals Mercedes and Eve had raised, but as they neared the bedroom, Brogan heard all the proof he needed.

Pausing outside the door, Brogan listened to them gloating about the blood the rabbits had shed and the mess they made. They had often seen Eve petting them and letting them out into the wire enclosure where she played with them.

That made their crime much worse, because they believed the rabbits were Eve's pets.

"Did you see how horrified she was?" Sandi drawled. "I thought she was going to puke." The obviously fake sympathy in her tone had his fists clenching in rage.

"Now, that would have been a real mess," Donny drawled.

Brogan could feel fury boiling inside him, white-hot and destructive; Eve would have never struck out at Sandi in such a way, no matter what she had done.

But Sandi had killed what she believed were pets, because Eve had bested her in a fight.

Pulling his mask into place, Brogan looked at Jed and Eli where they had taken position across from him. Holding up three fingers to indicate three seconds before bursting into the room, he counted down.

Three.

Two.

One.

Eli went in first.

With a hard kick from Eli's size-twelve boot, the bedroom door flew off the hinges as he and Jed rushed into the room and grabbed a nearly naked, clearly shocked Sandi from the bed.

In a second flat Sandi was restrained, her hands secured to the wooden arms of a nearby chair, her eyes wide as she stared up at Eli in mortal fear while Jed took his position on the far wall, the short, lethal barrel of the automatic weapon trained on her.

Donny just played stupid.

The little bastard actually thought he was tough enough to take his attackers on, and threw a punch at Brogan's jaw.

Brogan bitch-smacked him—an insulting backhanded slap across the face, as Sandi had used on Eve. He'd been enraged when he'd seen Sandi deliver that blow to Eve's face. He wondered how well Donny enjoyed the same insult.

The other man fell against the wall from the slight force. Hell, this wasn't going to be any fun—

Brogan smiled in delight as Donny straightened.

Maybe the little bastard had some fight in him after all. He damn sure had a wicked as hell bowie knife. Brogan had half suspected he'd gotten his nickname from Poppa Bear for just this reason.

"I know who you are," Donny screeched, the high-pitched cry sounding a little girlish. "I'm gonna cut you, Brogan; I'm gonna cut you bad."

Give me a break.

Chuckling, Brogan smiled back at the other man with confident mockery before lifting his hand and curling his fingers in an insulting "come on" wave.

"Fucking cunt," Donny screamed as he took a swipe at Brogan's midsection.

Brogan moved back easily, testing Donny's abilities once or twice. The blade actually came a little too close for comfort as he got a feel for Donny's actual experience.

Brogan had certainly fought much better opponents with a much higher level of experience. But Donny was piss-his-pants scared, and that made a hell of a difference.

Pressing forward only to step to the side, Brogan caught the other man in midswipe with the knife before striking out himself. With the flat of his hand he slapped Donny again, laughing as the other man's nose started to bleed.

"Motherfucker!" Sandi screamed out as Donny growled like an enraged bull.

Dancing back from the blade, Brogan waited, feigning one way, then dancing back, staying on the move as Donny let rage and fear drive him.

Donny jabbed the knife toward his belly.

Brogan jabbed his fist into Donny's face, busting both lips and laughing as Donny spit out pieces of his teeth.

He swiped at Brogan's arm, and the blade actually managed to skim the material of the black shirt he wore. The long sleeve covered his arm to the wrist, the protective weave of the material holding out against the glancing brush of the blade.

Donny snarled, enraged.

Brogan grinned, waited, then boxed both Donny's ears as the other man took his next swipe before Brogan spun away.

This was fun and all, but he was getting bored. Donny was actually shedding tears and snot, he was so pissed at being unable to shed blood.

Besides, Brogan wanted to get at least a few hours' sleep tonight. If he kept fucking around with this little weasel, then there was no way he would have time for it.

Brogan waited.

When Donny moved to slice out at his midsection again, Brogan caught his fist and twisted it hard as he angled the hand back forcefully and collected the knife from Donny's suddenly numb fingers.

Donny emitted a screech that would have done Sandi proud if she had made it herself.

Before he could struggle or attempt to get away, Brogan thrust his arm behind his back and laid the razor-sharp blade at Donny's throat.

"I like the sight of blood, too," Brogan rasped, his voice well disguised by the electronic box secured at his throat. "Tonight I want your blood."

"Please don't. Oh, God, please don't hurt him!" Sandi cried out, real tears filling her voice and falling from her eyes.

Hell, she might really love the bastard, Brogan thought as she sobbed out Donny's name and pleaded for his life.

"Muzzle that shit," he ordered Eli as he stroked the knife against Donny's throat warningly.

Glancing in the mirror across the room, he saw Donny as he watched Eli's black-clad form tear a strip of duct tape from the roll he'd pulled out of the mission pack on his back.

Rage burned in Donny's eyes as Eli taped his lover's mouth, then patted her cheek with gentle mockery.

"Shall I have him slice her throat, or do I slice yours?" Brogan asked softly at Donny's ear, still watching the other man's face in the mirror.

Donny swallowed tightly, and Brogan was certain what his answer would be.

The regret, the seeming apology as he stared back at his lover was all a dead giveaway that Donny would save himself.

Sandi was shaking her head desperately, sobbing through the tape, no doubt certain she was going to die.

"Answer me, Donny," he demanded, rubbing the blade against his throat in whispery strokes, "One of you is going to die. You or her?"

Tears fell from Donny's eyes as Sandi became almost hysterical.

"Me," he answered.

Sandi's chair almost tipped over before Eli could catch it as hysteria overtook her.

"I don't think I heard you, Donny." He held the knife motionless against the man's throat. "Say it again."

Donny was staring at his lover in misery as she screamed through the tape again, still sobbing uncontrollably. He hadn't even noticed that Brogan was watching him through the mirror.

"Me," Donny answered, his voice louder, strangely devoid of fear. "Kill me; don't hurt her."

Sandi bent forward, sobbing, screaming through the tape, jerking hysterically against the ropes that held her as jagged cries tore from her chest.

Brogan looked at Eli, the other man's eyes reflecting the same shock Brogan felt. Sandi was protesting so hysterically Eli actually had to hold the chair in place.

"You're going to sacrifice yourself for her?" Brogan asked in mocking disbelief. "Why? She's not faithful. She whores around on you—"

"Don't call her that," Donny protested raggedly as Brogan watched his expression thoughtfully while watching Sandi from the corner of his eye.

Hell, they loved each other.

"Tell me why," Brogan demanded again.

"Because I'll die anyway if you kill her," he stated, confusing Brogan with his suddenly calm demeanor. "I couldn't live without her."

"So you risk her life thieving? You pimp her out and keep her in harm's way here while committing treason?" he probed while he had the chance. "That's not love, Donny."

"I love her." It wasn't a protest or an argument. It was a statement. Then he frowned, confused. "I ain't no traitor, man."

"So you love the woman you let other men screw for money?" Brogan ignored the protest.

"I love her," Donny snapped, meeting his gaze directly. "And she's no whore. Sandi screws no man but me. I know what she does. She flirts and she teases a little. Then she gives them a few sleeping pills while I steal their money. She doesn't screw them."

"You endanger her in whatever moneymaking schemes you can come up with. That's not love."

"I love her."

Brogan whispered the next accusation sneeringly. "You use her; you don't want to die for her."

"I love her." Donny's voice cracked in misery. "I love her."

Son of a bitch, go figure.

"Donny?"

"What?" He sniffed, swallowing tightly.

"Do you want to live another day with the woman you love?"

Donny nodded slowly. "Yes."

"Then listen to me carefully." Brogan hardened his voice. "If either of you, at any time—tomorrow, next week, next year, fucking next lifetime," he snarled, "should verbally or physically or through someone else strike out at Eve Mackay again, I won't give you a choice; I'll just come after your woman."

Donny's eyes widened in shock.

"If you so much as breathe Eve's air, brush against her, or even think to insult her, her family, her friends, hell, her fucking enemies, then I'll come after your lover. When I do, I'll make what happened to those rabbits seem humane. You read me, asshole?"

"I hear." He snarled as Brogan nicked his neck with the blade.

"If Eve Mackay or Brogan Campbell learns anyone was here tonight, learns you were threatened in any way, coerced to act decent, then I'll come for her," he whispered insidiously. "And if I hear so much as a breath that you have information concerning thieves and traitors and didn't tell me, then I'm coming after her. Read me."

"I hear you." Donny's voice was barely a whisper now.

"If I find out you heard any of the above and you didn't contact me, I'll bathe in her blood. You got it?"

"How?" Donny swallowed tightly. "Contact you how?"

"You left your cell phone in the kitchen," Brogan reminded

him. "There's a new number in it. Now I'll ask you one more time: Do you know anything?"

Donny and Sandi stared at each other for long moments. Nodding to Eli, Brogan watched as he pulled the long, wickedly sharp knife from the sheath at his thigh and laid it against Sandi's neck.

"Wait. Wait," Donny whispered.

Eli lifted the knife marginally from Sandi's throat—just enough that it wasn't touching her skin.

"Come on, Donny," Brogan urged him. "What do you know?"

"The thieves are part of the touring club," he revealed. "Some say it's Brogan Campbell."

"Is it?" Brogan asked.

Fear flickered in Donny's eyes. "I don't think so. I think it's someone else, but I don't know who. Someone who used to be in that group with Chandler and Dayle Mackay."

"The Freedom League?" Brogan asked, his gaze flickering to Eli. This was the first they had heard this.

"Yeah, that Freedom League." Donny swallowed again, obviously terrified, but more terrified of losing his lover.

Luck was with him tonight, Brogan thought. He'd never imagined that coming here to beat the shit out of the little bastard over some rabbits would end up with information on the very investigation he'd been working for two and a half years now.

"You know something else, Donny," Brogan stated smoothly, confidently.

He could see it in the other man's eyes every time his gaze met his lover's.

"Just talk, that's all," Donny wheezed. "There's talk that the files Brogan Campbell stole are really important. They have coordinates in them for something. Something that the League wants."

"And where did you hear this talk?"

"I was outside at the bar one night, snortin' a little somethin'—somethin'," he said nervously.

"I don't care what you were doing," Brogan stated softly. "What did you hear?"

"Some dude was takin' a call." Donny's voice lowered as though he were afraid others might hear him. "I don't know who it was. He was pissed; he said Brogan had to be behind it because they were searching for the same thing. He said he knew it was Brogan Campbell. That only Campbell had a reason to want those files or the information in them."

Sandi was still crying, though not as hard.

"What's Brogan Campbell searching for?" he asked as though he didn't know.

Desperation filled Donny's gaze now. "I don't know," he rasped. "I swear to God, I don't know."

"What have you heard, then?" Brogan asked.

Donny licked his lips nervously, his gaze seeking Sandi's again. Sandi gave the barest nod.

"Come on, Donny; don't make my friend over there hurt her, okay? Neither you nor Sandi would like it."

Donny's gaze flickered nervously. "When Brogan showed up he got real interested in this motorcycle touring club we have. The dude said who they were lookin' for was there. They just don't know who he is. But he can read some files they have, and they think Brogan has the other files. He said Brogan was the only one with the background and experience to steal them, too. He said this dude they want can read them. Then, when I was in Fort Knox a few weeks later, there were these dudes at the bar I

went to, they was talkin' 'bout Dawg and Eve's daddy. They said
there was talk circulatin' heavy that there were files their daddy
worked on while he was in some federal agency he worked for
that hid the location on somethin', and those files were stolen.
Talk was maybe Dawg would know what that somethin' was,
and the only way to find out would be to use his sisters to scare
him, but no one can go after a Mackay, 'cause if they did, then
whoever that dude is that can read those files also has lots of
information on that Freedom League and if any Mackay, or anyone that any Mackay loves is threatened, then he's gonna talk.
And he's gonna tell all these secrets he has on that Freedom
League. And they don't want him talkin' 'cause word is, he
knows everything. Who wasn't caught, who's still hidin', and lots
of other stuff."

Bingo. So that's why Doogan wants Eve.

"Anything else, Donny?" he questioned softly. "Come on,
anything else?"

"I swear that's all." He whimpered. "I swear that's all. I
swear."

Brogan lifted the knife from Donny's neck and released him
slowly.

Donny stepped back quickly, his gaze seeking his lover's.

"You hear anything else, Donny, use the number," Brogan
growled. "Don't make me come back."

Donny gave a quick, short nod.

Hell, Brogan expected both of them to be gone within hours.

"One more thing, Donny."

"No one will know you were here," he promised, then gave a
bitter, mirthless laugh. "Trust me; I don't want anyone to know."

Brogan strode quickly from the room, Eli and Jed following
close behind as they left the house and disappeared into the trees.

The four-wheelers they'd used to get into the mountains were still waiting where they'd left them. Brogan mounted the rugged machine as Eli and Jed did the same, and they started the engines and headed for the enclosed trailer several miles down the mountain and the pickup it was attached to.

The night—or morning, he should say—had yielded far more information than he had ever expected.

Pulling the four-wheeler into the covered trailer as Eli and Jed pulled in behind him, Brogan knew he finally had a direction to move in. Something other than just a list of files currently under review by the military for destruction. Brogan hadn't seen a location for anything when he'd gone through the files, but that didn't mean it wasn't there. It meant he was going to have to go over them much more closely. According to the information Donny had, the files were evidently encrypted, if whoever he'd overheard talking that night, was right. So it made sense Brogan hadn't found it. What he needed was someone with the ability to read and crack military code.

Otherwise, there would be no keeping Eve out of this.

His director thought they had one asset no one else could touch.

That asset was Eve.

Because whoever cared enough for Eve that they would only come out if Eve needed them or would only trust whoever she was with, evidently had the ability to not just decode the encryption, but also had information on a militia that Homeland Security believed had been disbanded more than five years before.

He'd been trying to find someone Eve was close to in his search for this informant. Maybe the way to go about this was to see whom Eve and her father, Chandler Mackay, now had in common.

That was where the answers lay.

To get those answers he would have to make Eve break a promise and betray the brother she loved.

He would be risking his soul, but he knew the plans the Freedom League had when it had been disbanded. They had been only months away from assassinating the president and ensuring the vice president, who had been a part of the militia, took his place. From there, they would have ensured the government officials they'd been amassing information on, would fall in with their plans. If they succeeded, the world as he knew it would be over forever. The Freedom League's ultimate plan was the destruction of free enterprise, freedom of speech, and race equality. The nation would have been broken apart from the inside out, and before the American citizens even realized the danger they were in, it would have been too late.

According to Donny, the League was still in place, and that meant their plans were still in place as well.

And that, he couldn't accept.

EIGHT

Eve often helped not just at the bar, but also at
Janey Mackay Jansen's restaurant, Mackay's Fine Dining. She
helped Natches at the garage and in the office, and sometimes at
Dawg's lumber and building supplies store, or, if needed, on the
farm he had bought.

When she wasn't working for various cousins or their friends,
then she worked for her mother.

Fortunately, John and Sierra had hired two experienced waitresses within a few nights of her confrontation with Sandi
Mikels. Unfortunately, that left Eve at loose ends for a few
days—until her sisters learned she was currently jobless.

They saw that as extra time off from the inn to enjoy their
summers more. Before she knew it Eve found herself working two straight twelve-hour days until she managed to put the
skids on Piper and Lyrica.

Eight hours she didn't mind. Twelve hours she had a bit more of a problem with.

On the third day she found herself on cleaning duty after Zoey disappeared to "paint" again. Piper and Lyrica had made plans, leaving her mother without the extra help at the same time that dinner preparation began.

There were eight guest suites, four to each wing at the side of the converted two-story farmhouse. The suites weren't overly large, though Eve's was smaller than the others. Each suite consisted of a bedroom, bathroom, and small sitting room with a reasonable-size flat screened television.

That morning after the guests left, she went through each room that had the service tag hanging on the outside of the door to clean or just refresh the rooms. On the back of each tag the guest had written what services were required. Changing the bed, extra towels, or a variety of other services listed to check off on the back of the card.

Armed with cleaning supplies, clean sheets, pillowcases, and towels, she made her way from the rooms on the opposite wing from her own and worked her way around to the side she shared with Brogan, Elijah Grant, and Jedediah Booker.

Her plan was to finish in her room and sneak in a nap. Her evening was free, and she intended to keep it that way. She'd worked two weeks straight without a day off, and she was determined to make certain she had a break.

When she reached Brogan's room, nerves began to attack her normally calm demeanor.

Her hands were shaking as she unlocked the door and slowly stepped inside. The butterflies were beating at her stomach while her pussy decided it was a fine time to go from aching to all-out clenching in need.

And all it had taken was stepping into his suite.

She was pathetic.

Carrying the clean bedclothes to his bedroom, she was happy to see he wasn't a slob. There wasn't so much as a stray hair in the bathroom.

The same for the sitting area of the small suite. All it really required was a quick run across the floors with a vacuum and dusting the furniture before she returned to the bedroom to make the bed.

She had every intention of making the bed quickly, too.

Pulling the first pillow from the neatly straightened blanket, Eve stared at it for long seconds before slowly pulling it to her and burying her face against the ultrasoft cotton of the pillowcase covering it.

His scent was there: a clean, midnight scent that forcibly pulled the memory of his touch to the forefront of her mind.

Once again she could feel the heavy weight of his body against her own, his lips traveling down her neck, moving steadily closer to her hard, aching nipples.

She hadn't slept worth anything since that night. She tossed and turned, aching for him, and too wary of his warning of what would happen if he heard her masturbating again to risk it.

It was so tempting, though. The need for release was like a hunger she couldn't assuage. She couldn't forget it, and even if she could masturbate, she wouldn't be able to satisfy it.

Been there, done that, she thought wearily. She couldn't allow herself to take Brogan as a lover.

She had to get over it. This hunger for him was going to make her crazy.

Getting over it would be easier said than done, though.

For the first time in nearly eight months she had finally

accepted one of the numerous invitations to dinner that she received. While picking up her check from the bar the night before, one of John and Sierra's friends had come into town from Boston and stopped by.

Before the evening was over he had invited her to have dinner with him that night, and with a sense of desperation she had accepted.

Chatham Bromleah Doogan III, tall, dark haired, and dark eyed. He had a steady, confident aura about him, and John and Sierra both really liked him.

She was thankful that Brogan had left with the motorcycle touring group he was a part of that afternoon and wasn't due back until sometime in the hours before dawn.

The group went most weekends sightseeing on the bikes. A group of over a dozen couples, riding their motorcycles along the scenic mountain highways and byways of Kentucky, West Virginia, and Ohio.

Plenty of time, she thought to herself, to have dinner with Chatham, or Doogan as he'd told her to call him, and to figure out whether she truly was ruined for another man.

Not that she intended to do more than have dinner, because she didn't. But there was always the chance her body would see the error of aching for Brogan and decide to ache for someone else instead.

It was a long shot, she admitted, but worth trying.

Tossing Brogan's pillow to the bed, she quickly stripped the blankets while laying the pillowcases carefully aside before making the bed. Gathering the bedclothes together, she moved first to her own room and tossed the pillowcases to her bed, then took the bedclothes to the laundry room at the end of the hall.

Throwing the blankets in the wash, she moved back to her own room, locked the doors, then placed the pillowcases on her own pillows before returning to the shower.

Since walking from the shower to find Brogan in her room, it seemed she now expected him to be there each time she stepped into her bedroom.

Disappointment assailed her when she realized he wasn't. Even though she had known even before she entered the room that he wasn't there, still, the regret ached inside her.

The motorcycle touring club Brogan had been leading for the past year had been used to taking weekly trips several times a summer. They toured the States on their motorcycles, often riding to scenic, out-of-the-way areas, where civilization still hadn't marred nature's beauty. This last summer, they'd stuck closer to Pulaski County, though. Their trips usually lasted no more than twelve to sixteen hours between leaving then returning.

Oh, civilization was creeping closer by the day, she admitted, even in Pulaski County.

Removing the towel she'd wrapped around her and climbing onto her bed for a nap, she was surprised she fell asleep as quickly as she did.

A deep, luckily dreamless sleep.

No dreams of Brogan and sex, or the dream that often visited her of watching him, aching for him, only to see him leave with one of the local women she'd known him to see in the past.

Today, though, there was only peaceful sleep.

Something she hadn't had in far longer than she could re-member.

Brogan pulled into the rest stop, parking the Harley in front of the concession building as Eli and Jed pulled in to one side of him.

The two other agents, despite renting suites at the bed-and-breakfast, were only rarely seen in his presence. The only time they spoke or even came in contact with one another was during the rides the touring club made.

Luckily, there were fewer rides this summer than there had been in summers past. After the former "president" was arrested for drug possession, it was learned that the club's riding account was at nearly zero. They would be making a lot shorter trips until the monthly membership fees added enough for them to resume their normal summer schedule.

Dismounting the bike and hanging his helmet on the handlebars, Brogan watched as the rest of the group pulled in. Behind Eli and Jed, Poppa Bear and his wife pulled in, sharing a cycle the size of a small car. Their daughter rode her own Harley next to them and managed to make many of the trips her parents went on.

Behind them, surprisingly, rode and Donny and Sandi. They had been unusually quiet since their ordeal. Donny hadn't gotten into any fights, and Sandi hadn't instigated any. They were up each other's asses like Siamese twins, impossible to separate. The one time Brogan had heard one of the club members comment on the change, Donny had replied only that he was getting too damned old to be fighting and carousing all damned night long.

The number Brogan had programmed into his phone hadn't yet been called either. He'd hoped the happy couple would be eager to get some useful information, just in case. Not that he'd really kill either of them in cold blood, but he was fine with the fact that they believed he would.

"Brogan, I have to admit, you know some damned fine scenery," Poppa Bear boomed as he helped his slender wife from the back of their cycle. "It's nice to finally see something besides the interstates we were seeing when your predecessor was running things."

"I'm glad you're enjoying it, Poppa Bear." He inclined his head in acknowledgment.

"When are you gonna invite that little Mackay girl to join us?" the Santa-looking Poppa Bear questioned him with a suggestive wink. "There's nothing like having your gal sittin' behind ya."

Hooking his thumbs into his belt, Brogan grinned back at him. "Hell, her brother might shoot me."

"Naw, ol' Dawg loves his baby sisters. He might snap and snarl, but he'd not kill you over her."

Brogan wasn't so certain of that.

"Better claim that pretty little thang afore it's too late," Poppa Bear claimed. "There's a lot of nice-lookin' boys that'll snap her right up 'fore you know it."

"Yeah, like the one who asked her out last night."

Brogan's head jerked around to Donny's unusually quiet tone of voice as Poppa Bear and his family headed to the restrooms.

"Do what?" Brogan asked.

He didn't have to force the vein of surprise in his voice.

"There was a guy at the bar who asked her out to dinner last night." Donny shifted on his feet, moving with a nervous rhythm that made Brogan want to order him to stand still.

"What did she say?" He frowned.

"Well, she accepted." Donny scratched nervously at his cheek. "They're having dinner at Mackay's tonight at seven."

The hell they were.

Brogan could feel the blood suddenly boiling in his veins.

Glaring at Donny, he wondered whether the little bastard would have the nerve to lie to him.

"Man, I wouldn't lie to you about it." Donny lifted his hands helplessly as Brogan silently cursed the other man's ability to read him, if only for a second.

"How the hell would you know?" Brogan snapped. "I thought you and Sandi were barred from Walker's Run."

Donny shook his head and shrugged his shoulders uncomfortably as he cleared his throat. "Just Sandi. But I doubt I'll be around much without her."

Yeah, he felt real sorry for them. When hell froze over.

"Sorry, man." Brogan grimaced. "I guess it was more than I expected. Thanks for letting me know." He gave the other man a short, tight nod before turning back to the Harley and jerking his helmet from the handlebars.

"Brogan?" Donny spoke again, his voice lower.

Turning to him with a frown, Brogan waited impatiently.

"I'm like Poppa Bear; I don't think Dawg would kill ya because you're sleepin' with his sister. Break her heart, though, and Natches might."

Yeah, yeah, yeah, he was getting damned tired of that refrain.

Securing the helmet beneath his chin, Brogan mounted the Harley, kicked the stand back, and turned the key. The engine purred instantly.

Ignoring the confused summons from the riders returning from the concession building and bathrooms, Brogan sped from the rest stop. Pulling onto the two-lane road, he pointed the motorcycle toward Somerset and the woman who just might have it in her head to see whether Brogan could be pushed from her life.

Brogan had no intentions of being pushed out.

He'd made a mistake in waiting. He should have never given some bastard the opportunity to slip in.

It was a mistake he would rectify.

NINE

He absolutely couldn't believe Doogan would do something so damned underhanded.

Chatham Bromleah Doogan, director of special operations of the Federal Protective Service, had actually dragged his ass out of his D.C. office to come poke his nose into Brogan's operation.

It was unbelievable.

As he drove the three hours back to Somerset, Brogan tried to figure out exactly what was in the director's mind.

There was no figuring it out.

Doogan was known for his oddities, but Brogan had never known him to physically interfere in an investigation. Especially as he was now.

He was a known player when it came to women. The man had no heart and no belief in a woman's tender emotions.

The son of a bitch would take Eve's innocence as though he

had a right to it. Then he would ride off into the sunset and never give her another thought. And there was no doubt of Eve's innocence. Brogan knew from the investigation report Doogan had shown him that Eve had no lovers in Somerset since she had arrived. Brogan's investigation into her life in Texas revealed there had been none there.

Mercedes had kept a tight rein on her daughters and raised them to understand their responsibilities to themselves and one another. Survival had been uppermost, juvenile sex had been highly frowned upon. Mercedes, he had heard, had tried to instruct her daughters often on the dangers of sex and the chances of conceiving a child they were far too young to care for. Seeing their mother's example, living the hardships and the weariness their mother had suffered had obviously convinced the girls that she was right.

As he pushed the speed limit as far as he dared, Brogan found himself gritting his teeth.

Dammit, at this rate he'd wear his back teeth to nubs.

Knowing what Doogan would do to her tender heart brought another realization, though. Brogan had never taken Eve out. He'd almost taken her virginity in her own bed, but he hadn't taken her out or shown the world she was worth far more than the pleasure he would find in her body.

Doogan thought he could wine and dine her, but the ruse had nothing to do with showing the world a damned thing. Getting lucky after he took her home was all he would care about.

That, and ensuring that he pulled Eve Mackay in on an operation she had no business being a part of.

Brogan made one stop.

Driving into the back parking lot of the inn, he pulled a spare set of keys from the magnet beneath the four-by-four truck parked there, unlocked it, and a second later slid it into drive.

It was well after seven that evening before he pulled into valet parking at Mackay's Fine Dining, and gave the young man, Mark Carlson, a hard look and a fifty-dollar bill as he growled, "The truck stays here."

"You gonna be long?" Mark eyed the fifty-dollar bill dubiously, making Brogan wonder when a fifty stopped impressing kids.

He slapped another in the young man's hand. "Mark, that truck moves and I'm going to kick your ass and take both these fifties back," he promised softly. "You got me?"

"Alls I can say is, as long as Declan, Rogue, Janey, or Alex don't yell at me."

Brogan wasn't worried about Declan for sure.

Declan Mackay, formerly Faisal Mackay, the Afghani whom Natches Mackay had adopted more than five years before, was the floor manager of the restaurant.

"Just tell them whose truck it is; they'll be fine with it," Brogan promised as he turned and entered the restaurant.

He strode past the well-dressed customers waiting for a table, knowing damned good and well that he was far from the dress code in his biker boots and khaki shirt tucked into his jeans.

He'd been riding for more than six hours. The bandanna skullcap was still tied around his head, and Brogan didn't give a damn.

Striding past the sputtering hostess, he looked around quickly, caught sight of Eve, and strode toward her.

Damn, she sure looked pretty, too, he thought.

She wasn't dressed in her customary jeans and snug cami.

Tonight she wore a sundress with thin straps at her shoulders. The bodice cupped and loved her breasts. It skimmed to her hips and fell to her knees in shimmering chiffon.

The soft blue color brought out the green of her eyes and made her look like a tempting little sorceress.

A sorceress he was set and ready to claim.

Eve could feel her heart racing, pounding in her chest as she watched Brogan stalk across the room.

It was obvious he'd just returned from the ride. She had understood, based on listening to other members of the touring club, that the riders wouldn't be arriving back until late into the night.

He looked hot, though: rough, tough, dangerous, and so damned sexy she almost caught her breath in excitement.

Jeans, a road dust–stained khaki shirt, rider's boots, and a dark blue bandanna skullcap wasn't exactly adhering to the restaurant's dress code, though.

She was aware of the other diners watching curiously. She could almost feel them waiting to see what Brogan Campbell would do with his woman, who was obviously enjoying an evening with another man. Eve just wished there had actually been enjoyment.

Chatham Bromleah Doogan was a player, and he didn't try to hide it. He was nice about it. He was damned charming about it. But Chatham was unapologetically a playboy.

Brogan was unapologetically all man. Wild, tough, dangerous. He was willing to be tame, but only under his own conditions, and only at those times that he chose to be.

He wasn't willing to be tamed at this moment, though.

His gaze locked on hers, the blue-gray depths a sliver of color behind the lashes of his narrowed gaze, he came to a stop at the table, glowering down at her.

Chatham never lifted his gaze from the dessert menu.

"Ah, the maître d'," Chatham murmured dismissively. "Isn't it about time?"

Eve almost groaned in rising trepidation.

This could get ugly fast.

Brogan lifted a red-gold brow mockingly as he stared down at her. The arch conveyed such deliberate intent that she could feel her knees almost trembling.

How the hell was she supposed to handle this?

Chatham lifted his head then, gazing up at Brogan arrogantly.

"He's not the maître d'," she commented as Brogan completely ignored him.

"Really?" Chatham drawled in amusement. "My dear, I would have never guessed. Friend of yours?"

It could end gracefully, she thought.

Without bloodshed.

She hoped.

Eve cleared her throat. "Sometimes, I guess."

Chatham chuckled. "A friend is not a friend, my dear, unless he is a friend at all times."

"So I've heard." She couldn't break the hold Brogan had on her gaze. She wanted to. She tried to. Yet she couldn't turn away.

"What happened to the ride?" she asked, fighting the tremble in her voice as something flickered in Brogan's gaze.

"I canceled it," he growled as he slowly lifted his hands from where he'd had his thumbs hooked in the front pockets of his jeans.

Almost immediately his hands flattened against the top of the table, his upper body bending to her. He was almost nose-to-nose with her so fast she could only stare up at him in surprise.

"Are you coming peacefully, or will I have to discuss the situation with your date?"

Eve's gaze flickered in Chatham's direction. He sat back in his chair, completely at ease as he, too, seemed to await her decision. His dark brown eyes mocked her dilemma, and for a second Eve swore he appeared as self-satisfied as the proverbial cat with the canary.

"I'm not waiting much longer," Brogan warned her softly.

"I believe we should leave this decision up to Ms. Mackay, without undue coercion," Chatham advised, causing Eve to flick a horrified glance in his direction.

Didn't he know a dangerous situation when he saw one? Brogan was in no way willing to endure advice at the moment.

"I'm sorry about this, Chatham." Lifting the napkin from her lap, Eve laid it on the table as she apologized.

Rising, she quickly opened her small clutch purse and pulled several bills free before laying them on the table.

"That is entirely unnecessary." Chatham looked almost horrified as he glanced at the bills before his gaze lifted to her again. "My dear, your company was well worth the meal."

Brogan jerked her money from the table.

"Brogan?" she hissed, outraged by the action.

"He looks like he can afford the damned meal." Brogan snorted.

Chatham rose to his feet, the amusement in his gaze intensifying.

Turning to Brogan, she said querulously, "I hope you brought something besides that Harley."

"I came prepared."

There was something about the way he said it and the words he used that sent a rush of heat flooding her body.

Before Brogan turned away, though, he reached into his pocket, pulled two hundreds free, and tossed them to the table.

"I can pay for the meal." Chatham chuckled.

"Take the money and count yourself lucky," Brogan suggested, his tone dark and forbidding. "My ancestors castrated poachers. With great satisfaction."

Chatham lifted a brow as the diners around them snickered in amusement.

Gripping her upper arm, Brogan led her unhurriedly through the restaurant and out the front door as outrage rushed through her.

"That was completely uncalled-for, Brogan." She turned to face him as he stepped into the driver's seat after helping her into the truck. Glaring up at the brooding anger burning in his gaze, she ignored the butterfly excitement in her stomach.

"You had absolutely no right whatsoever to barge in on my date in such a way."

"A date, was it?" Silky, dangerous, his voice lowered and his expression tightened savagely as he started the truck. "I'd change the description of that little outing if I were you, Eve. Because you knew better than to date until this relationship thing of ours has been settled, one way or the other."

"That's what you think," she snapped back at him, so offended by his attitude she could barely tolerate it. "We have no relationship, remember? I told you, I can't do this."

It was killing her—the need for his touch, for his kiss. It raged inside her, hotter even than the anger now coursing inside her.

"Because of you my brother is probably getting calls from everyone in that restaurant about now. He's going to end up at my door again—God forbid, while you're in my bed. And before the night is over I'm going to feel like the worst sister to live, because I find it completely impossible to tell you no."

She was only barely aware of the tightening of Brogan's knuckles on the steering wheel, as though he were fighting desperately to keep his hands off her.

"You tell me no all the damned time," he argued, his tone rasping with irritation. "Your damned brother can just be proud as hell of you, can't he, Eve?"

"Not if he shows up and you're in my bed." Turning to face forward again, her arms crossing over her breasts, she glared into the evening traffic.

Until the chain swinging on the rearview mirror drew her gaze. She recognized the small gold cross Timothy Cranston had told her belonged to his daughter. She had been wearing it the day a bomb had killed her and her mother.

"Timothy let you use his truck?" she questioned in disbelief. "He doesn't even like you."

"I stole it," he informed her with such a look of triumph she was momentarily taken aback. "I knew where he kept the spare key and I just took it."

Pure disbelief filled her as she shook her head and returned her gaze forward. She had to grit her teeth to keep herself from completely losing her temper. That lasted all of the time it took him to pass the turnoff that led to the inn.

"Where are you going? You just missed the turn to the house," she reminded him as he continued through town.

"I borrowed a place for the night." He shocked her with

the statement. "I don't intend to have Dawg Mackay disturb me again while we're together, Eve. I may end up forgetting he's your brother."

"The only friend you have in this county who would have something to loan is Billy Ray, and all he has is that ragged houseboat of his. You think Dawg won't know the minute we pull into the marina and go onto that alley cat's boat? Are you trying to rub his nose in the fact that I can't stay away from you?"

Where had his mind gone? There wasn't a chance in hell that she was getting on a houseboat with him. Especially Billy Ray Chauncey's. The man was a dog when it came to women.

"For God's sake, give me a little credit here, Eve." The look he shot her was rife with simmering lust and banked frustration. "Do you really think I'm going to give Dawg Mackay the opportunity to try to beat the shit out of me?"

"Try?" She looked back at him doubtfully, determined to make him as crazy as he made her.

She was pushing him, and she knew she was, but this was the first time she had seen so much emotion in him. He wasn't as controlled as he normally was, and the knowledge of that had adrenaline crashing through her system.

She could get used to this. The excitement was addictive.

Brogan snorted. "Don't fool yourself, sweet pea. The Mackay cousins are hitting their forties. They're not exactly as spry as they used to be."

Eve almost laughed. For a second—well, maybe a millisecond—she had the insane urge to share with him the fact that the cousins' wives often made that claim themselves. But it was only after the cousins proved otherwise.

"Maybe your confidence is just enough to ensure that he does kick your ass," she suggested. "Be careful there, Brogan; you could be a little overconfident."

"That's possible." Surprising her with the agreement as he cast her a hard, mocking look, he continued. "Personally, I'd just as soon not find out, though, so I've made certain he'll be completely unaware of our location."

She doubted that. Dawg seemed to know exactly where each of his sisters was and what they were doing at any given time of the day. Or night.

"So what have you borrowed and who did you borrow it off of?" she asked, rubbing at the sensation almost of static electricity that raced over her arms at the thought of being alone with Brogan right now. Sensual intensity and male confidence seemed to bleed from every pore of his body. Sexual intent and erotic heat filled the cab of the truck, raising her heart rate and sending excitement crashing through her bloodstream.

"Does it matter who I borrowed it from?" he answered her as he turned up a narrow, unlined paved road.

It was one of the few she and her sisters hadn't explored—for a reason.

"The property up this road is gated," she told him. "There used to be a guard at the gate, too."

"Only when it's being used by certain people," he informed her cryptically.

"What sort of people?" Eve probed as the truck pulled up to the locked gate and the guard post.

The guard post was empty. Surprisingly, Brogan pulled his wallet from his jeans back pocket, extracted what appeared to be a key card from one of the credit card slots, and slid it through the security scanner.

The gate swung open slowly in the bright lights of the truck as a green light flashed next to the gate's support post.

Driving through, he stopped at the mounted control box on the other side, opened the weatherproof door as he stuck his arm through the open window of the truck, and pushed in a code. The gate swung closed behind them.

The entirety of the property was fenced in, though it was fenced at different heights as it moved up the mountain, to allow larger wildlife to clear it. As the cabin came into view, Eve glimpsed the eight-foot fence about two hundred feet from the house and another gate. Like the control box that closed the first gate, this one took only a code that Brogan pushed into it.

There were rumors . . .

Eve stared through the windshield as she propped her elbow on the door and rubbed at her temple. "Who does this cabin belong to, Brogan?"

"Tonight it belongs to me. I told you: I have a friend."

"Did Timothy give you the key and access code into it?" she asked. "I know there's a rumor this cabin belongs to the government, and Timothy's the only former agent I know who you talk to."

"As you said, though, Timothy and I aren't exactly friends," he reminded her.

"Yeah, well, Timothy has friends no one knows anything about, and often treats the friends he does associate with like suspects or enemies rather than friends. So who the hell knows?"

Brogan chuckled, a low, sensual sound that sent heat skipping up her spine.

Stepping from the truck, Eve stared around the small clearing before turning to the cabin and staring up at it.

She'd thought the fence surrounded all four sides of the large cabin until she stepped from the truck. To the side, instead, the waters of the lake lapped at the sandy ground, while a dock extended out into the water.

Lights had flipped on from the front porch as the truck pulled up to it, revealing the elegant wilderness retreat.

She'd heard the cabin hidden in the wide canyon above the lake was a luxurious retreat often used by government officials, senators, governors, and megarich hunters with the right political ties.

From the back of the truck Brogan pulled two overnight bags free. Eve's brows lifted in disbelief as she recognized her own bag.

"You packed my clothes?" Propping her hands on her hips, she stared back at him incredulously. "Before or after you stole the truck?"

"Let's just say I had help." He growled.

"You had no right to go through my things, Brogan," she informed him, furious that he'd taken such liberties. It was one thing to practically kidnap her, but packing her clothes? Going through her drawers? That was uncalled-for.

"You weren't there," he stated, as though that made it just fine.

"So? That doesn't give you the right to paw through my clothes." Or anything else she kept in her drawers.

"Don't worry, sweetie; your little toys didn't offend me in the least," he promised good-naturedly as he stepped up on the porch, set the bags on the wide bench beside the door, and pulled the key card from his shirt pocket before swiping it through the reader.

"I can't believe you," she bit out furiously as she followed him into the cabin. "Brogan, what gives you the right to do any of this? First you barge in on my date—"

He turned on her so fast she stepped back, startled that he was facing her so quickly, no more than inches from her where less than a second before he had been a good three feet away.

"Eve, sweetheart, don't make me tell you again not to call that farce of a dinner you were having with that jackass a date," he ordered fiercely rather than furiously. "My patience is wearing thin with the people who seem to be standing between us. I can deal with your brother, your sisters, your cousins. Hell, I can even deal with your mother if she decides to protest. But if you dare to put a *date* between us, then I might not hold on to my patience much longer."

Her arms lifted, her hands propping on her hips as she lifted her chin defiantly. "Are you threatening me, Brogan Campbell?"

"No, Eve, I'm not threatening you." He was closer, his head lowering, his gaze holding hers as the blue-gray appeared more a steel gray now than the light blue it sometimes seemed. "I'm telling you: My dick is harder than titanium, my control is all but shot, and I'm so damned hungry for you I'm about to lose my fucking mind. So please, for both our sakes, don't refer to that man as your date again."

Her lips thinned.

She could feel her nostrils flaring as she drew in air, fighting to control the racing, adrenaline-laced blood surging and thundering through her. That small movement was her first warning that her own control was thin. That her ability to access her common sense was endangered.

"Now, I'm going to take our clothes to the bedroom," he stated as he stepped back from her. "If you want something to drink, there's a bar in the living area and one in the kitchen. The fridge should have drinks, as well as the walk-in pantry. I'll be right back."

She nodded silently, her gaze still narrowed on him, her fingers so tight on the purse she expected her nails to pierce the soft leather.

Her cell phone was in her purse; she should call her mother—no, she should call Dawg. She should show Brogan he didn't have the option of ordering her around.

There was a part of her—the independent fighter who used to worry her mother to distraction—that assured her she didn't need Dawg's help. If he showed up he'd drag her from the house and probably camp on her doorstep to ensure Brogan didn't come around her again.

She could handle this.

Besides, if Dawg dragged her off, then there was no way she would end up in Brogan's bed. And Brogan's bed was exactly where she wanted to be.

Well, that was where she wanted to be once she and Brogan set a few ground rules, that was.

Nothing strenuous for him, just a few concerning free will, her own choices, and dates.

TEN

Brogan stared around the bedroom, making a mental note to himself to thank Timothy for everything he'd managed to arrange in a few short hours.

If the DHS agent survived his little chat with Dawg, that was.

The bedroom was exactly as he had requested.

The huge custom-made, larger than a king-and-a-half bed was surrounded by ivory netting that hung from the ceiling and draped around the thick, ultracomfortable mattress situated on the platform beneath it.

Candles by the dozen, from thick pillars to slender tapers and everything in between, were positioned around the large room. The property's caretaker had slipped in and lit them just before Brogan and Eve arrived.

The hot tub just outside the glass patio doors steamed invitingly, while candles were positioned around the deck that surrounded it, flickering with warmth.

Opening Eve's overnight bag he'd had Piper pack for him, he grinned as he pulled free the white lace-and-chiffon gown he knew would fall to Eve's pretty toes, and the matching robe. She did love her chiffon.

Beneath that were jeans, camis, socks, and sneakers. He'd told Piper to pack for her sister enough clothes to last the weekend. Piper had been more than happy to do so. It was high time Brogan decided to finally do something about all the sexual tension burning between him and Eve, Piper had laughed.

He stared around the room again.

Hell, he'd never taken a virgin before, but he knew his sister had once claimed her girlfriend would forgive her anything if she treated her like a virgin and put some effort into seducing her. Brogan had snorted in amusement at the claim, while Samantha had stared back at him with a confident smile.

Picking up his own overnight bag, he moved to the shower in the next room. The damned thing was the size of two of his bathroom at the inn, let alone the shower. It was much too large for one person.

If Eve was there with him, though . . . The bench on the other side of the shower was easily six feet long and nearly as wide. Hell, the things he could do to her luscious little body on that bench as the rain showerhead poured down on them.

Showering quickly, all he could think about was the fact that she was still a virgin. Twenty-four years old, beautiful, social, yet she had saved herself for some reason—until now.

Drying quickly, he dressed in clean jeans and a white shirt.

Buttoning the shirt, then tucking it into his jeans before securing a belt around his hips, Brogan moved back into the living room, his gaze searching the room before he found her curled up on the wide hanging chair on the screened-in patio outside.

Padding barefoot to the open patio doors, Brogan stepped out on the stone flooring and leaned against the teak bar just outside the doors.

"You look like a teenager curled up in that chair like that," he told her with a soft smile.

"Oh, really." The sassiness and defiance in her voice had his balls throbbing, his dick threatening to swell impossibly wider. "Well, that just makes you a dirty old man then. Feeling the guilt yet?"

He wanted to laugh. Damn her, she could have the sharpest tongue.

"I picked out my bedroom while you were freshening up," she told him with a little arch of her brow. "It's not nearly as nice as yours, of course, but it's still pretty swanky."

She'd obviously explored the house some while he had been showering.

Lifting a glass to her lips, she sipped at the white wine she'd obviously found in the large walk-in refrigerator. The house had an actual walk-in refrigerator, which had amazed Brogan the first time he had been there.

Propping one arm on the bar, he just watched her, biding his time. She was sitting over there trying to convince herself she could control what was going to happen this weekend and how it was going to happen. And he would give anything to allow her the opportunity to see whether she could use all those very perceptive instincts and feminine wiles to control him. Unfortunately, in the middle of an operation with the potential to turn nasty fast was no place to allow himself to be that distracted.

"Are you ready to tell me who owns this place yet?" she asked when he said nothing more.

"I'll tell you everything before we leave Sunday," he promised her. "Hold your questions until then."

"How very ominous," she murmured as she brought the wineglass to her lips once again. "Let me guess: You're waiting until Sunday because you know once you explain everything, I'm going to be either so pissed, so brokenhearted, or both that you won't have a chance in hell of getting me into your bed."

She was good; he had to give her that.

He merely grinned back at her, and kept his opinion to himself. His opinion and his confessions. It was the confessions that were going to get him in trouble. Or might piss her off for a while.

Of course, sometimes she was so much like her brother she might actually shoot him.

"I'm going to bed; I'm tired." Sliding from the chair, still wearing those strappy four-inch peep-toe heels and carrying her glass of wine, she strolled toward him with such sensual grace and sleepy-eyed arousal, he had to clench his teeth, grinding off yet more enamel, to keep from throwing her to the couch and taking her with all the finesse of a callow, inexperienced teen.

He waited until she was ready to pass him. Until he was confident she actually thought she was going to get past him.

Then he stepped in front of her.

"You haven't seen all the rooms yet," he told her softly. "How can you be certain you've chosen the right one if you've missed any?"

Her heart was pounding. He could see the proof of it at her throat, where her vein pulsed at a rapid pace beneath her flesh.

It was there in the hard, quick rise and fall of her breasts and the fine trembling of her body.

"The room I chose is fine, I'm sure."

God help him, her nipples were as tight and hard beneath the material of her dress as little pebbles.

He lifted his hand and stroked the backs of his fingers down her cheek as her breath caught before she exhaled with a rough little sigh.

"You know what's going to happen," he told her as her lips parted to facilitate her breathing.

"That doesn't mean it's going to happen right now," she informed him. He let her lift the wineglass and take a healthy sip before he spoke.

"I don't heel worth shit," he told her then. "You won't control me, Eve, you won't tame me, and you won't dominate me. Now, that's a warning I've never given another woman, and I won't waste my time telling you again. So if that's what you think you're going to do, then I highly suggest you reconsider your options."

Eve stared back at him silently, careful to keep her mouth firmly shut until she was certain she had a handle on the anger ready to burst past her lips.

When she felt she could speak civilly she smiled back at him with cool disdain.

"Brogan. Number one." She held her forefinger up to him imperiously. "I am not now, nor have I ever been, some bitch who needs to be warned how arrogant, controlling, dominant, and manipulative men such as you can be until you realize just how it can potentially damage a relationship you decide you don't want to lose."

"Eve—"

"I listened to the bullshit spilling from your lips, Brogan; you can take a few precious minutes of your time to listen to common sense now."

That finger pointed up toward his face imperiously.

"Number two," she continued. "Not only am I not a bitch to jump at your command, neither am I some whore you bought for fifty bucks, or the mistress you support. Just because you all but kidnapped me does not mean I owe you so much as my company, let alone my virginity."

She watched as his eyes narrowed on her, the blue-gray definitely turning steel gray at the mention of her virginity.

"And number three," she snapped, unable to hold back the anger caused by so much adrenaline with no place to go. "If you can't respect me, Brogan, and see me as your equal, then I'll be damned if you're even in the running for my virginity."

She was finished now.

Stepping back, she propped her hands on her hips and glared at him. He smiled. And that smile sent trepidation surging through her.

"My equal?" he asked. "Sweet pea, when you can work a ten-hour day in the freezing rain, take down four drug-crazed dealers intent on having your head, keep up with my daily workout, and show me you've grown a ten-inch dick at some point, then I will most gladly drop all my dominant, manipulating schemes to rid you of your virginity and will then consider you my equal." His hand shot out, grabbed her wrist, and, before she could jerk it back, he used it to drag her to him, his other arm locking around her back to hold her to him. Eve found herself up and close and personal.

"Ten . . ." she squeaked as his hips pressed against her firmly while he held her close enough that there was no escaping the fact that he might not be lying.

"Outside our bed, outside what is sure to be some damned fucking mind-blowing sex, you can attempt to tame me until hell freezes over, if that's what you want." His head lowered, and the erotic demand and white-hot lust that tightened his features completely stole her breath as he continued. "But you will not control nor tame the dominance and sexual tastes that are as much a part of me as the color of my eyes or the sound of my voice. And I'm still damned sure going to accept your virginity."

She didn't remember offering it, and he didn't give her a chance to offer or refuse.

Brogan lifted her closer as his lips slanted over hers, heated and hungry, the rough velvet feel of them staking a claim on her senses that she'd always known was coming.

The kisses they had shared before now were nothing compared to this one.

Eve whimpered in rising pleasure as her hands slid from where they were pressed against his chest to grip his shoulders. Sensation swirled inside her, around her, threatening to destroy any hope she ever had of escaping the hold she could feel he was taking of her soul.

As he lifted her closer, bringing her feet off the floor and urging her knees to his hips, Eve moaned at the implications of the position. She gripped his hips anyway, because she couldn't help herself. Because the feel of his erection, heavy with lust and pressing tight against his jeans, was driving her crazy with need.

Using his hips as leverage, she rose and fell against the wedge of heat between her thighs, grinding it against her pussy, rubbing the denim covering it against the silk of her panties, and pressing it against the swollen, too-sensitive bud of her clit.

Suddenly she could feel things she had never felt before where her own body was concerned. She was feeling things she had never known she could feel until Brogan.

The emptiness of her vagina, clenched and aching; she could feel the desperate need to be filled. To be possessed.

His lips continued to devour hers; he took deep, stinging kisses and licked at the burn before deepening the kiss again. His tongue pressed between her lips, licked and teased hers. His lips slanted over hers as his tongue tasted against hers, and the taste of them together became intoxicating.

She was only barely aware of him moving, walking the distance from the patio to the bedroom, she assumed as he lowered her to the incredibly lush support of a mattress. His lips slid to the curve of her jaw before he lowered himself to his knees.

Her knees were still gripping his thighs. As he lifted from her, hurriedly unbuttoning his shirt, Eve stared around them in awe, taking in the incredibly romantic candlelit bedroom. The soft light cast a dreamy quality through the netting draped over the bed in several layers.

Like a scene out of one of the naughty romance books she liked to read, the candlelight gleamed against the bronzed flesh of his chest and shoulders as he shed the shirt. He was living proof that redheads could indeed tan to that gorgeous bronze color.

Lifting her hands, she ran them down his chest, past his flexing abdomen, to the leather belt cinching his hard waist.

Loosening the leather, she smothered a cry at the feel of his hands pushing the chiffon of her dress above her thighs. His gaze locked with hers as she struggled with the metal tabs securing his jeans.

When she eased up until she was sitting in front him, he let her have her way. When she released the last tab, he caught her hands, holding her from her prize.

"What?" she demanded desperately, her hands secured by his.

"Undress for me, Eve." The demand in his voice should have pissed her off, rather than making her wet between her thighs.

Swallowing tightly as he eased back and helped her from the bed, Eve found herself standing before him, suddenly uncertain, trembling.

"I don't . . ." She swallowed again, her hands lifting helplessly.

"Shh, baby," he whispered, catching her hands, and as she watched he brought her hands to his lips, turned them, then pressed a kiss to each palm before he released them.

"I fantasize about watching you undress," he said softly as he rose before her and shed his jeans. "Every time I jack off it's to the images of you." He sat back down on the bed, his fingers gripping the broad length of his cock, and began stroking it slowly as she watched, mesmerized.

The wide, engorged crest throbbed demandingly as a creamy bead of pre-come formed at the tip. Eve licked her lips nervously, unable to draw her gaze from the heavily veined shaft and throbbing head.

"How does that pretty dress come off, Eve?" he asked, the low, caressing murmur of his voice drawing free a sensuality she hadn't known burned within her.

Lifting her hands, her gaze locked on his fingers as he caressed himself, Eve slowly reached behind her back and slid the zipper down. She knew what she wore beneath the dress. She had worn what she dreamed of wearing for him.

After releasing the zipper, Eve lifted her shoulders and slowly lowered the material over the black lace bra and matching bikini panties. The chiffon fell to her feet, revealing the silk thigh-high stockings gripping her thighs with a band of lacy elastic, while the four-inch heels made her legs look incredibly long.

Brogan's fingers stilled on his cock, his gaze glittering with lust as it went over the lacy underthings.

Reaching back, Eve moved to unclip the fastening of the bra. Once the tiny hook released, she shrugged the straps from her shoulders and let it fall to the floor.

He was stroking his erection again, his fingers tightening at the base as she bent to loosen the heels she wore.

"Leave the shoes and the stockings," he growled, reaching out to thread his fingers through her hair before she lifted her head.

"Eve," he whispered her name, but the command, the dominance in his tone left her trembling. "If I ask for something and you're uncomfortable, make certain the discomfort is because you're not certain you want it rather than because of your innocence."

He was trying to still the demand in his tone and give the statement more of the appearance of a request, but she knew what he was doing, just as she knew what he wanted.

He held her head, staring back at her as he stroked his erection, and Eve felt a shudder race through her as he slowly released his grip on her hair.

She straightened, restraining a low groan as he rose and held her shoulders, slowly turning her to the bed as his lips lowered to hers once again, moving against them, sipping at her lips, tasting her as his hands stroked down her back to her hips.

His lips shifted to her neck, stimulating and exciting the sensitive flesh as Eve trembled beneath him. She tipped her neck to the side, arching against him, and the hard, engorged shaft of his cock pressed against her lower stomach. Heat and steely strength throbbed against her, dragging a whimpering cry from her lips as need overcame hesitancy.

Eve's lips found his chest, brushed the small disk of a male nipple, and she gloried in the sudden tension that tightened his body. One hand buried itself in her hair as the other gripped her thigh, holding her to him.

Easing her lips lower, Eve caressed the broad expanse of his chest one kiss at a time until the fingers buried in her hair tightened, easing her lips lower.

She knew what he wanted. She could feel it in the press of his fingers in her hair, the waiting stillness of his body.

Gripping his lean hips with trembling hands, Eve lowered her head down his torso, her tongue peeking out to sample the dark male taste of him. Slowly easing lower, she paused inches above the broad, throbbing crest awaiting her attention.

She'd never done this before. She'd dreamed about it, but she never actually tasted a man so intimately. And she found herself so nervous now, so uncertain.

Brogan pulled back.

Staring up at him in surprise, she gripped his hips, not ready quite yet to admit to failure. Her lips pressed against the strength of his abdomen, she closed her eyes, uncertain what to do.

"Sit on the bed." The growl in his voice was a rasp of pure hunger.

Eve sat on the bed, finding herself at the perfect level now for what he wanted. His hand slid into her hair again as his fingers wrapped around the pulsing shaft.

There was no request, no apology. Her gaze jerked up to his as the broad head was slowly pushing against her lips.

"Open your mouth over it." He groaned, his expression demanding. "Suck it into your mouth."

Her lips parted over the bulging crest, a whimper escaping her as the slow penetration of her mouth sent a surge of sensation racing to the depths of her pussy.

Her clit was a swollen knot of sensual agony, aching with a force she hadn't expected as her lips finally closed over the full breadth of his cock head.

It was a powerful feeling, the intimacy of holding such erotic strength with nothing but the pleasure her mouth could bring him.

The second her lips closed around the width of the throbbing crest, instinct seemed to take over. Everything she had read, every time she had tried to practice what she read with the erotic toy she had bought, came to her rescue. Her natural sensuality and the hungry need filling her did the rest.

Caressing him, her nails rasping against his flesh, Eve lowered her hands from his hips to his thighs. The fingers of one hand curled around the heavy shaft throbbing beneath her lips, while the fingers of the other found the taut sac drawn tight to the base of his cock.

Forcing her gaze to meet his, Eve watched the steely depths of his eyes flare, the color darkening as his hard jaw tightened with a noticeable clench.

She sucked the fierce heat of the broad crest into her mouth. Eve flicked her tongue beneath the flared head, rubbing at the sensitive underside with her tongue. Caressing and sucking the throbbing head, she closed her eyes. She stroked the hard shaft, her nails rasping over the tightened flesh of his balls before she cupped them, weighted it as a harsh groan sounded above her.

Brogan watched her face, the flushed, delicate features absorbed, suffused with sensuality as the heated dampness of her mouth tightened on the head of his cock. His fingers fisted in her hair, the silky midnight length like living warmth in his hand. Holding the soft strands, clutching them, he fought to keep from pushing her faster than she was ready; he wanted to let her find her own rhythm, her own pleasure in him.

And she was killing him with that pleasure. Each heated stroke of her hot little mouth, the silken glide of her delicate fingers, lanced his balls with heat. His shaft throbbed furiously as her mouth destroyed him with each sweet draw, with each stroke of her fingers and lash of her tongue.

She was pushing him to an edge he'd never known before, one no other woman had ever pushed him to. As inexperienced as she was, as nervous as she had been starting out, she was destroying him now, moving her mouth up and down, suckling and licking and sending pulsing flares of incredible sensation racing through his cock.

"Fuck, Eve." He couldn't hold back the rough groan as the sensations threatened to send him exploding into her mouth. "Sweet baby. Sweet, sweet fucking Eve."

Holding her head in place as his hands tightened in her hair, Brogan watched her face, watched the lush beauty of her mouth as he fucked it with slow, shallow thrusts.

"Ah, yeah. Suck it, sweetheart. That's it." His teeth clenched as her hold on his cock head tightened, the heat of her mouth drawing him closer to the edge of control.

If he didn't pull back he was going to come. He'd fill her mouth with every hot pulse of semen building in his balls. And though he would love nothing better than watching her take every spurt of his release, he wasn't quite ready to give in to the sensations whipping through his senses.

Pulling back from her, forcing her to release her hold on the engorged head of his cock, Brogan forced himself to ignore her moan of protest. If he heeded it, if he gave in to her, then the pleasure he had in store for her might well have to come another night.

He had only one more night to give her before he had to tell her the truth.

Cupping the back of her neck in his hand and pulling her to him, Brogan covered her lips with his again and consumed her kiss. Tilting his head, slanting his lips over hers, and devouring the pleasure to be found in her, he gave the lust burning in his veins full rein for just a second.

God, he loved kissing her. Loved the way her lips moved beneath his, the way her fingers slid into his hair, gripping and holding tight to him. She trembled in his arms and moaned into his kiss, lost to the pleasure building between them.

He loved her—no, he loved her kiss. He loved her touch. He loved her— He pushed the thought away, kissing his way from her lips, along her jaw, to the delicate line of her throat.

Eve's head tilted to the side, granting access to the graceful line as her lips found his shoulder and her nails dug into his biceps. He kissed, licked, marked the base of her neck, shocked by the groan of satisfaction that escaped his lips at the sight of the reddened love bite where her neck and shoulder met.

Leaning back, Brogan framed her face with his hands and stared into her dazed expression.

"So pretty," he whispered, stroking his hands along her neck, shoulders, and then down her arms to her wrists. Slowly pulling her wrists behind her back, he lowered his lips to the upper curves of her breasts.

Hunger, lust, and something more—something he didn't recognize and couldn't define—threatened to pull him under. Threatened to destroy his control and the pleasure he insisted on giving her.

When this night was over he would have to tell her the truth. He had no choice. Pulling her into his life required that she know what his life was, and her part in it. And the chances of losing her once he did so were high. High enough that he had to attempt to tie her to him with pleasure.

Brushing his beard over the hard tips of her breasts, he allowed his tongue to take a quick, flickering taste. Restraining her gently, he watched her expression, watched the pleasure building inside her.

This was a high that could never be duplicated. It was a high more dangerous to a man's soul than any found in a drug. Because this high chanced an addiction to not just the pleasure, but to the woman. And he was beginning to fear he had found the woman and the pleasure that could become an addiction impossible to live without.

Parting his lips, still watching her, he lowered his mouth to the pebble-hard tip of her nipple.

"Oh, God, Brogan," she cried out, arching into him as desperation filled her voice and aching, imperative need filled her gaze.

Ah, yes, he knew that pleasure rising inside her. The same pleasure he'd felt lashing at his cock as her mouth surrounded it and sucked it inside the damp heat.

He drew on the engorged peak of her nipple, licking at it, watching her expression and feeling the tension rising in her—ah, God, yes. She could definitely become his addiction.

His weakness.

She could become his destruction.

ELEVEN

Explosive pleasure, flaring through her senses and rasping over sensitive nerve endings, screamed through her body. The feel of Brogan's lips surrounding the tender tip of her nipple was throwing her senses into chaos. Whipping pinpoints of sensation struck at her clit, at the sensitive depths of her pussy. They burned through her, flickered across her flesh, and sent electric bursts of impending ecstasy rocketing through her.

She arched to him, desperation filling her with the need to get closer to the heat of his body. She needed more, needed her nipple deeper in the fiery heat of his mouth. She couldn't get close enough. She couldn't still the demand raging through her body. Frantic, hungry lust built and burned to furious peaks, spilling her juices from the clenched depths of her pussy and drawing her body tight with pleasure.

"Please. Oh, God. Brogan, please," she cried out, feeling her senses spinning as her breath caught at the sensations thrumming through her clit and making her pussy clench.

Releasing her nipple from the devouring grip of his mouth, Brogan turned his attention to its mate.

"I love your nipples," he crooned, brushing his beard against the hard, incredibly sensitive peak. "The feel of them, the sweet taste of them."

He surrounded the hard tip with his mouth, and heat shot from the throbbing peak to pierce her womb before striking at the pulsing bud of her clitoris.

"Brogan. Damn you . . ." Straining at the hold he had on her, Eve felt herself becoming consumed by the needs racing through her body.

Excitement and adrenaline pumped through her bloodstream and laid waste to her ability to hold any part of herself back; pleasure rushed through her system again. Holding her relentlessly in his grip, Brogan sent torturous pleasure whipping through her with his touch, melting her, consuming her ability to function without him.

When his head drew back she could only moan at the loss of his touch as she attempted to push her breasts to him once again.

"I'm going to release your arms, Eve," he told her, staring into her eyes as she forced them open. "Don't touch me, understand?"

She could only shake her head, confused now.

"I need to touch you, Brogan," she whispered, breathless and aching with such force it was like being tortured from the inside out.

She loved the feel of his body. The warmth and strength of him were a stable port in a chaotic storm of sensation.

"Not tonight." He grimaced. "My control is shot, Eve."

"Then don't wait." She reached for him, pouting when he caught her hands again.

Holding them at the wrists, he stared back at her with dominant intent. "Eve, I could always tie you to the bed."

Her eyes widened. "You wouldn't dare!"

Gripping her wrists in one hand again, he lowered the other, trailing it along her thigh before sliding it between them and quickly wedging them apart.

"I've dreamed of eating your hot little pussy," he growled. "So yes, sweetheart, I damned well would tie you to the bed."

The first sentence hadn't passed his lips before Eve was breathing roughly, more of her juices flooding her pussy and spilling to the swollen folds beyond.

"Want me to do that to you, Eve?" he asked softly, knowingly, as his finger touched her, slowly easing through the saturated slit.

Her hips jerked, the sensations tearing through her pussy, jerking through her body like bolts of electric energy.

"Ah, you do like that," he crooned.

Holding her gaze, he returned his finger to where it had been, the tip stroking upward this time to circle the swollen bud of her clit and dragging a harsh, desperate cry from her lips.

A second later he removed his touch again, staring up at her, demand filling his expression. "No touching me, agreed?"

"Fine. Agreed," she breathed out roughly.

He released her slowly. "Lie back on the bed."

Oh, God, oh, God. This was going to be so good. She could feel excitement racing through her veins and searing her body.

Lying back, lifting her arms above her head, she breathed in hard and deep.

"Come to the edge of the bed," he urged her, his hands at her hips to help her scoot forward until her hips were braced on the side of the bed.

Slowly he opened her thighs, spreading them wide as Eve fought to breathe through the anticipation.

"So fucking pretty," he whispered, his finger easing through the bare folds again, sliding heatedly through the gathering juices.

"Brogan, please don't torture me," she whispered, her fingers clenching in the blanket above her head. "I've waited too long."

She'd waited so long for him.

"I'm going to enjoy this," he promised, his lips pressing to her thigh as she jerked in reaction. "Just let it have you, Eve. Let *me* have you. Let me give you all the pleasure you've waited for."

All the pleasure she'd waited for?

Could she bear it?

No.

She couldn't.

The first heated kiss to the swollen bud of her clit had her crying out as his head lifted. Her hips jerked, lifting to him as the first warning pulse of her orgasm began rippling through her.

"No. Damn you, Brogan, don't stop." The breathless demand came out as a desperate cry.

Gripping her hips, he controlled her movements easily as she tried to press closer to his mouth once again.

Easing his tongue through the swollen folds, he licked at her flesh, tasting the slick, wet heat spilling from her. Heated kisses along the bare folds stole her breath. As he lifted her feet to the narrow edge of the platform to open her more fully to him, her breath caught.

His tongue glided through the narrow slit, licking and probing as he moved lower. The rasp of his licking strokes moving over the sensitive flesh had her hips lifting to him. The needs assailing her were so unfamiliar they were impossible to anticipate. She couldn't hold back. Second by second she could feel more and more of herself becoming lost to this man.

Gasping, fighting to breathe through the building sensations, Eve couldn't help the cries falling from her lips. She couldn't hold back the burning, building pleasure of her cries.

Her pussy contracted in spasming waves as his tongue flicked around the clenched, weeping entrance of her sex. Quick, heated licks of his tongue lapped at the juices falling from her.

She screamed.

Brogan's tongue plunged inside her pussy, suddenly fucking into the delicate tissue, rasping around it as the sensitive flesh and clenched muscles clamped down in an effort to keep him inside her. The fierce impalement, the heated internal licks and sure stimulation of her nerve endings sent her hurtling through an explosion that completely devastated her senses.

Ecstasy tore through her. Her hips lifted, her hands jerking from above her head to bury themselves in his hair, clutching the strands, holding on tight, holding him to her. Eve's release swept through her.

His tongue pumped inside her, even through the brilliant explosions tearing her apart. Her pussy clenched and rippled, clamped down as heat surged from the depths of her cunt. Ecstasy sent her juices spilling to his tongue, explosions radiating through her as she cried out his name.

Shuddering, fighting to breathe, Eve sobbed beneath the overwhelming release, barely aware of Brogan moving, his hands forcing her fingers from his hair as she shuddered again.

She couldn't imagine a greater pleasure, a more sweeping release. She didn't believe she could survive it—until she became aware of the fiery, stretching invasion of her sex.

Her eyes opened, her gaze centering between her thighs. There, the head of his cock buried inside her as the slick folds of her flesh embraced the wide shaft.

"So fucking tight. Like a living vise clamped around my dick," Brogan growled as her gaze jerked up to his.

His eyes were a cloudy gray now, his face savagely hewn and pulled into lines of agonizing pleasure. Perspiration dotted his forehead, but a bead slid slowly down his neck. The muscles of his chest tightened, the exertion of holding back reflected plainly on his face.

Her gaze fell to her thighs again. Eve watched as he eased back, dragging the engorged crest from the spasming entrance of her pussy.

Throbbing, slick from her juices, the dark crest gleamed beneath the candlelight for a second, until he was pressing into her again, entering the flexing entrance and working into the snug muscles.

Eve's breath caught, the fiery heat blooming in the delicate tissue he slowly forced to part, stretching them until she was certain she could take no more. Until he pulled back and pressed inside again, stretching her further.

"Fuck, baby . . . Eve, it's so fucking good." He groaned, taking more of her, giving her more of himself.

With each inward stroke he filled her further, burying himself deeper and deeper inside the fierce clasp of her inner muscles.

"Brogan. More." She gasped. "Please, please, more."

More sensation. More pleasure. Enough sensation to send her hurtling into release again.

The incredible pleasure bordered on pain, crossed the line

only to ease back before building again. Each thrust was a stroke of pure, lancing sensation. Agony and ecstasy burned and flamed and kept her poised on such a brink of incredible rapture that she began to fear flying from the peak.

Each stroke buried him to the depths of her sex, the thrusts gaining in pace until the sound of their flesh slapping together filled her senses. She was so sensitive she swore she could feel the air brushing across it, the flickering warmth of the candles like a lick of flames.

Her internal muscles stretched around the impaling flesh, nerve endings so sensitive, so responsive that each thrust only pushed her higher.

She was screaming, yet only barely aware of it.

She was begging, terrified of the coming onslaught, desperate to weaken her release when it came. She could feel it building to a critical point. The sensations were flaming higher inside her as her pussy clamped on his cock. With each forward thrust he began fucking her harder, shafting inside her faster as he surged over her. His head lowered to her breasts, his lips covering a nipple and sucking it inside, tipping her over the edge.

Eve felt the explosions tear through her senses. The force and fury of her release flung her so high, so deep into ecstasy Eve swore she felt her soul open and merge. . . .

Felt it embraced and sheltered . . .

Brogan felt Eve's release as her pussy clamped down on his shuttling dick. Her eyes were open, her lips parted on a silent cry as he was taken unaware.

It happened so fast. It hit him with such force, with such impact, there was no saving either of them.

He knew the second it slipped his control and began blazing through him. The moment he realized the condom he wore had split, the latex folding back from the head of his cock. For the first time in his life he felt the full sensation of the lush, silken depths of his lover's pussy. He felt the heat of her slick cream as it surrounded his engorged cock head.

For the first time in his life he lost that last measure of control.

Eve exploded with the initial stroke of his bare cock. Her internal muscles rippled and stroked the wildly throbbing crest, then clamped down on it like an internal fist, milking it until his release began spurting furiously into her fiery depths.

A shattered groan tore from his chest as complete rapture drove spikes of ecstasy through his soul.

He had no idea what happened or how. As his release began spurting inside, the muscles of her pussy clamping and rippling over his dick, Brogan lifted his head, staring into her pleasure-dazed eyes, and he felt her. . . .

The ecstasy and the fear—the uncertainty and the—

God, no, he swore he could feel her heart, step into her soul. He could feel an emotion he couldn't allow himself to acknowledge as he buried his head at her shoulder and felt the last of his seed spurting inside her.

It had to be an aberration. Shock at the realization that he was spilling into her unprotected. That he was risking not just their lives, but possibly one more innocent than he could ever imagine.

Yet the thought of that hadn't been enough for him to pull free of the grip she had on him. It wasn't enough to hold back his release, or the need to give her all of himself once the condom ruptured. Nothing on the face of the earth could have held him back once he felt the unprotected depths of her pussy and the rich heat surrounding his bare cock.

And nothing could change the fact that he had given in to the urge to do just that.

As the last pulses of her waning orgasm caressed his cock, Brogan fought just to catch his breath. Beneath him, Eve was motionless, her own breathing hard, her heart racing in her breast beneath him as he forced himself to ease from her.

A shudder raced up his spine at the incredible pleasure of her snug grip as he pulled free of her. The overly sensitive head of his cock pulsed at the silky stroke of her slick inner muscles that had the shaft throbbing in renewed interest before he managed to pull free.

Hell, his knees were weak.

As he stood before her, his lips kicked up in a grin at the sight of her legs as they sprawled off the bed, her feet resting against the floor.

Picking her up, he laid her fully on the bed, brushed the tangled length of her hair back from her face, and wondered what the hell they were going to do now.

It was bad enough that he'd allowed her to be pulled into something that could possibly risk her safety. But now he'd done something she could find even more unforgivable. Something he didn't know whether he could even forgive himself for.

Yet he also knew he would do it again if he could.

If it happened again, if he once more found himself bare inside her that second before release, then he would give in to it. Because the pleasure had been astounding; the sensations, the intimacy of it had been more than he had ever imagined it would be.

Pulling back, he strode to the bathroom and quickly cleaned

and dried the proof of their release from his flesh before wetting
a clean cloth and grabbing a fresh towel. Returning to the bed he
had to grin at the sight of her as she slept. Sated, exhausted, she'd
given in to the weariness and slipped into sleep. He cleaned her
gently, easing the cloth between her legs, then through the soft
folds of her pussy before he quickly finished with her thighs.

Drying the dampness from her, he pulled the comforter and
sheet over her body before collapsing in the large chair by the
bed. Staring at her, watching her sleep, he couldn't help but wonder at this new joke fate seemed to be playing on him.

He had a woman whose qualities were exactly those he'd
once told friends he dreamed of finding in a woman: innocence,
honor, humor, and strength. She knew how to find amusement in
herself as well as the world around her, but she also knew compassion. She'd saved herself far longer than he had ever imagined
a woman of such beauty could have, and she had given herself
completely to him.

Because she loved him.

The thought smacked him like a blow to the head and rattled
his senses.

That was what he had felt as he stared into her dazed eyes,
feeling her release spill along the bare crest of his cock.

She believed she loved him, he amended. She couldn't truly
love him, because she didn't truly know him.

And once she did?

He sighed at the thought. Once she did, would she still believe
she loved him?

He highly doubted it.

TWELVE

Brogan stood next to the water, watching as bass jumped and frolicked playfully in the first morning light. It wasn't the bass that held his attention, though, any more than it was the beauty of the fog rising from the water and twisting around the trees growing along the bank. It was the unfamiliar emotions twisting and churning in his chest that held his attention.

He was thirty-four years old; there shouldn't be emotions he hadn't felt before, but these feelings were completely alien to him.

The possessiveness he knew and he understood. He wasn't a man who appreciated or practiced casual sex. One-night stands had never been his thing. It had always been his intention to develop a relationship with Eve. It had just been his intention to complete this operation first.

He'd never meant to drag her into whatever the hell was

going on in the Lake Cumberland area. And it had never, ever been his intention to risk the creation of a child.

Rubbing at the back of his neck, he paced at the edge of the lake, the sound of the water lapping at the bank joining the soft, early morning symphony as the memory of spilling his release inside Eve tormented his mind.

It had happened only one other time in his life, when he had been much younger. The condom hadn't ripped with such force, and he hadn't known the pleasure of finding his release as his bare cock sank inside the heated depths of his lover's pussy.

Rather, the small tear at the tip of the condom had allowed a small amount of his release free.

Brogan hadn't been ready to be a parent, but he'd accepted the responsibility of it. The day his fiancée had taken the home pregnancy test four weeks later, his heart had melted at the thought of their child when he'd seen the positive result.

They hadn't discussed it. She had never mentioned not wanting the child, but neither had she mentioned plans to abort the baby. Until he'd returned home from the law enforcement academy after officially being offered a position in the Department of Homeland Security.

He'd bought a teddy bear for the child, and had made plans to build a house on a piece of property outside his hometown. When he'd stepped in the door of the apartment Candy met him with a happy squeal as she threw herself in his arms. Pulling back, she'd looked at the teddy bear that had fallen at his feet and laughed. She wasn't ready for a child to blow her figure out of shape, and she definitely wasn't ready to settle down to the ties of motherhood.

And Brogan had never forgiven her.

The moment the admission of the abortion had slipped past

her lips, he was finished with her. He had felt grief wrap around his heart, felt the guilt and shame of it sear his soul. Their child had been innocent of its creation, and she hadn't been able to give nine months of her life to giving it birth?

He would have taken the child and raised it himself. Hell, he would have paid her to have the baby.

He'd broken their engagement immediately. As she cried, screamed, pretended confusion, and then raged in fury that it was her choice, he had packed.

The child hadn't just been hers; that baby had been his, too. It should have never been just her choice. He should have had a choice as well. Their child should have had a choice, he had raged at her as he left her life and never looked back.

What would Eve do? he wondered. Would she kill their child or would she shelter it? Could he take the chance that she would at least discuss the options with him?

He was torn, and holding the knowledge of what had happened the night before bothered him more as he thought of it. He'd raged at Candy for not giving him a choice in their child's birth, yet here he was, holding the truth of a possible conception from Eve, fearing the same result. What he was doing was no better than what Candy had done. He was refusing to give her a choice.

As the internal debate raged inside him, the muffled sound of a boat's motor moving closer to the cabin reached him. The narrow water lane leading to the hidden cabin wasn't one that could be accidentally taken. The safeguards set at the entrance of the tributary, the warnings placed farther up it, combined with strategically placed cables stretching across several points, the metal signs attached to them warning boaters back. It normally turned innocent curiosity seekers back.

Whoever his visitors were, they weren't there by accident. Pulling his weapon from where he'd tucked it at the small of his back, Brogan stepped behind the huge oak growing close to the water. From here, he could identify any threat and make his way back to the cabin before the boat could reach the beach. He would have time to pull Eve out if he had to, and to ensure her protection.

As the boat came into view, clearing the fog, the trolling motor easing it through the water, Brogan grimaced in irritation. This was definitely one of those uncalled-for occurrences in his life.

At the controls was Eli. Riding in the back of the expensive bass boat was Jed, cradling an automatic rifle. Sitting cool and comfortable in the seat next to Elijah was Chatham Bromleah Doogan III, director of operations and all-around fucking bastard.

There were opinions that he and Timothy Cranston were cut from the same cloth.

That wasn't exactly true. Cranston had a heart. He had compassion. Doogan had neither. Brogan was convinced pure ice water ran through his veins. That or oil. All good robots had to run on something.

As the boat pulled up to the small dock and Jed jumped out to secure it, Brogan stepped from behind the tree and strolled out to the boardwalk that led from the beach to the dock farther out in the water.

What the hell were they doing there cramping his day?

Doogan pulled off his dark glasses, amusement filling his dark brown eyes as a grin curled his lips.

"Dawg Mackay's looking for his sister and he's fit to be tied," Doogan stated, mockery filling his gaze. "He's a little overprotective, wouldn't you think?"

What would Doogan know about protectiveness?

"You don't have a sister, do you, Doogan?" Brogan asked.

Doogan shuddered, his gaze flashing in mock horror. "My parents were actually humane enough to stop with me," he said. "So I can't say I do."

"It shows," Brogan retorted.

Doogan scowled back at him. "Nevertheless, Dawg didn't care much for Timothy's explanation, nor mine. The fact that Dawg knew I was in Somerset still greatly concerns me. I was unaware he knew my full name." As opposed to the codename Doogan had insisted be listed instead. The only reason Brogan, Eli, and Booker were aware of it was because they'd trained with him, drank with him, and listened to his drunken ramblings before he'd begun his climb up the federal ladder.

"It should," Brogan assured him. "My question is, how did you find us?"

Doogan smiled complacently. "This is a political retreat, Brogan. All those nasty politicians with their young mistresses need someplace safe to hide. And someone has to make sure the place doesn't get overcrowded. That job falls to me."

"And if it does? Get overcrowded, that is," Brogan asked mockingly.

Doogan shrugged. "Federal Protective Service has a houseboat stored along a nearby tributary and another cabin hidden along the lake. But overcrowding doesn't happen if one is diligent."

"Regular little caretaker, aren't you?" Brogan taunted him.

Doogan tilted his head to the side. "Why do I keep seeing a real dishonorable discharge in your future?"

Brogan shrugged. "Wishful thinking maybe? Because we both know John David Bryce isn't going to allow that."

Doogan's eyes flashed with rueful laughter rather than the offense Brogan had intended.

"There is that," Doogan agreed. "It's kind of hard to fire the director of Homeland Security's bastard son, I would imagine."

"Well, a few have tried." Brogan shrugged. "I'm still here."

"Unfortunately, unfortunately," Doogan lamented on a sigh. "But I didn't come up here to trade insults, as much as I do enjoy the opportunity. And neither did I come up here to warn you about Dawg. Though I would enjoy being present when he finds you."

Brogan only snorted at the comment as he waited to see why Doogan had shown up.

Stepping from the boat, Doogan started around the small clearing. "It's really rather pretty here," he commented.

"Get to the point, Doogan," Brogan growled. "I have things to do."

Concern flashed in Doogan's eyes for a second before the brown depths were once again icy and emotionless.

"We need to seriously discuss this operation," he warned Brogan. "I know you; you intend to tell her your purpose for being here, and the fact that you were ordered to develop a friendship with her."

Brogan's brow lifted as he noticed the amused amazement on Elijah's and Jed's faces.

"A friendship?" Brogan questioned him. "Doogan, you've been playing pimp from afar for more than two years in your attempt to get me to invite myself into her bed. It was only your dumb luck that I wasn't able to stay the hell away from her any longer."

Doogan slid one hand casually into the pocket of his slacks as he stared back at Brogan coolly.

"I did you a favor, actually," he drawled. "You'll thank me for it later."

"Get the hell out of here before I have to shoot you." Brogan glowered back at him. "I don't have time to deal with you."

"Not until we discuss what you intend to tell Ms. Mackay."

"The truth," Brogan snapped. "I won't lie to her."

"I would highly suggest doing just that," his boss ordered. "She hasn't been cleared for this operation, and her brother and cousins sure as hell haven't been cleared for it." He swiped his fingers through his hair as he glared at Brogan now. "I'm ordering you not to inform her of your true purpose for being here. You will stick to the parameters of your cover and tell her nothing more."

Brogan almost laughed. Doogan liked to think he had some measure of control over his agents, but they'd all learned how to deal with his manipulations.

"Go to hell, Doogan. Tell me something I want to hear or get the hell out of here," he warned, hostile.

Brogan might not know what he was up to yet, but he'd figure it out. When he did . . . well, it wouldn't be the first time the two of them had fought.

"There are a few details we need to go over," Doogan began.

"Like the one where someone slipped into Eve's room last night," Elijah spoke up. "We saw it on the cameras when we returned to the inn. The same intruders tried to get into your room, but the new dead bolt you put on it kept them out long enough that they were forced to leave when Timothy made his rounds. That's why Dawg's trying to find you two. Timothy found her door unlocked, stepped inside to see the suite wrecked, and called her brother."

Brogan slid his gaze to Doogan slowly.

The other man stared back at him coolly before turning to Elijah and Jed. "I could have taken care of that."

"I was trying to help you out, boss." Elijah shrugged with a tight grin.

Doogan snorted in disbelief as he turned to Brogan. "You inspire insubordination," he accused irritably.

"You're welcome." Brogan inclined his head in a gesture of gracious accomplishment before turning back to Jed and Elijah. "Did they take anything from her room?"

Elijah shook his head in the negative. "They searched the hell out of it, though. She won't be happy."

She wasn't going to be happy to begin with.

"Why search her room?" he asked thoughtfully. "I can understand searching mine, but why hers?"

"Maybe to be certain you hadn't hidden anything there," Doogan pointed out. "You would expect your room to be searched, but not that of a woman you hadn't even made your lover yet."

Brogan frowned, turning to Eli. "Did anyone leave the trip yesterday after I did?"

Eli grimaced. "Poppa Bear called it off after you left. He said he wasn't going searching for scenic destinations or those caves the group was heading to see without the leader of the pack." He chuckled.

Doogan snickered at the comment.

"This happened before we arrived back at the inn," Elijah told him. "We were almost there when Donny asked exactly where the caves were, and Sambo commented that it would have been nice to have you there to make sure they were at the right place. That's when Poppa Bear called us all to pull into the parking lot of a grocery store and suggested coming back."

Sambo was a bear of a man and often pretended he didn't know his own ass from a hole in the mountain, let alone how to find some of the most popular caves in Kentucky.

"Did anyone know why I left?"

Jed and Elijah shook their heads. "I don't know if Donny and Sandi called anyone later or not, but they played real dumb after you left."

"You know, Brogan, that boy's acting damned strange anyway after the two of them went ape shit thinking one of them might die. If I didn't know better, I'd say they might love each other. A lot." Jed shook his head at the thought.

"That little strike was unsanctioned as hell," Doogan reminded them all before glaring at Brogan. "You don't use agency resources to get vengeance over a perceived slight to a potential girlfriend, Agent Campbell."

Brogan found it strange that Doogan knew about it to begin with. And he'd had to have said something to Jed or Eli about it first for either of them to have discussed it with him.

Brogan turned to the other two men. "Is that everything Doogan needed to tell me?"

Eli grinned as the director shot a silencing look at him and then at Jed. Brogan knew that if there was more, one of them would call or text the moment they had the chance.

"Anything else I need to know before you leave?"

"Don't tell her what you're doing here, Brogan," Doogan warned him again. "She'll tell her brother, her brother will tell his cousins, and then I'll have to start arresting Mackays."

"I'll consider your argument. . . ."

"No, damn you, you won't consider shit," Doogan burst out furiously as he stepped closer. "I'm giving you a direct order, you little son of a bitch. If you want to keep your job, you'll obey it."

Brogan's eyes narrowed, though he was very damn careful to hold back the suspicion he could feel churning in his gut.

"Feel that strongly about it, do you?" he asked softly.

"I feel that strongly about your deliberate, constant insubordination," Doogan snapped. "Get a handle on it before I take care of it myself."

Stepping onto the bow of the fishing boat, Doogan stepped back into the boat and took his seat as he shot Brogan a deliberately superior look.

"Move out, Agent Grant," he ordered Eli.

Eli did as ordered as Jed rolled his eyes and gave Brogan a quick, short shake of his head.

This was why he preferred working with Jed and Eli instead of the two agents over those in the regional office. He could trust them to cover his back, both in and out of the field. His gut was already telling him Doogan's reaction was way off base.

He'd come out there specifically to piss Brogan off. All he'd done was make him highly suspicious. The other man was a manipulator. And he was trying to ensure that Brogan did as he wanted him to do, not as he was telling him to do.

Doogan wanted the Mackays in on this operation, and he'd wanted them there from the beginning.

From the first day Brogan had set foot in Pulaski County, Doogan had been pushing him toward Eve.

Walking back to the house as the last of dawn began to slip away, he knew Doogan was only pushing him, or Eve, into informing her brother of Brogan's mission. And Brogan couldn't figure out why the other man didn't say so. Brogan had finally put Doogan's manipulations together. He was salivating to get the Mackays on this operation.

Doogan was a hell of a manipulator, but usually he was only this bad when he had no other choice. And if he wanted the Mackays so badly, why not just ask them himself? Or he could have gone to Timothy. There were few things Timothy enjoyed more than manipulating Mackays; he would have loved to have pulled Dawg and his cousins into the operation himself.

There were few things Doogan loved more than the chance to do his own manipulating, too, though. Once he saw that pulling the Mackays in would actually take some effort, he would have done exactly as he did: rushed straight to Somerset and set his plans in motion. Plans that would get him killed if they managed to harm even the first silken hair on Eve's head.

Eve stood in the large bathroom staring through the window that looked out onto the water and the small beach with its long dock extending out to deeper water.

It was the faint sound of the boat's trolling motor moving up the waterway that had urged Eve to crawl from the bed and go to the bathroom, where she could see the beach more clearly. And boy, had she gotten an eyeful that she hadn't expected.

It was easy to recognize the three men Brogan had just been talking to. Jedediah Booker and Elijah Grant, the two building contractors staying at her mother's inn, along with Chatham Doogan, were meeting with Brogan.

She couldn't hear what they were saying, but she'd been able to follow their expressions. Brogan had been trying to hide his irritation and suspicion, where both Jedediah and Elijah looked more amused than anything else.

The one thing that had clearly come across, though, and really pissed her off was the fact that Brogan and Doogan obviously knew each other very, very well.

Liars. She hated them. There was something about deliberate lies and deceit that reminded her far too much of Chandler Mackay.

As Brogan moved toward the house, Eve turned and rushed back to the bed, knowing he would come straight to her. He wouldn't wait; he wouldn't find anything else to do.

Crawling back into the huge, obviously custom-made bed, she pulled the sheet to her breasts just as Brogan entered the room. He came to an immediate stop as he saw she was awake and waiting for him.

Instantly wariness seemed to settle around him, though his expression didn't change. It didn't flicker in his gaze, and there was no tension in his body. So she had no clue how she knew he was suddenly unsettled by the fact that she was waiting for him.

"You're awake," he stated softly, moving toward her as she watched him closely.

"For a while now," she agreed. "I wondered where you were."

"I had some business that couldn't wait." He grimaced as he rubbed at his jaw. "We'll discuss it later. Are you ready for breakfast yet, or would you like a hot bath first?"

They would discuss it later?

Eve could feel an impending sense of panic settling in her stomach.

"I'd rather discuss the business first," she argued.

Brogan shook his head, his lips tilting in that little partial grin she thought was so sexy.

"Breakfast or bath." Evidently, those were her only choices. "Which do you prefer first? There are some bath salts to ease the soreness in your muscles, imported all the way from China." Rueful amusement tinged the blue-gray depths of his gaze.

"Bath, I guess." She shrugged. "Brogan?"

He paused as he moved to turn to the bathroom, staring down at her questioningly instead.

"This business we're going to discuss," she asked as her heart began beating hard and sluggishly. "Is it something bad?"

"No, it's nothing bad." He shook his head. "Don't worry, sweetheart; everything will be okay. I promise."

But he didn't really believe that. He wanted to, she thought. He might be trying to convince himself it would be, but she could sense his uneasiness, and that was freaking her out just a bit. She shouldn't be able to sense anything that he wasn't showing the obvious signs to.

"I'll start your water." Turning, he headed back to the bathroom before pausing at the door and glancing back at her. "You have several changes of clothes; wear whatever you like. I thought we'd take a walk after breakfast, but the path is easy enough for sandals or sneakers."

A walk sounded nice. Or was that when he was going to discuss the business of Chatham, Elijah, and Jedediah's morning visit?

Checking the bag he had brought, Eve pulled out one of the heavy plastic hair clips she used to pin her hair up. Twisting the long strands to the top of her head, she clipped it in place before moving to the bathroom when he left.

True to his word, he had started her bath. The water was deliciously warm without being too hot. The bath salts gave it a silky, caressing feel as she settled into it, sighing at the luscious sensation of the water easing overused muscles.

The tub itself was large enough for two or three people. There was an open shower larger than her entire bathroom. The vanity and sleek modern overlarge sink sat on one side of the room, a pair of heavy padded chairs beside it. The toilet was in a room by itself, separated from the bathing area with a sliding wooden door that pushed into the wall. Heated ceramic tiles covered the floor, while more tile covered the walls and gave the bathroom an elegant, charming feel. It was luxurious and ultrarich, with enough wasted space to house two more regular-size bathrooms.

The entire house was a rich person's play den, nothing more. One of those places the megarich kept as a hidden sex spot: wild parties, mistresses, booze, and drugs. Hell, in the other bathroom there had been an eight-ball of cocaine sitting in the medicine cabinet in plain view.

She hadn't checked this bathroom that well yet.

Finishing her bath with the fragrant soap Brogan had laid out for her, Eve stepped from the tub nearly half an hour later. Drying herself, she brushed her hair until the silky sheen gleamed a blue-black, then dressed quickly.

The white lace panties and matching bra she'd found in the bag comprised one of her nicer sets. Trust Brogan to pick out the best she had.

The short cream-colored chiffon skirt and matching sleeveless top slid over her skin as she dressed, caressing it with cool silkiness.

The top was held up by fragile straps over her shoulders, while the shallow vee cut of the bodice revealed the upper curves of her breasts. The skirt fell just below her thighs, the soft flare of the material making her legs appear much longer and sexier.

She was dressed now and ready to face whatever lies or perhaps explanations Brogan might have.

Nervously she left the bedroom and headed to the main part of the house. There she found Brogan in the large open kitchen sliding pancakes onto a plate with steaming eggs. Beside it sat another plate, while bacon, sausage, and fluffy biscuits filled a platter.

"I thought we'd sit on the breakfast patio." Grabbing the two plates and silverware, Brogan nodded to the platter. "Grab that. The coffee's already out there."

The breakfast patio held a wide table and seating for six. Sitting across from Brogan at one end, she stared at the tall picture windows that surrounded them on three sides.

Eve enjoyed the view outside as they ate in silence. At one point, a doe moved through the trees beyond the glass, and a thought piqued her curiosity.

"What happens if hunters accidently shoot this way?" Hunting season would be coming around in a few months.

"The windows are actually bullet resistant. The glass itself has a special coating that blocks anyone outside from looking in." He volunteered more information. "All the windows in the house are similarly secured. The basement has a security room with its own backup generator, and that wall"—he indicated the mural painted on the wall leading into the living area—"has a hidden panel to a safe room. There are satellite phones, cell phones, and a landline. The wires to the landline are buried nearly six feet deep and run through metal pipes. The phone and electrical wiring runs through the house in titanium tubing, and it's almost impossible to open the access panels without the proper key."

"Wow." Sipping her coffee, she turned back to him. "All the comforts of home, huh?" She grinned.

"Just about," he agreed as he bit into a sausage link.

"So, which ultrabillionaire does it belong to?"

"The government." He finished his coffee before placing the cup on the table. "Are you ready for that walk now?"

"I don't know," she answered, staring back at him with a sense of nervous awareness. "Are we taking a walk to avoid the questions I'm going to ask?"

"To answer your questions, Eve," he promised her softly. "Whatever you want to ask. As soon as I tell you a few things, then you can ask all the questions you like."

Rising from the table, he held his hand out to her, his expression closed and guarded. "Walk with me, baby."

Placing her hand in his, Eve let him draw her to her feet and lead her through the open kitchen and living area to the wide patio she'd sat on the night before. Opening the glass patio doors, Brogan stood aside, allowing her to step into the cool mountain air before he closed the doors behind them. Eve couldn't help but feel she should have stayed where she was.

She should have waited.

She should have begged him to make love to her one more time before she learned something that could destroy every possibility of her staying with him.

She should have never gotten out of the bed at the sound of the boat motor and taken a chance on seeing the men who had arrived. If she hadn't, she would have never known he was hiding anything. And that, she thought, was her biggest mistake.

Getting out of the bed.

If she had just stayed, then when he returned to the bedroom she would have done as she had been fantasizing. She would have tempted him to lie down with her again, perhaps convinced him to allow her the exploration of his body before he took her again.

But no, Eve had to be nosy.

She had a feeling she wasn't going to like the consequences of that nosiness now.

THIRTEEN

Stepping from the cool interior of the luxurious house to the heated summer warmth of the sun was a comforting feeling. This was the part of Kentucky that Eve loved so much: the heat overhead, the cool, sheltered shadows of the surrounding trees, and the lush vibrancy of the mountains.

"It's so pretty here," she said as he led her along a decorative gravel path that wound through the trees. "And peaceful."

He settled his palm against the small of her back as they followed the path, and Eve swore she could feel a sense of hesitancy filling him.

"It's not very peaceful when the parties get started up here." He sighed. "Sometimes it's been a veritable den of iniquity for days at a time."

He was giving her the perfect opportunity to delve into the questions she'd claimed to want to ask.

"You can't tell it's been anything but this peaceful," she commented as they continued along the path. "I remember when we first came to Somerset. Timothy flew us in and pretty much surprised Dawg with our existence. But I remember the drive to the house Timothy was living in at the time. The mountains were so beautiful and so green. After spending most of our lives in northern Texas, it was like an alien world."

She was aware of him glancing down at her thoughtfully. She rarely talked about their arrival in Kentucky. The years in Texas hadn't always been pleasant, and remembering them was something she rarely enjoyed.

"How did Dawg react to meeting four sisters and their mother? Hell, Mercedes is younger than he is, isn't she?" he questioned her curiously.

Eve nodded as she pushed her hands into the hidden pockets at the side of the skirt. "He's older by several years. The day we arrived at the marina, Momma was sick. Timothy was trying to explain to Dawg who we were when Zoey rushed in accusing him of not wanting us." She grinned at the memory. "The rest of us were in the truck with Momma, but I remember seeing his face when he came out to where we were. He looked completely stricken."

"Good God." Brogan gave a surprised laugh. "There's no way in hell he could deny he's related to Zoey. Look at her and you're looking at the image of his daughter in a few more years."

"They're the image of each other now." Eve laughed lightly. "Christa thinks it's a hoot when people mistake Zoey for Laken's mother."

"And how did Dawg react to Zoey?" he asked her, his tone husky with amusement.

"Zoey swears he looked like he was going to cry. She says his hands were shaking. But as soon as she mentioned Momma was sick again, Timothy rushed outside to the truck where we were waiting. After that, it was like Dawg had always been there watching over us."

She glanced up at Brogan, seeing the understanding in his eyes. "He made sure Momma got the tests and medication she needed. He moved us in with him and Christa while Momma was in the hospital. When he learned Momma had always wanted her own bed-and-breakfast inn, he had one waiting for her when she came out of the hospital. He'd completely remodeled it and had everything perfect for her. He told her he didn't have just four sisters; he had five. And he had to take care of her, too."

Rounding a bend in the path, Eve came to a surprised stop, delight racing through her at the sight of the small trickling stream flowing past a nearly hidden grotto.

Beneath the canopy of wisteria and honeysuckle was a wide padded bench almost half the size of a bed.

"Can we go in?" she asked, the urge to stretch out on the padded bench nearly overwhelming.

"Of course." Catching her hand, he held it with his own as he led her beneath the wide opening.

Releasing her to explore, Brogan leaned against the heavy support post as she sat on the padded stone bench before stretching out on it and staring up at the fragrant, colorful clusters of flowers hanging above her from amid the leafy green.

"It's so beautiful," she said wistfully, wishing she could hold back time just a little longer. That she could still the questions raging inside her.

Turning her head, she stared back at him. His gaze met and

locked with hers, regret flickering in the blue-gray depths. Did he wish time could be held back as well? That they could have just a few more hours before reality had to be dealt with?

Sitting up slowly and tucking her legs to the side, she took a deep breath.

"Are you going to lie to me?" she asked, somehow knowing she would sense it if he did.

"I won't lie to you," he promised. "I may not be able to answer some questions, but I won't lie."

Eve looked away. She gazed down at her lap and watched her fingers for long moments as they twisted together. When she lifted her gaze to his once again, it was to see the regret he made no effort to hide now.

"Why did you wait so long?" she finally asked. "And why now?" She had flirted with him since she had first met him the day he arrived in Somerset two and a half years before.

"I waited because I didn't believe it was fair to drag you into my world," he explained, his voice heavy as he crossed his arms over his chest. "Why now? Because I couldn't stand it any longer, Eve. I've wanted you since that first day, and waiting simply wasn't any option any longer."

His answer only made her next question harder. Twisting her fingers together in her lap, she watched his eyes as she asked, "How do you know Chatham Doogan, and why did you show up at the restaurant last night?"

"Fuck, we couldn't start with the easy questions first, could we?" He grimaced before his eyes narrowed on her. "I'm going to be honest with you, Eve, but I'm telling you now: No one— not your brother, your sisters, or your mother—can know about this. It goes no further, no matter what."

"It won't go any further," she promised. She knew his answers weren't going to be easy to hear, though.

"Chatham Bromleah Doogan the third." He gave a short, bitter laugh. "He's my boss, sort of. He's the operations director for the regional office of the Federal Protective Service. It's a division of Homeland Security that deals with the protection and security of federal buildings, employees, assets, and possessions. And if you tell anyone what I'm telling you today, then Doogan is going to jump on it like a dog on a bone and drag your brother and cousins into something I don't think they want to be a part of."

Eve stared back at him, expecting him to declare, "April Fools'," despite the fact that it was already June. If not that, then, "psych," or, "joke," or some declaration to indicate that he certainly wasn't serious. But the longer she stared at him, the more she knew it wasn't coming. The more sense it made.

"You're not a traitor then?" she finally asked. "You haven't been stealing government files left and right or attempting to weaken the pillars of society?"

A bitter smile pulled at his lips. "I don't know about the pillars of society, but sorry, baby, the thieving is pretty much true. For the past two and a half years I've been a thieving son of a bitch."

Her hands were shaking. As Eve stared at her hands in her lap she realized they were trembling like leaves in a storm.

"Why?" she asked, keeping her gaze on her hands, wondering whether she could will them to be still.

"It's part of the investigation FPS is conducting to catch the thieves actually stealing government files from independent analysts who were contracted to study them," he explained.

Okay, so he was pretending to be a thieving son of a bitch, she thought as her gaze lifted to him again. That was the easy part. There was much more than this going on; Chatham's presence at the boat dock proved that.

"Before you ask this next question be damned sure you want the answer," he warned her as her lips parted.

"How do you know what I'm going to ask?" Her voice was faint, cautious.

She could feel things she didn't understand. Feelings and suspicions she wasn't certain were hers.

"The hell if I know, but I can tell," he growled in annoyance.

"So tell me." No. She really didn't want to know. She needed to know, but she didn't want to. The truth truly could hurt.

Brogan's jaw clenched savagely. "You want to know why Doogan asked you to dinner and why I came back and dragged you out of there. That's what you're ready to ask."

She wasn't exactly ready, but . . .

She stared at him in shock before turning away for long moments. How had he known? The same way she knew he didn't want to tell her? The way she knew he'd never intended for her to ever have the opportunity to ask even the questions she was asking?

She turned back to him and nodded slowly.

"Doogan asked you to dinner to force me to do exactly what I did," he revealed. "Donny heard him invite you to dinner, heard the location and your answer. The bastard let me get three hours out of town before he was good enough to tell me. And I came back for you, by God, because you're mine! And that's besides the fact that I've never fucking cared for Doogan's poaching tendencies. Coming back for you was a hell of a lot easier than trying to get out of a murder charge."

Eve could feel her insides shaking now as well. She was trembling from the inside out, shaking with the desperate need to deny what he was telling her.

"That doesn't make sense, Brogan," she whispered. "How could I be of any use to Homeland Security or to Chatham?"

"Not so much you as your brother and cousins. Doogan wants the Mackays to solve this for him, without his asking. If he has to ask and they solve it, then he owes them major. They solve it because you're possibly in danger or your lover endangers you, then it's just a freebie and he doesn't owe them a damned thing."

There had to be more, though. She could feel it, sense he was holding back. But if she didn't ask the right question, then he wouldn't tell her. But she knew it wasn't just a case of pulling her brother and cousins into some conniving bastard's operation.

Staring back at him, she whispered, "Is everyone in Homeland Security manipulating bastards with nothing better to do than scheme and interfere in innocent people's lives?"

Brogan shook his head. "Timothy and Doogan are freaks of nature best avoided."

"So Chatham Doogan asked me out knowing you would return once you found out about it and then make me your lover?" she asked dubiously. "How could he be so certain it would work?"

"Because he's a freak of nature," he repeated. "Men like that can calculate the odds and then find ways to turn the situation to their favor. That's what Doogan is best at."

"All of this just so Dawg, Rowdy, and Natches would help solve a case for him?"

Brogan nodded.

"How are they supposed to accomplish something you've not yet managed?" she bit out, her fingers forming fists as offended anger began to surge through her senses.

Brogan's lips tilted in a smile, more rueful than mocking. "They know this county and the people in it," he told her. "Even more, they know which rocks to turn over and the heads to knock together to get the answers they need."

"And you think they haven't gotten tired of waiting and are doing it anyway?" she asked in disbelief. "Brogan, this is their home, and they wouldn't let this go on without helping if they knew about it."

He shook his head, his arms dropping from his chest.

"No, Eve, I don't think that's what they're doing," he said acerbically. "There's doing what's required because the director of operations of the Federal Protective Service threatened to imprison you if you stuck your nose in another agency operation. Then there's active determination to finish the job before something happens to the baby sister you swore you would protect. The first kind of man steps in only when asked to. The second doesn't wait to be asked."

And Dawg wouldn't wait to be asked if he thought Eve, Piper, Lyrica, or Zoey were in danger.

"And you think Dawg won't figure it out?" she questioned him harshly. "For God's sake, Brogan, I promised him I would stay away from you. That I wouldn't take as a lover the only man he couldn't bear to see me with. Trust me; Dawg will question me. He'll want to know why I broke my promise when I've never done it before."

What had she done to betray her brother?

Disbelief crashed through her system as the reality of it, of the fact that she had done the one thing Dawg, her brother, had asked her not to do. The only thing he had ever asked her not to do.

"He should have never made you promise to stay away from me." His brow arched, mockery gleaming in his eyes, but Eve could feel the thread of anger emanating from him.

"You're a suspected traitor, Brogan," she reminded him.

"Living in the same house as a former Homeland Security special agent," he reminded her. "Don't fool yourself, sweet pea. Dawg Mackay knows a traitor when he's in the presence of one. Just as he knows an agent when one's around."

Eve stared back at him, hurting, her heart aching so fiercely she reached up to rub at her chest, trying to ease the burning tightness.

He was right. Dawg would have known Brogan was no traitor, so why would he deceive her? Make her believe he suspected Brogan of being exactly that?

"Maybe it's because everyone else believes you're one?" she questioned him, her voice rough. "Or maybe it's because he suspected what your boss is capable of doing."

Still, Dawg had led her to believe he, too, suspected Brogan of treason, or acting against his country. And because he had believed it, Eve had questioned her own instincts where Brogan was concerned.

"Tell me, Eve, when you made that promise, did you intend to keep it?" The look in his eyes warned her he wasn't happy she had given in to Dawg's demand.

Had she intended to keep it?

Eve had never lied to herself, but she realized she had lied to her brother.

"My head did," she finally whispered. "But my heart wasn't so certain."

Staring up at him, Eve realized that even when Dawg had asked for her promise, she had known it was unfair. Just as she had known it would be impossible for her to keep.

Rising to her feet, she had every intention of returning to the lake house, gathering her things together, and leaving. There were too many emotions swirling inside her. Too many that she could sense were coming from Brogan, and too many of her own that she didn't understand.

Then there was the hunger.

Through the conversation, each question and answer, there had been an unspoken hunger building, growing between them: needs she didn't understand, hungers that raged and built until she was certain she wasn't sensing just her own, but his as well.

"Where are you going?" he demanded as she moved past him.

"I have to leave, Brogan." Staring up at him, she felt torn, so torn she couldn't make sense of it. "I need time to think."

"Time to think about what?" he demanded, his hands catching her hips and pulling her into him. "About us? Or about keeping a promise you should have never made to begin with?"

"Maybe I need to think about the fact that I really don't like being controlled," she burst out. "Not by my brother, your boss, or you."

She faced him, her chin lifting proudly as she tried—hell, she fought—to ignore the needs raging through her.

Hard and erect, his cock pressed into her stomach.

She was wet, slick, and hot, the weeping heat spilling to the bare folds of her pussy and dampening her panties.

"And I already warned you that was something you should

have already considered. It's too damned late to think you can just walk away, Eve," he warned her.

"I can do whatever I want to do," she informed him defiantly.

"Then maybe I need to remind you why you don't want to," he stated, his tone rasping, assuring her that the thought of her leaving was one Brogan was refusing to entertain.

"Why?" she cried out, the uncertainties assailing her driving home the fact that maybe she really didn't know the man she had allowed herself to sleep with the night before.

No, she hadn't known him, something protested inside her, but she knew him now. She could stare into his face, into his eyes, and she could see him now. She could see the man staring down at her and recognize the emotions swirling beneath the chilly surface of his gaze.

What she sensed there had her body instantly priming for sex. Her clit swelled; her pussy began heating, the slick dampness preparing her vagina for his invasion. She could feel the fierce determination swirling in the depths of his gaze reaching out to her. And being able to read him so well now was a little freaky.

"I can fucking feel you." He grimaced, his blue-gray eyes darkening, flashing with frustration. "It's like you're slapping me with your hurt feelings and uncertainty. Stop it!"

"Stop it?" Shooting him a withering look, she propped her hands on her hips in vexation. "Fine, Brogan, I'll stop slapping you with the fact that everyone around me seems to be using me, for some reason, and you can stop slapping me with all that arrogance and distrust I can feel rushing from you." She started to turn away before turning back to him. "And while you're at it, stop fucking me in your mind. It was bad enough before, when all I had to worry about was changing my panties because of my own dirty thoughts, but yours are just plain depraved." Her arms crossed beneath her breasts as she stared back at him, incensed.

His gaze became shuttered, brooding as she watched him, her heart racing with anger and excitement.

"You've never felt this before either, have you?" That certainty was as clear as the knowledge that the arousal hardening his body was only burning hotter inside him by the minute.

"Felt what?" Guarded, cautious, he watched her almost impassively.

"Forget it." Shaking her head, she refused to allow herself to be drawn into an argument he would only find ways to refute. "Just mark it down to my overactive imagination. But remember, Brogan, you're the one who told me to stop slapping you with my emotions first. I was keeping my mouth shut about it."

That was what she sensed, felt. As though a part of her had opened up to him, making her completely empathic when it came to him.

And, it seemed, him to her.

"Chatham Doogan spoke to me first at the bar," she gritted out between clenched teeth, determined to steer the conversation well away from what they were feeling. "John Walker introduced him as an old friend of his and Sierra's."

"Sierra's a distant cousin," he admitted grudgingly.

"He asked me to dinner; I accepted. Why did the two of you pretend you didn't know each other at the restaurant?"

"Because it was the wrong place and time for explanations." His tone was clipped as the curve of his jaw tightened into unyielding lines.

Complete denial filled his expression and his gaze, but that did nothing to change what she could feel—or what she could sense, perhaps.

She wasn't certain what it was. Staring back at him, she could feel his anger, his sudden distrust, but also his arousal. And that was building by the second.

"I'm ready to go home, Brogan. . . ."

"No, you're not. You're as damned ready to fuck as I am." Dripping with carnality, his voice roughened, lowering insinuatingly. "What do you want, Eve? My tongue filling your tight little pussy again? My cock fucking your mouth until you can taste my release?" As he spoke, his sharp, almost insulting tone became hoarse, heated.

And he was right; she wanted that and more.

Warily, she watched as he moved closer, his head tilting as he stared down at her, his gaze becoming dark, stormy as it glittered almost feverishly.

"And you want it here," he stated provocatively. "Don't you, Eve? Right here within this grotto, spread out on that bench." His head lowered, his lips brushing at her ear. "You want my tongue and my cock so deep inside your pussy that you can't bear any more. But you want more than that, don't you?" he whispered then, surprise and rapacious anticipation growling in his voice. "You want it to hurt just that little bit again. You liked it, didn't you? Fuck, no." His breathing was heavy, harsh. "You loved it."

"Stop." She couldn't fight this battle. She didn't have the experience or the knowledge to combat what he was sensing.

"Do you know what I would love to do to you?" His hand lifted, the calloused tips of his fingers running up her arm. "I'd love to turn you over on your stomach, prop that pretty rounded ass up to me, and spank it until it flushes cherry red. Until your pussy is so wet your thighs are damp with your cream. And when you're begging, so desperate to be fucked that nothing else matters, I want to watch my dick stretch your ass, watch as that tiny, tiny little entrance blooms around my cock and sucks it inside."

She couldn't breathe.

Eroticism rushed through her, weakening her knees and accelerating her breathing as he gripped her hip with his other hand while the fingers stroking her arm slid to the curve of her rear.

Cupping the rounded flesh of her rear cheeks beneath the soft chiffon of her skirt, he clenched the rounded flesh, pulling at it, igniting a tiny burst of heated sensation in her anus.

"I could make that hurt so good, Eve. You won't know if it's agony or ecstasy. All you'll know is that you want more. That you have to have more."

She was shaking in his arms, trembling as his hand moved between them, obviously loosening his belt, then his jeans.

"Brogan." Protest or pleasure?

She had no idea what she was feeling or how she should react. She had no idea how to handle the wicked, carnal animal Brogan was unleashing on her.

Or the one he was unleashing in her.

"I can't take your ass here." Grudging regret filled his voice. "Unfortunately, the lube and toys are all back at the house, baby. But I can give you part of what you want."

His jeans parted and a second later she could feel him stroking the hard, heated length of his cock as her nails curled against the shirt covering his wide chest.

"Why . . . why are you doing this . . . ?" Why was he using his ability to sense only her sexual needs and not the rest of her?

The sexuality, the hunger for him, was rooted in something much deeper than lust.

"Because I'm just as hungry to do it as you are to have it done," he admitted, his tone ragged. "And I'm going to do it, Eve. Just like you're going to suck my dick, right here. Right now."

His gaze was narrowed as her gaze jerked to his in sudden nervous awareness.

"Go to your knees," he demanded, though his tone gentled at the last second. "Show me how badly you want to come for me, sweetheart. Show me how badly you want me to come in your hot little mouth."

Sensation erupted in her womb, spasming through it as his gaze suddenly gleamed with avid hunger and awareness.

"On your knees." The erotic command sent wanton excitement exploding through her senses.

Slowly, her gaze held by his, she went to her knees.

His fingers slid into her hair, clenching it and holding her in place as he gripped the base of his cock and rubbed it against her lips.

"I love watching my dick slide between your lips," he confessed, his voice thick and rough. "Watching you suck it in as that hot little tongue licks over it. Suck it in, Eve. Show me how much you want it."

Her lips parted, her tongue curling over the engorged crest as he pressed inside, filling her mouth with the throbbing heat of his cock head.

She wrapped the fingers of both hands around the thick shaft as she began to milk it slowly, her mouth tightening on the crest, sucking it deep as it filled the damp interior.

Brogan's hands clenched in her hair, his hips suddenly tense, the need to thrust inside her mouth filling him.

Fuck. How had this happened? He'd been certain he'd never convince his sexually inexperienced little Eve to become so brazen and wanton.

Eyes closed, her face flushed and absorbed in the complete sexuality overtaking her, Brogan watched as her lips stretched to take the broad crest.

Her mouth suckled at the iron-hard flared head; she milked it with her mouth and hands as each draw sent brutal lashes of pleasure striking at his balls, surrounding his dick. Her delicate hands moved on the wide shaft, masturbating it in rhythm to the hungry draws of her mouth.

"Sweet Eve." He groaned, his body taut with the sweeping pleasure. "That hot little mouth makes me crazy." His hips moved, thrusting shallowly against her stretched lips. "Your fucking mouth is so damned good. Watching my dick take your mouth is so damned hot."

Her lips tightened, her mouth drawing on the fiercely erect cock head. Her tongue lashed beneath the flared head, rubbing at the highly sensitive, nerve-laden area just beneath the crest.

Exquisite pleasure tightened around the taut sac of his balls. Clenched tight beneath the base of his cock, his testicles throbbed, ached for release. He watched her lips surrounding the throbbing crest as he fucked in, pulling free, the glistening moisture followed by the lash of her tongue around the crest.

His fingers held her hair, keeping her head firmly in place as he pressed deeper.

"Take it, baby," he crooned, encouraging her hunger. "Just relax. Breathe out and swallow."

His cock slid to the back of her mouth, and the feel of her swallowing against the tip sent jagged forks of sensation rushing straight to his balls.

Brogan knew he wasn't going to last much longer. Hell, he didn't want to last much longer. He wanted to watch her face, see her take his release as he filled her mouth with it.

His thrusts increased, a ragged groan escaping his chest as he swore he could feel something more. He swore he could feel wild hunger, fierce pleasure, and a tempting adventurousness that he knew had to belong to her.

He could sense her pleasure.

He could sense her hunger.

His cock slid faster inside her gripping mouth, sinking to the depths of it, feeling her moan ripple against the sensitive head. Each sensation, each strike of pleasure that began in the flared, responsive crest echoed stronger, hotter in his balls. Her hands stroked and milked the shaft; her tongue licked and lashed; her mouth sucked and tightened around it. Pleasure whipped through the hardened flesh, coalesced in his steadily tightening testicles before it exploded through his system.

"Suck it. Fuck. Suck it deep, baby." He surged to the back of her mouth as his head tilted back in furious rapture. Brogan felt the ecstasy explode in his balls before it rushed in furious release to the broad head of his cock.

Throbbing, expanding in rapture, Brogan felt the first heavy gush of his semen spurting into her mouth as she struggled to take it.

Each subsequent explosive eruption drew a ragged groan from his throat. With each pulse of semen blasting to her throat, she swallowed, sending spikes of ragged pleasure shooting through his system.

Each spurt of his release jetting into her mouth, Brogan realized he felt more than he had ever felt before at the point of orgasm. He could feel his own release, feel it tearing through him, weakening his knees and draining his balls. But he felt hunger. A wild, tempestuous hunger that blazed with a heat that he knew could belong only to Eve.

A heat he had a feeling would turn into a conflagration and burn them both to cinders.

FOURTEEN

Eve was shaking, arousal and pure white-hot need flooding her bloodstream and pounding through her veins. As she stood before him, her knees shaking and weak, her senses dazed from the excitement surging through her system, she watched as Brogan toed off his sneakers, then slipped his jeans from his powerful legs.

He was still wearing the white, luxuriously soft cotton shirt buttoned to his chest. Those buttons were falling open beneath his fingers, though, revealing his powerful chest with its mat of red-gold curls and the almost invisible freckles she'd glimpsed the night before as the candlelight had gleamed off the powerful muscles.

He was so incredibly tall and strong. It was one of the first things Eve had noticed about him: that strength and easy power that he wore so effortlessly.

Moving to her, his hands framed her face, and though she hadn't expected it, she watched in surprise as his head lowered to cover her lips with his.

The kiss was deep, searing, and intimate.

His tongue brushed over her lips, then over her tongue. He sipped at her lips, kissed them, drew her deeper into the twisting storm of sensation rushing through her.

"God, how pretty you are," he whispered, reaching out to touch her. "Come here, baby."

He sat down on the padded bench and his hand wrapped around the back of her neck. He pulled her to him. This time the feel of his lips moving over hers dragged a cry from her. The sound was so ragged it startled her, so filled with hunger it was shocking, even to her.

Running his hands down her back to her thighs, Brogan pressed her legs apart before he moved one to make her straddle him before pulling her closer to him.

She found herself straddling his lap, her rear resting on his knees as he kissed her with pure carnal demand. His hands gripped her rear, slowly pulling the curves apart until Eve felt the tingles of heat as the nerve endings in her puckered rear entrance revealed themselves.

Was she insane to have pushed him as she had? To have revealed how much she had enjoyed the pleasure-pain sensations he had given her the night before? But how could she have hidden the knowledge of it from him when she responded so readily to the more intense pleasure?

Whatever had happened the night before to bind them together hadn't been the aberration she had thought it to be. It was still there, and she wasn't the only one feeling it.

As he urged her closer she knew where he wanted her, knew he wanted her as he helped her remove the cami and her bra.

Easing his lips from hers, he kissed the line of her jaw, moving lower, drawing a cry from her as pleasure began washing through her.

Kissing his way from her lips to her neck, he laid more of the stinging kisses to the base of her neck, where he paused, caressing the skin there with a sharp, fiery kiss that dragged a startled moan from her lips.

Then one hand moved from her rear, slid beneath her breast, and lifted it, and he surrounded the small, pebbled tip with the heat of his mouth.

"Brogan," she cried out, her arms wrapping around his neck as she arched against him. "Oh, yes, please."

As he suckled at her nipple, his hand moved back to her rear, pressing beneath the fragile material of her skirt to find the naked flesh revealed by her thong panties.

The hardened width of his cock was pressed between them, the heated stalk grinding against her clit as her hips moved, rubbing the tortured bud against the fierce heat of the iron-hard flesh.

As she did she felt the hidden zipper at the side of her skirt release, easing down before Brogan pushed the material down her hips and let it puddle on the ground.

She was all but naked in his arms now. The cool mountain air touched her body, stroking it as the breeze drifted over it.

His hands moved to her rear again, caressing and cupping the curves as his lips moved to her other nipple. He sucked it inside as well, laving the tip with his tongue and sending starbursts of pleasure exploding in her womb.

One of his hands lifted, though she wasn't certain what he was doing, because he didn't move it to caress any other part of her body.

Then it landed against the rounded curve of her rear in a firm, heated little tap of his fingers.

"Oh, God!" Eve jerked in his hold, the muscles of her rear clenching, a shudder working through her body at the sensations flooding her system now.

It wasn't a hard blow. There was nothing painful about it, just a little startling.

Then another landed.

His lips drew on her nipples, first one, then the other. His teeth rasped against them, tugging at the taut tips as she arched in his hold. Her nails bit into his shoulders now, her head tipping back, her hair flowing around her and caressing her naked skin.

The tap came again, this one just a little firmer, just a little heated against flesh that had already grown warm from the taps before it. With each heated caress a flame began to lick beneath her flesh and spread outward.

With each firm, quick little tap to each cheek of her ass, Eve felt the heat blooming in her rear spread to her clit, to the delicate muscles and tissue in the clenched emptiness of her pussy.

Sensations as shocking as they were arousing began to consume her, drawing muted, muffled little cries from her lips that she fought to contain.

The next tap was followed by his fingers slipping between her thighs, gathering the slick, heated moisture flowing from her vagina. Drawing her juices back from her pussy, he used the tip of a finger on the other hand to rub against the clenched entrance of her anus.

Another solid tap to her rear heated the flesh more, the sensation a stinging pleasure she was beginning to crave. She couldn't get enough. It wasn't burning enough. It wasn't firm enough.

His fingers slipped between her thighs again, drawing even more of the slick heat from her pussy and easing it to her anus. As his hand delivered another hot little tap, a fingertip rubbed more firmly against her back entrance.

No more than two taps later he was able to use the same hand to gather the moisture outside her pussy to lubricate her anus further. His fingertip pressed against the little hole, pushing the slick moisture just inside the snug entrance.

The next little slap had his fingertip pressing further inside as she ground her clit against the stalk of his cock. The hard shaft pressed against her pussy, the iron-hard, iron-hot flesh torturing her with the awareness of how desperately she needed to be fucked.

With the next little blow to her rear cheek, Brogan gathered more of her juices as they spilled to his fingers, lubricated her anus further.

"Push against my finger with your muscles here," he ordered her roughly as he began rubbing the little hole. "Open for me, baby; I'll do the rest."

His hand landed again; more of her juices were used to slick the little hole further; then, as his fingertip pressed against it, Eve fought to relax the muscles he caressed, pushing against the pressure.

His finger slipped inside.

Instantly the little hole clamped shut, shocking electrical flares of heat suddenly erupting in the nerve endings being stretched around the digit. He'd already penetrated the tight entrance, though. Her body's instinct to clench around the intruder and then to try to push it out only aided in allowing his heavily lubricated finger to push farther inside.

His hand delivered another firm, heated pat, the gentle slaps driving her crazy with the burning heat flaring beneath her flesh. Between the cheeks of her ass his finger moved inside her, stretching the tight entrance around it and burying inside her again.

Pulling free, he dragged more of the juices collecting outside her pussy back to the tender entrance, pressed two fingertips against it, and began working them inside the tender channel.

Rising and falling against him, Eve worked her hips against the broad heat of his cock, her clit on fire. Her pussy clenched and wept the slick lubrication he was using to penetrate her rear; she was desperate to be filled by the throbbing shaft pulsing between them.

The two fingers penetrated her again, sliding inside her in one smooth thrust as Eve cried out, stilling against him as shudders raced through her body.

"Lift," he ordered harshly.

She lifted against him, her knees braced on the padded edge of the bench as he used his free hand to maneuver his cock between them.

"More." The sexual roughness of his voice had her fighting to breathe as she lifted further.

The flared crest of his cock pressed against the entrance to her vagina then, stretching it as another little slap landed on her rear and his fingers thrust inside her ass again.

The penetration, the pressure against her pussy had her bearing down, feeling the thick crest penetrate her muscles with a suddenness that had her head falling against his shoulder and a cry tearing from her throat.

"Brogan." She sobbed, the demands her body was putting on her both confusing and frightening. "Fuck me now. Please. I can't stand this."

"Just a little more, baby." He groaned, his fingers pulling back, working more of the natural lubrication inside her before penetrating her again. "Just a little more."

She couldn't wait just a little more.

His hand fell against her rear again and Eve lost her mind amid the shattering sensations tearing through her body.

The fact that he wasn't wearing a condom registered only in the most distant part of her mind. The fact that his cock was inside her, working too slowly past the clenched muscles, wasn't lost on her.

Lifting against him, feeling the flared crest of his cock throbbing inside her, Eve lowered herself against the impalement, forcing him deeper, harder.

His fingers pushed deeper into her rear, driving her to work her hips harder, to take more of him. His hand landed against her ass again in a firm little tap, almost a little slap, and sent a flare of such wicked heat racing through her system that nothing mattered but her desperation to reach her orgasm.

The dual penetrations were building a pleasure so hot, so wild inside her that Eve couldn't bear the rising tension whipping through her. Her thighs clenched his, straddling them as she rode the fierce length of his cock with desperate movements.

She rose and fell, the heavy width stretching her pussy, stroking inside her as Brogan fucked her rear with his fingers and had her panting for air, fighting to scream out his name but unable to find the breath to do more than gasp.

Perspiration gathered on her body as the heat inside her begged for relief.

Brogan released the nipple he'd held in his mouth, his arm wrapped around her back as the fingers of the other hand thrust in an increased rhythm into the tender rear entrance and his hips began moving, driving his cock harder inside her, faster.

The heat of the morning gathered around them; the heat burning in their bodies began to flare and flame with sensation, burning their senses. Eve felt the conflagration as it happened as though in slow motion: The rake of her clitoris against his flesh as he drove inside her. The brutal pleasure that seared delicate nerve endings revealed by the thick width of his cock stretching her with burning pleasure. His fingers stroking inside her anus, stimulating nerve endings that responded with a strident clamoring for more.

Each sensation tightened, flamed, then erupted into an orgasm that shook her to her core.

It imploded inside her before exploding outward, sending her juices gushing against the rapidly thrusting movement of his cock and the sudden, heavy spurts of his release spilling inside her.

Her eyes opened wide in shock, met his, and that feeling of being a part of him was there again. As though time stopped and stilled for precious moments. As though nothing existed but the sensation of hurtling through space, locked in an ecstasy that neither of them could escape, and both of them shared— merging, melding, ecstasy that sealed them together for an impossible moment in time before hurtling them from an edge of such rapture that nothing else mattered.

Eve collapsed against him, only barely aware of the moment he fell backward on the bench, cushioned by the pad beneath them as Eve's body was cushioned by his.

One arm locked around her, ensuring that she stayed in place, as they both fought to catch their breath.

Their hearts raced; their breathing was ragged, frantic.

Nothing existed outside the place they'd found for this one fragile moment. There was no danger; there was no anger or pain, confusion or impending heartache. There was nothing but the two of them, the pleasure that had bound them, and the certainty that, like an addiction, the need to touch, to taste, to hold each other again would be one for which denial would not be an option.

Finding the strength to pull themselves from the bench and dress took a while. As Eve pulled the thin silken camisole shell over her head and adjusted the thin straps over her shoulders, she looked up at Brogan.

Securing the dark leather of the belt at his hips, he hadn't yet straightened his hair. The coarse, red-gold strands had fallen over his forehead and now lay disheveled around his head.

Scratching at his chest, he leaned down, snagged his shirt from the rug that lay over the stones, and pulled it over his arms. As he began securing the buttons, his gaze lifted as though drawn by the thought that suddenly seared her mind.

"What?" he asked absently, snagging his sneakers and untying them before propping himself against the heavy support column and pulling them over his feet.

"You didn't use a condom," she stated, watching him closely.

He paused for a moment before resuming with his shoes. Pulling the other one on, he tied them quickly before straightening and staring back at her.

"No, I didn't," he admitted—a little too calmly to suit her.

"You didn't pull out either."

His fingers raked through his hair, pushing it back, if not neatly, then at least into some kind of order.

"I know," he admitted again.

She stared back at him, feeling a sudden disquiet begin to settle around her. "Why?"

He sighed heavily. "Because whatever's going to happen began last night. The condom split, and before I could think to pull free, I was already spilling inside you. This morning isn't going to make a difference."

"You didn't tell me this morning," she stated, wondering why.

His jaw clenched brutally, a sudden feeling that he was pushing back something angry and bitter filling her senses.

"I was waiting to make certain it would be too late to use the morning-after pill," he finally snapped, his eyes turning a dark gray as he glared back at her. "I don't believe in it, Eve."

She looked away, frowning heavily.

She couldn't believe he had just said that. She couldn't believe he would even suspect she would do something so horrible. That she would abort her baby, just get rid of it as though it were trash. Damn, he sure did have a hell of an opinion of her, didn't he?

What hurt more, though, was the fact that he seemed to think it was okay to make that decision for her. That he thought she would be so easy to control and to maneuver.

He may not have lied to her, but what he had done was by far much worse: He had tried to take her free will, her right to a choice away from her.

"What?" he growled.

She rose from the bench, smoothed her skirt, then stared back at him painfully. "At what point, Brogan, did you begin to believe that you were entitled to make any decisions for me? Let alone one so important?"

Didn't he know her any better than that?

There had been a few moments over the years when she had sworn she had known what he was going to do or say, or what his opinion would be even before he voiced it. Yet after all this time, he believed he needed to hide something so important from her rather than trusting her?

"When the decision involves me or mine, then I have some say in it," he growled.

She laughed, a mirthless, angry sound that she didn't bother to hide.

"No, Brogan, you only have the right to discuss it, and you just made damned certain you no longer have even that right."

She moved from the grotto, aware of him following behind her, silent, a dark shadow keeping pace with her as she moved quickly back to the house.

Stepping inside the glass doors and hurrying through the living room, she suddenly came to a hard, surprised stop. Behind her, she heard Brogan curse, and she would have seconded the explicit word if it weren't for the fact that she knew it was a word her brother was attempting to erase from his vocabulary.

And there he stood, along with Rowdy and Natches, all three men staring at Brogan with an animosity that would be impossible to miss.

"I'm fairly certain you were told that I was fine, Dawg." She crossed her arms over her breasts and glared back at the three men.

"I was told," he growled.

"You didn't believe it?"

"Physically," he offered, "I believed you were fine."

"Then can I ask why you're here? Tell me, have you decided to take it upon yourself to make some decisions for me that have absolutely nothing to do with you, as well?" she asked sarcastically.

"Told you so," Rowdy muttered aside to Dawg as he lifted his hand and covered his mouth.

"Shut up, Rowdy," Dawg ordered, his gaze still locked with hers.

"I told you so, too," Natches offered.

Dawg didn't bother to give the same order to his younger cousin.

"I'll tell the four of you what." She included Brogan in the offer. "You can stay here and beat one another to a bruised pulp, scream, yell, curse, or whatever, and I'll just get my things and roll." She looked over at Natches. "You were smart enough to drive yourself, right?"

"Yeah," he answered warily as he hooked his thumbs in the belt cinching his lean hips. "Why?"

"You owe me," she reminded him. "I want your ride."

"Ah, hell, now, come on, Eve." He frowned, protesting the order as he glanced at the other three. "I don't like their company." He hooked a thumb over his shoulder to indicate Dawg and Rowdy.

"You're not leaving, Eve," Brogan stated behind her.

She turned slowly, drew in a hard, deep breath, and met the anger burning in his gaze. "You don't want to do this," she told him softly. "I won't be manipulated, ordered, or deceived, Brogan. If you learned anything about me in the past two and a half years, then you know that."

Fury burned in his eyes, but his lips thinned as he only continued to glare at her.

Turning to her brother once again, she stared at him until his gaze flickered. No one, but no one could make Dawg flinch when he believed he was completely in the right.

"This is none of your business," she told him. "I'm not six; nor am I sixteen. I'm a grown woman and I can make a grown woman's decisions."

"Can you?" His arms went across his chest as his brows lowered broodingly. "Even if he's a damned criminal?"

"Even if I'm wrong about the fact that everything inside me tells me he's not a criminal," she amended, "I can't live my life by your instincts and your rules, Dawg. I have to live by my own."

"You made me a promise, Eve," he reminded her. "I thought you understood the stakes."

"Are you going to disown me, Dawg?" she asked curiously. "You once said we'd get along fine as long as I didn't betray family, country, or myself. I haven't betrayed any of the three. But you skirted the line when you manipulated a promise from me that you knew I'd never be able to keep."

Rowdy and Natches both turned a look of disgust on their cousin.

"Man, you know Christa's gonna find out," Natches warned him.

"Not if you keep your fat mouth shut," he growled.

Natches frowned and turned to Eve. "Is my mouth fat?" He was suddenly fingering his lips as though worried before turning on Dawg. "I'm going to give you a fat lip in a minute."

Dawg snorted. "Yeah, and go home all bruised to Chaya? I don't think so."

Natches grinned. "I won't get in near as much trouble as you will."

Eve shook her head. "You three just work that out on your own." She turned her attention to Natches. "Give me your keys."

"That's the last time I play cards with you," he threatened her, clearly annoyed that the promise he owed her from the poker game months before had resulted in losing his ride for the day.

"You said anytime, anywhere," she reminded him with a shrug as he tossed her the keys.

"Eve." Brogan moved in front of her. "We need to discuss this."

She shook her head, steely determination and offended pride clawing at her emotions. "No, Brogan, we don't," she told him softly, distancing herself from the frustration and the edge of desperation she felt emanating from him. "Not now. Not until you decide that controlling me may not be as important as you seem to think it is." She turned to Dawg then. "You knew he wasn't a traitor. Hell, your instincts are better than mine. You all but lied to me, Dawg. And I would have sworn that was something you would have never done to me. You knew all along he was an agent, didn't you?"

Facing him, seeing the brooding guilt in his gaze, she knew beyond a shadow of a doubt that he had been aware of what he was doing when he did it.

Her eyes filled with tears.

She couldn't stop them. She couldn't stop the sudden, brutal sense of betrayal as it exploded inside her any more than she could have stopped the sun from rising that morning.

"Why did you do it?" Her voice cracked with the tears suddenly filling her eyes. "I wouldn't have done that to you, Dawg.

I wouldn't have lied to you about Christa to keep you away from her."

"Ah, hell." It was Natches who emitted the low exclamation as he and Rowdy both turned on Dawg.

"He's going to hurt you," Dawg stated, so certain of it, so determined he was right that pure arrogant stubbornness filled his face.

"So what if he does." A tear slipped free as she suddenly realized just how much she and her sisters, even her mother, had allowed Dawg to shelter them. "Can't I live, Dawg? Do I have to have your permission?"

He frowned at the question. "No . . ."

"Evidently I do," she cried. "You made me swear I wouldn't take him as a lover by telling me he was the only man you couldn't abide my being with. That you believed he was a traitor." Her breathing hitched as astonishment filled the cousins' expressions as they turned to Dawg.

"There's no proof that says he's not a traitor," Dawg accused Brogan, his fingers clenching at his sides as his expression turned wrathful and centered on the other man.

Eve shook her head as a sob escaped her. "Momma once told me that even good men had the power to be bad," she whispered. "And I didn't believe that of you, Dawg. I really didn't. I believed there was nothing bad or deceitful in you. That all I had to do was find a man like you and I'd always be safe and loved."

He reached up and rubbed the back of his neck in agitation.

"Come on, Eve," he cajoled gently. "I'm not perfect, honey."

"Ain't that the truth," Natches bit out.

"Shut the fuck up, Natches," Dawg snarled, silencing them all in surprise as he said the hated F-word before turning back to Eve. "Look, I never meant I would disown you or anything else if you broke a promise. I just meant that you know he's going to hurt you. You know it, if he hasn't already." He shot Brogan a look of promised retribution. "That's all I meant."

"And you left me feeling like I had betrayed you. Like I was no more than a criminal myself, Dawg, because you couldn't let me follow my own instincts. You couldn't let me follow my heart."

"Dammit, Eve, whatever the hell he's into could get you killed," he yelled back at her.

"And that was just too hard to tell me at the time, wasn't it," she cried out, furious and hurt, and feeling her heart breaking in two. "You lied to me, Dawg. You may not have said the words, but you still lied."

Gripping Natches's keys in her hand, she turned to Brogan, seeing for the first time the heavy, dark emotion that filled his gaze, and feeling something hesitant, something distant shutting that door on what had been forming between them.

His eyes were that unique blue-gray. The color was no longer shifting with emotion, just as his emotions were no longer reaching out to her.

Her lips twisted bitterly as she suddenly felt so bereft, so alone without that connection she'd had for such a few short hours.

Another sob escaped before she forced the others back and quickly dashed the tears from her cheek.

"You should have known I would have never done something so vile," she whispered for his ears only. "I believed in you, Brogan." She shook her head bitterly, painfully. "I believed in you."

Turning away from him, she strode quickly to the front door, glancing back at her brother and her cousins as they stared back at Brogan with the same expression.

Disappointment.

Pushing through the front door, she ran to the car Natches had driven, surprised that he hadn't driven his truck, hit the automatic lock, and slid inside the low-slung sports car quickly.

She had to adjust her seat so she could reach the gas pedal, but once she did she pushed the start button and felt the throbbing vibration of the powerful little Mercedes before reversing and turning, then sliding the vehicle into drive and roaring away from the cabin.

She should have kept her promise to Dawg, she thought.

She should have never given in to Brogan. She should have never given in to her own needs. If she hadn't, then perhaps her heart would still be in one unbroken piece.

FIFTEEN

Dawg shook his head as the door slammed behind his sister's livid form, his gaze locking on Brogan accusingly as the other man stared at the door with a piercing, intent look.

"Man, you are one stupid fucker," he stated, pitiless. "I could almost feel sorry for you, but you brought every damned bit of it on yourself, and you know it."

"No." Brogan shook his head slowly, his gaze still locked on the door.

He was watching the heavy wood panel as though he actually thought Eve would walk back through the doorway at any moment.

"No?" Dawg glanced at his cousins before his gaze moved back to Brogan. "No what?" He looked back to Natches and Rowdy again. "Is he okay?"

Natches gave a brief, amused chuckle as they all watched Brogan take a step toward the door before pulling back almost immediately.

He raked his fingers through his hair.

"Knew better," he mumbled peevishly as he left a spike of red-gold hair standing on end. "Fucking knew better. She's a fucking Mackay."

Dawg actually growled.

Now, that was just damned uncalled-for.

"He's in love." Natches snickered behind Dawg.

Dawg glowered back at his cousin. "I already fucking knew that. Thanks for the news flash, cuz."

"Then why get Eve to promise to stay away from him?" Rowdy was the one who asked that question.

Dawg wished he'd kept his damned mouth shut now.

"Fucking knew better. She's a Mackay," Brogan mumbled, drawing their attention back to him as he glared at the door again.

Brogan turned his gaze to the Mackays then.

"It's your fucking fault," Brogan accused Dawg. "You son of a bitch, if you had just left her the fuck alone."

"My fault?" Dawg would have shown him the business end of his fist if Rowdy hadn't grabbed his arm and pulled him back.

"You." Brogan's lips pulled back from his teeth in a snarl. "Why didn't you stay the fuck out of it?"

"Because she's my sister, asshole!" he bellowed back at him.

"Someone needs to have a talk with your wife," Brogan suggested snidely then. "I have a feeling she'd put a stop to your fucking meddling."

Dawg snorted, though he knew that was way too close to the truth. Behind him, Natches snickered.

"I warned you last year," Dawg reminded him. "Didn't I warn you, Brogan? You could step the hell out of what you were doing or you could stay away from my sister; it was your choice."

Yeah, Rowdy and Natches were both staring at him now as though he were crazy, but Dawg figured Brogan would end up letting the truth slip out of his mouth anyway, so he might as well strike first.

Brogan's eyes narrowed in contempt before he turned and stalked across the house to the patio room, where he stood with his back to them, obviously staring out into the woods beyond the house.

"What have you done, Dawg?" Rowdy muttered.

Dawg grimaced at the question. "Protected my sister."

"I wonder how you would react to it if Christa's brother Alex up and decided to protect his sister in the same way?"

"Kill him." He shrugged as though he would do just that.

He wouldn't, but hell, it would be damned close.

"What was the threat?" Rowdy bit out, obviously pissed now. "You had to have had a threat to go with it."

Dawg shifted uncomfortably beneath his cousin's glare as he dropped his arms from across his chest and gave the other man a scorching look. "What threat? What do I have to threaten him with?" he muttered.

Brogan turned back to them then, and Dawg wondered whether he had been unlucky enough that the other man had heard the question.

"Dawg, what the fuck did you do?" Rowdy's no-nonsense tone had him breathing out roughly.

The threat had been a simple one. Dawg still had connections, major connections at the Department of Homeland Security and among the politicians that could make or break a man's career in law enforcement. Dawg had simply told Brogan that if he was an agent, and if he did care anything about his career, then he'd understand the ramifications of Eve's heart getting broken.

His father might well be the director of Homeland Security, but that wouldn't save Brogan's place in the Federal Protective Service if Dawg wanted him out of there.

Brogan chose that moment to stalk through the house and disappeared into a room up the short hall. The bedroom, no doubt, Dawg thought.

"Maybe I should just tell Kelly what happened today and see if she wants to ask Christa if she knows what's going on," Rowdy suggested.

Hell, he was getting tired of this. Every time his two yahoo cousins went blabbing on him, Dawg managed to do without his wife's tender touch for far too long. At this rate, they were going to cause him to have to just start knocking heads together again instead of trying to be nice about things.

"We didn't come up here to hurt Eve or piss Brogan off," Rowdy reminded him as the door slammed behind Brogan with enough force that Dawg swore the windows rattled.

"He's not going to listen to us right now," Dawg reminded him testily. "He's going to be too busy feeling sorry for himself."

"And whose fault is that?" Natches questioned behind him.

"Would you two stop acting as though this is all my fault?" Dawg questioned them incredulously. "I didn't do anything."

"You breathe, Dawg," Rowdy accused him bluntly. "You breathe. Some days that's seriously all it takes."

The bedroom door jerked open so hard it crashed against the inside wall as they turned and stared at Brogan in surprise.

He was carrying two small bags; one was obviously Eve's.

"Where the hell do you think you're going?" Dawg inquired sarcastically.

"Wherever she went," Brogan informed them ruthlessly as he stalked to the door. "Stay as long as you like. There's nothing here that's mine."

"We didn't show up here to watch you stalk off, asshole," Dawg called out as they followed close on his heels until he reached Timothy's pickup.

"No, you accomplished what you showed up to do," Brogan informed them, keeping his voice calm. He'd caused Eve enough heartache and pain; he wouldn't compound it by sending her brother and cousins to the hospital. Not unless they forced him to it.

"Well, there was that," Dawg agreed with a vein of amusement behind the words. "But that's not the only reason we're here."

"I'm already aware someone tried to break into her room." Thank God for Eli and Jed. Brogan wasn't certain Doogan would have told him, if it had been left up to him.

"Well, there was that," Dawg repeated. "But once again, not the only reason we're here."

"Then why the fuck are you here, Dawg?" he snarled back, his hand clenching on the truck door to keep from ramming his fist in the other man's face.

He'd get the first strike, but he doubted he'd leave unscathed. Then Eve would just be pissed as hell at him. And if he did manage to get her to let him touch her again, he'd be too sore to do much.

Dawg chuckled. "You see that look on his face, Rowdy?"

Rowdy grinned, his arms crossed over his chest, the smile amused and mocking.

"That's the 'I'd love to try to kick his ass, but if I do, she's gonna be too pissed and I'm gonna be too sore to love her later' look." Natches snickered knowingly. "I'd tell him to join the club, but he's not quite paid his dues yet; what do you think?"

Rowdy shook his head. "Nah, not yet. We'll make him wait awhile just for being a prick about us showing up and all."

"The three of you are fucking insane." Brogan moved to step into the truck.

"Pull out before we're finished and I promise you, I'll make your life such hell that you'll beg me to let up on you. And I can do it, Brogan. I promise you I can do it." Arrogant assurance and self-confidence filled Dawg's expression as well as his voice.

Brogan gripped the door hard enough that he could feel his knuckles turning white as he glared back at the three men.

"I don't like your endangering my sister's life, and if I could have steered her toward some nice, safe, simpleminded little farmer or accountant to ensure her safety, then I would have done it. But you're what she wants. So I'm trying my damnedest to help you here."

"You made her promise to stay the hell away from me," Brogan accused him furiously. "That's not helping me, Mackay. And that was only after threatening my fucking career if I didn't stay the hell away from her."

Rowdy and Natches turned to Dawg incredulously.

Brogan bit back a curse as he just ignored them.

"And I knew damned good and well she wasn't going to keep that promise."

The acknowledgment had Brogan narrowing his gaze on the other man.

"Then why do it?"

"Because she's my sister," Dawg grumbled irately. "And I

needed time to finish what I was doing to protect her before she drew any more attention to the fact that she was most likely the only weakness you had. You weren't doing anything to keep her out of your bed."

"But you couldn't come to me." Mackay's arrogance and stubborn independence reminded Brogan of a crazed bull staring at a red flag.

"You're too close to Doogan. And if you weren't, then we knew your partners definitely were," Dawg informed him, his tone hardening. "Until Doogan asks one of us for help, then he's getting nothing from me that he can use to pull me into his bullshit without a hell of a compensation package, Brogan. You know that bastard as well as I do, and you know damned good and well he'd use us up, then throw us to the wolves when he was finished."

Brogan had no idea Dawg knew Doogan, let alone that he knew him so well.

"Agreed," Brogan growled.

"What I've done instead is work from where it counts," Dawg informed him. "That motorcycle touring club is bullshit. A bunch of veterans riding around sightseeing? Give me a fucking break," he jeered. "I know exactly what it is, what it was started as, and what it will always be now that it's established. Just as I know there's not a chance in hell you're going to be pulled into the inner circle of that group, no matter how long they let you carry that title of 'leader,' without our help."

Brogan stiffened, his gaze going between the three men as suspicion rose inside him.

"Tell me what's going on," he demanded, suddenly certain these three men were the exact reason he'd never been able to break the ice where the club was concerned.

Brogan had known there was far more to that club than he'd ever been able to figure out. Just as he'd known that many of the tours they'd taken came far too close to the known locations of small militia groups rumored to be operating from those areas.

"Not without that compensation package," Dawg growled.

Brogan shook his head. "Fuck Doogan. He'll come to you; I promise you that. I don't need Doogan to do my job or to protect Eve any more than you need him to tell me what I need to know."

Dawg glanced at his cousins, each man meeting his gaze, communicating as only men as close as they were, who had fought together and worked together in the operations that they had been conducting in the county, as long as they had, could communicate.

Finally Dawg nodded before turning to him. "Your thieves aren't in the motorcycle club, Brogan. And the files that have been stolen don't have a damned thing in them that tie them together. What they do have, though, is the ability to draw three men out of hiding who were working with Chandler and Dayle Mackay in the Freedom League. Twenty years ago, Chandler was stationed at Fort Knox when a transport hauling more than six million in gold bullion was hijacked. Rumor in the Freedom League was that the gold was hidden by one man and the location of it supposedly encoded in a set of files at Fort Knox in case something happened to him before it could be recovered and used to fund the League. Timothy managed to acquire the files and we found the gold. What we don't have are the three high-ranking military officers Chandler was working with."

Brogan stiffened in sudden outrage. "You mean I've been busting my ass for two and a half years for nothing?"

Dawg grinned. "Well, you did get Doogan here. And you obviously drew the attention of the three we're looking for. Unfortunately, now Eve's drawn their attention as well." He glared at Brogan for that. "It was suggested to Doogan that he pull us into this, because we're the only chance he has of recovering the gold or arresting the traitors involved in it. When Doogan refused to come to us, and decided to find the answers without us, then we let him. Don't doubt that you've done your part, despite his machinations. You've done exactly what we would have wanted you to do if we had been working together. But when Eve became involved, I had to adjust the plan a bit to ensure she was protected."

"You're the bastard Donny said has the information Doogan wants and will help only if Eve was involved with me?" Son of a bitch, and they called Timothy and Doogan game players?

"Not quite." Dawg rubbed at the back of his neck as he grimaced in irritation before propping his hands on his waist and blowing out a hard breath. "We didn't know who that was until last night, after Eve went missing from the restaurant. He came to us then."

Brogan looked between the three men, more amazed that they had been able to accomplish drawing that contact out without raising red flags with Doogan, or with him.

"Who is he?" Brogan demanded.

Dawg shook his head. "You have enough. Get Doogan on board with the program. We want those packages. Full immunity, no matter what we have to do from here on out, no matter the investigation or the agent conducting it. Because I'm telling you, we're getting damned sick of being pulled into the agency's bullshit, threatened, our families endangered, and our freedom placed on the line because the agents in charge are too damned arrogant to accept defeat, or to acknowledge that they don't know what the hell they're doing once they get in these mountains."

He was right, and the fact was that Doogan wasn't the only agent with the opinion that just because a man was from the backwoods Kentucky mountains, then he was somehow not as smart, as quick, or as capable as one born and raised in the city. Or in Doogan's case, the boardrooms and drawing rooms of the ultrarich.

Brogan shook his head. "Delaying risks Eve," he protested. "Wrap the case up; then play games with Doogan."

Dawg shook his head in the negative, his expression as well as Rowdy's and Natches's turning grim as they watched him.

"I have Eve covered, but that won't last forever," Dawg informed him, his voice tight. "Get those packages in place, Brogan; then we'll finish it."

"And if Eve gets hurt while we're fucking around with Doogan?" he snarled furiously. "What then, Dawg?"

"What if she gets hurt because our hands are fucking tied, or later one of the others is hurt because our hands were fucking tied or we didn't know they were pulling an operation beneath our noses?" Natches sneered, his eyes, so like Eve's, glittering in fury. "I don't think so, Brogan. We've told you enough; get it fucking taken care of; then we can finish this."

"If Doogan doesn't cooperate? What then?" Brogan questioned harshly, beginning to see exactly where this was going.

"If he doesn't want to play ball, then you have other connections," Dawg stated knowingly. "Use them."

"My father," Brogan surmised mockingly. "This is where it's been going all along. You want me to go to JD and have it taken care of." Brogan rarely called his father by anything other than "JD." "John David" if he was pissed with him.

Son of a bitch, just what he needed.

"I want you to do whatever it takes for me to see to my family's fucking protection. And if you care anything about Eve, then that's all you should want, too," Dawg retorted heatedly. "As long as DHS is using this county and the Mackays to do their dirty work, then we're all at risk. And that includes Eve, her sisters, and her mother. And trust me, you think she's pissed at me?" he warned with dark emphasis. "Then how will she feel if one of her baby sisters, or God forbid, her mother, who nearly died of a chemical infection trying to feed Eve and her sisters, or her brother and cousins who all but got on their knees and begged for your help." Dawg grinned mockingly. "If any of us end up hurt because you didn't go to daddy to ensure we were all protected, then how do you think she's going to feel?"

Brogan stepped into the truck, slammed the door, and started the engine.

Throwing the three men one last bitter, furious look, he reversed the truck and whipped it to the side of the parking lot before pushing it into drive and hitting the gas. Gravel spewed as the tires bit into the unfinished parking area and the truck shot forward and sped from the cabin.

Folding his arms over his chest, Dawg frowned before sliding his dark sunglasses over his eyes and turning back to his cousins. They, too, were watching the truck speed away, their expressions brooding.

"Are we doing the right thing?" Natches murmured.

Dawg could only shake his head. "Timothy and Chaya are right, Natches. As long we're alive and living here, DHS or some

other American alphabet agency is going to play games with us
for the simple fact that they know we love our homes, our families, and our country too much to stand back and just protect our
own asses. And if they get the urge to demand more from us, they
can always threaten our family's freedom to ensure they get it.
We have too much at stake and too much to lose not to do this
now, while we have the chance."

"And you really think Brogan will ensure that it happens?"
Rowdy muttered, unconvinced.

"He ensured that he had his own agreement and compensatory package before ever agreeing to work with Timothy Cranston and Chatham Doogan." He shrugged. "And I know Director
Bryce. He wants the gold. He has no idea it's been found, and
that's been okay until now, because he wants those traitors more.
They've been a thorn in his side since before DHS existed. I think
this is the best chance we have."

"Think Eve's going to forgive you for playing these games
with her?" Natches asked quietly, compassionately. "You should
have talked to us, cuz. Told us what was going on. We work better together, remember?"

Dawg turned away from his cousin's too-perceptive gaze to
stare into the beauty of the mountains for one long moment.
When he turned back, he took a shaky breath and said, "If she
can't forgive me, she'll need you and Rowdy. I couldn't chance
her hating all of us. She's too much of a Mackay, Natches. Too
much pride, too much spirit and fire, and when she hurts, she
hurts too deep. I didn't want her hurting and feeling she didn't
have one of us to come to."

Natches breathed out roughly and gave his head a hard
shake.

"It doesn't work that way, Dawg." It was Rowdy that chastised him quietly. "She wouldn't come to us. She'll go to our wives. And that's okay, because that's what makes them strong. They'll always have each other, and they'll never be alone if the unthinkable ever happens and we're not there anymore. And we have each other, Dawg. Our ladies take care of home and hearth, our babies and our hearts. We keep their lives, their families, friends, and homes safe. We do that together. No more hiding things, you got that?"

"I got that." He gave a hard, sharp nod of his head.

"What about Eve, Dawg?" Natches asked again.

Dawg knew he wasn't repeating his earlier question, but that earlier question was all Dawg could consider.

Would Eve forgive him?

Dawg's lips tightened. Shaking his head, he strode to the dual-cab pickup he'd driven in, and stepped into the driver's seat without answering.

He didn't have an answer because he simply didn't know.

What did he know?

If it were him, he knew he wouldn't forgive—no matter the reason, the explanation, or the circumstances. He wouldn't want platitudes and promises of protection. He'd want the trust and the ability to choose his own path and his own protection. And he knew Eve was often far too much like him and his cousins, just as the other girls were.

There was a chance, a very good chance, that she might never forgive any of them.

SIXTEEN

A week later, Eve entered the backyard of Ray and Maria Mackay's farmhouse and stared around at the gathering of family, relations, and scattered friends.

This year there were nearly a hundred family members who had confirmed attendance at the Mackay family reunion, and it looked as though every one of them had shown up.

The reunion was a yearly endeavor Ray and Maria—Grandpa Ray and Grandma Maria—had begun insisting on the year Rowdy and Kelly had become engaged. As he had explained it to his son and nephews, as children came, they would need traditions. And his "boys"—who comprised his own son as well as his two nephews—well, their children deserved a far better life than their father had had.

Not that Rowdy's life had been too hard, as Eve heard it. He'd had Ray, and then, once Ray had married Maria, he'd had a mother. The stories she'd heard of Rowdy's mother had never been pleasant, but there was no doubt Maria had loved Ray's son.

Just as Ray had taken her daughter, Kelly, in and loved her.

Eve had always found it amusing that Rowdy and Kelly had lived in the same house for so many years and then ended up married.

But Grandpa Ray had bragged that his boy, his Rowdy, hadn't been base or without honor. When his son had realized he was feeling things for Kelly, Rowdy had moved out. And even before he'd realized he was falling in love with her, Rowdy had made certain he'd taken care of her, his father bragged.

Once Rowdy and Kelly became engaged, Ray had begun the family reunions, even though the first "reunions" were only him, Maria, Kelly, Rowdy, Dawg, and Natches.

He said kids needed traditions. They needed to know and understand family.

Christmas, New Year's, church on Easter morning, then the egg hunt before dinner once the girls had been born. Ray made certain each holiday was celebrated for the meaning it was intended by the family, with the family. And every June, there was the Mackay family reunion.

That Saturday, Eve had no choice but to slow down, take a day off, and show up at Grandpa and Grandma's farm. The reunion had begun as a meal, and had turned into a daylong circus as years had gone by.

It was a day Eve and her family looked forward to every year. And each year it had only grown. With Dayle Mackay, Nadine and her son, Johnny Grace's, deaths eight years before, the separation of Ray, Dawg, Rowdy, and Natches from their relations had ended. Now, all the Mackay relations and their families had begun showing up. Among them were the Augusts from Madison, Texas—Cade, Brock, and Sam August—along with their wives and children.

The Mackays and their extended families were just as interesting and just as complicated as Eve had always imagined they were as she grew up. Living in northern Texas, so far away from the brother and cousins her father had told her mother about, Eve had often hungered for news of them. She'd built them up in her mind instead, and at times she could honestly say she hadn't done them justice.

Grandpa Ray and Grandma Maria, as they insisted they be called, were the grandparents Eve and her sisters had always dreamed of having. From day one, they had accepted Mercedes Mackay and her daughters with such warmth and acceptance that it often seemed her family had come home when they stepped foot in Kentucky.

That first family reunion, Eve and her family had cried. They had never been to such an event; they had never known family. All they'd ever known was one another. Having that tradition and then so many others as well had been a dream come true for them.

And having not just one big brother, but three, had always been so incredible to Eve. Rowdy and Natches never accepted being described or introduced as her cousins. They were her brothers, too, they promised.

Yeah, she had family now, and for the first time, Eve had no idea what to do with them. They were just as intimidating and as controlling as Timothy was rumored to be. They were just sneakier about it than Timothy.

Eve herself had never seen Timothy playing those games with her or her family. Of course, the Mackay sisters had never done anything to cause him to need to investigate them, or for him to have to maneuver them into protecting themselves.

For five years Eve had lived in a dream world that she was now terrified was no more than a lie.

Dawg loved her and her family; she knew that. But he was manipulating and controlling her, and she was suddenly afraid he had been controlling them all along. Especially her, where Brogan was concerned.

As she wandered through the backyard, stopping to talk to cousins, friends, and various Mackay relations, she looked around for Dawg, Rowdy, and Natches.

She found Dawg with Timothy, standing at the oversize barbecue grill, where Timothy was grilling the burgers and hot dogs. Eve couldn't help but wonder whether she was wrong about the man her mother was in love with, as she had been wrong about Dawg.

Watching them talk, though, she saw Timothy pause and glance up at Dawg disapprovingly. As Dawg continued to talk, Timothy frowned and, without so much as the flicker of an eyelash, froze so completely that Eve knew he was livid. She'd known Timothy long enough that sometimes, unless he was trying to hide what he thought and what he felt, she could detect his anger.

Her gaze moved to Dawg. As she watched, his arms crossed over his broad chest and a scowl darkened his face. Then Timothy shook his head.

Dawg began protesting, and Timothy was ignoring him.

She would love to be the fly on that wall rather than the one watching from afar. Except she doubted Timothy would have discussed her with Dawg if she was close enough to hear.

Eve forced herself to move away.

Dawg once warned her and her sisters of the rules of the Mackay house, so to speak: Don't betray yourself, your family, or your country, he'd told her. If they could adhere to those few rules, then they would always have family.

For the first time since she'd become a part of his family, she'd lied to him. And she was smart enough to know that part of her anger toward him had a lot to do with the fact that she had broken a promise, and now, she feared, she had risked not just her place with the Mackays, but also her sisters' and mother's places.

What Dawg had done was wrong. He'd played her in some way and she knew it. She just wasn't certain how yet, and that hurt her, just as it risked her trust in him. But never her trust in the fact that he loved her family.

Or he had loved her.

Would she do it again? she wondered as she slipped into the house to find a little privacy for a while.

Eve knew she would.

Brogan had broken her heart, but staying away from him was so impossible that she had forced herself to work until she collapsed into bed around daylight. The less time she spent anywhere close to him, the better.

Not that she had seen him around very often. He seemed to be gone more often than not. Even Jed and Eli hadn't been around much.

She couldn't stay busy enough to forget the night and the morning she had spent in his arms, though. The memory of it tormented her. She couldn't sleep without dreaming of it. She ached for him. She missed him.

And she was beginning to wonder whether perhaps he had lied to her in the worst possible way. Maybe he was one of those men who, once they'd had her, were just finished with a woman.

"Hey, Eve." Rogue Mayes, a friend of the family and, as Grandpa Mackay liked to call her, his adopted granddaughter, waved at Eve from a table set beneath the huge oak at the side of the yard.

Smiling whether she felt like it or not, Eve moved to the couple and stared at the baby Rogue was holding close to her breast.

Little Ezekiel Mayes Jr. was only three weeks old, and looked impossibly tiny to Eve. He was filling out wonderfully, though. The cap of red fuzz on his head reminded her too much of Brogan's red hair, while everything else about him was the image of his father.

"How gorgeous." She breathed out as Rogue handed the baby to her carefully. "I didn't think I'd ever get a chance to come out and see him." She sighed.

"Yeah, I did good, huh?" Rogue laughed.

"You did excellent," Eve assured her as she caressed the baby's soft, rounded head before turning to the father. "You didn't do too bad yourself, Sheriff."

Zeke chuckled at the compliment. "At least you acknowledge that I might have had a hand in him. Your brother and cousins seem to believe immaculate conception occurred."

"Eh, that's because they think Rogue's a sister, too," she assured him. "And you know all their sisters are pure, sweet, and completely innocent."

Zeke turned to his wife in surprise. "Has anyone told his sisters that yet? If they have, they've completely ignored the concept."

Eve couldn't help but laugh at the playful mockery as she handed the baby back to his mother. "He's gorgeous. He's going to break hearts right and left when he grows up."

Rogue beamed in pride, while Zeke's chest must have puffed out two feet.

As Eve turned to skirt the main part of the yard, she heard her name called out again.

"Auntie Evie. Auntie Evie." Erin Jansen, Natches's niece, was running through the yard, a smile covering her face as her long dark hair flew out behind her.

That child was going to have the boys worshiping at her feet, Eve thought as the six-year-old ran to her. Bending, Eve caught her, lifting her as Erin wrapped her arms around her neck for a tight hug.

"I missed you." Erin beamed as Eve set her back on her feet, then bent down in front of her.

"I missed you too, baby." Eve grinned as the little girl stared back at her with eyes an odd mix of green and gray. The world would label the color hazel, but there was no way such a tame description could describe it. At any time, there were at least two shades of green playing with the unusually dark gray color.

"I'm gonna go play with Bliss now." She jumped around like a little Mexican jumping bean on caffeine. "Love you, Auntie Eve."

"Love you, baby." Eve smiled back at her, watching as she skipped off, the pretty summer dress she wore bouncing around her.

At that second, the possibility of being pregnant slammed into her so hard, Eve lost her breath.

Pressing her hand to her stomach, she looked around wildly,

desperate to escape now, to find someplace to think, to ache in peace.

Someplace where so many people weren't around her and possibly watching her.

Entering the quiet house, Eve moved through the kitchen, remembering the years that the reunion had been held in the house, and the kitchen had been brimming with people, laughter, and food.

It had quickly outgrown the house, though—so much so that Grandpa Ray and his "boys" had gone in together and built the backyard kitchen, with its huge grill, gas stove, and a sink so big Eve had teased them that it could double as a tub.

The whole thing was built under a massive gazebo-style shelter with a fireplace at one end and sliding windows that allowed the whole interior to be open to the yard in the summer to catch the breeze that rolled out of the mountains. In the winter it could be enclosed and, with the warmth of the fireplace, made a wonderful gathering area.

Moving to the living room and sitting on the sofa, she slipped her sandals from her feet and curled her legs beside her. Resting her head in the corner of the furniture Eve stared into the shadowed room as she closed her eyes and fought her tears.

She'd been crying for a week and she was tired of it. She hated it.

Not that fighting the tears often did her any good. Just as they did now, there were those tears that escaped her control and eased down her cheek.

"I'll have to kill him if he's the reason you've been crying for a week." Dawg's declaration had her eyes flying open as she quickly swiped the tears from her cheek.

"I can't talk to you yet," she whispered, refusing to look at him.

She couldn't look at him. She felt too guilty. She'd made a promise, and no matter what he'd done, that didn't change the fact that she had broken her word to him.

Dawg let out a hard breath and a second later she felt him sit down beside her.

Leaning forward, his big hands clasped between his spread legs, he stared at the floor thoughtfully.

"Do you hate me now, little sister?"

Swinging her head around, she stared at him in surprise. "Hate you? For what? Caring enough for me that you tried to protect me?" She sniffed back more tears. "Wouldn't that just make me more awful than I already feel I am?"

Her voice was hoarse with the effort to hold back her emotions as she watched him, despising herself for the brooding look she saw in his eyes.

Finally he shook his head slowly. "You're not an awful person at all, Eve," he seemed to chide her gently. "What would make you think you are?"

Her breathing hitched as she pushed back a sob. "I lied to you. I didn't mean to, but I gave you my word and I broke it. I broke it and I blamed you for my own guilt when I knew, you may not have been able to explain why, but you were only trying to protect me."

His brows lowered, his expression becoming dangerously still.

"Eve, do you think I'd hold that against you?"

She couldn't maintain his look. Turning away, she whispered, "One of the few things asked is that we not betray family." She shrugged. "I lied . . ."

"And I think I'll kill Brogan and just have it done with," he threatened as her gaze swung back to him. "Because it's obvious that falling in love with him has somehow weakened your mind."

Never let it be said that Dawg Mackay was afraid to state his opinion.

Eve shook her head in confusion. "I promised . . ."

"Pretty much because I manipulated you into that promise and exerted as much guilt as I could to ensure you made it." He snorted. "Eve, sweetheart, you can't let the people you love do this to you." Reaching out, he wiped a tear from her face as his expression eased. "Honey, I never blamed you for breaking your promise. Hell, I knew you would break it."

"Then why did you come to the cabin?"

"Because the night before, someone had broken into your room and trashed it maybe?" He sighed. "It took several hours for me to find out you had left with Brogan. He wasn't answering his phone, and yours was going straight to voice mail. No one knew where the two of you were or where Brogan planned to go. If it hadn't been for Timothy and the fact that he knew the location of the cabin, then I would have driven myself wild thinking that you were hurt, or worse."

Lips parted, Eve stared back at him in surprise. "I hadn't known about my room until I returned home."

"I was going to tell you before you left the cabin." He sighed. "It's just . . . Hell, sis, I took one look at Brogan that morning and I knew you'd slept with him. Then all I could think was, 'That bastard was sleeping with my baby sister.' Sometimes I forget you're an adult. I still see that wary, uncertain teenager who watched me with that sure and certain knowledge I was going to let her and her family fend for themselves."

Eve looked away from him.

She'd been terrified when she'd returned home to find her suite trashed. So terrified she'd accepted her mother's offer to move into the extra bedroom above the inn.

She was still in that bedroom.

"Come on; you're not crying because you broke a promise I knew you'd never be able to keep," he chided.

She was almost amused. Sliding a sideways look toward him, she caught the concerned look on his face.

"Then why did you ask me to promise, Dawg?" She didn't know how to feel about anything this week. Or how to deal with such strong, stubborn men.

"Because I was fighting to find a way to protect you, Eve." He reached back and rubbed his neck with an air of weariness. "I could see what was going on between you and Brogan. I've watched it building between the two of you, and when I saw it was going to happen, and it was going to happen soon, I needed time to finish some things."

Did he know?

Her eyes narrowed on him. "What are you talking about?"

He sat back on the sofa and watched her quietly. "I know Brogan's an agent for DHS, Eve. I suspected at first, but then I knew what he was doing here. You don't have to keep that secret for him, from me."

"I never asked to be told." She picked at a loose thread on the knee of her jeans as her throat thickened with emotion. "Is he okay?"

"Why do you ask?"

"He's not been at the inn in a few days," she revealed. "I was just wondering."

"You've been worried as hell," he corrected her. "Timothy says you've been pacing your bedroom."

She shrugged again. "I was just wondering."

"He had some things to take care of in D.C.," he told her. "He should be back in a few more days, from what I understand." *Thank God.*

Eve felt a sense of relief expand inside her. She hadn't realized how worried she had been until Dawg had confirmed that Brogan was okay.

"Do you love him, Eve?" he asked, his gaze so heavy she felt her lips tremble.

"Does it matter?" She had asked herself that question all week.

"You don't think it does?"

"It didn't seem to matter to him." A bitter laugh escaped past her lips as the ache in her chest echoed to her soul. "He had a job to do. I was a way to do that job."

"Hmm," Dawg murmured. "I guess that was why he waited two and a half years to do it, if that's true? Strange, if I knew that there was an asset that could help me solve a case, I believe I'd be on her ass first thing out."

She picked at the thread on her jeans again, not certain what to say now.

"Eve, do you know what having you meant for him?" Dawg pressed.

Eve shook her head.

"It meant dragging you into a case and endangering you for the very fact that you were there. I may be pissed at him for not keeping his hands off you until this was over, but I'm not a stupid man, honey. You want him as much as he wants you. You didn't know why he was there; all you knew was that you couldn't believe the rumor that he could do anything illegal. A man can fight himself, but he can't fight the woman who can break down his defenses with a smile. Or a tear." Lifting his hand, he used his thumb to wipe away another tear. "I don't know the man as much as I know his history, but I do know he was engaged once, years ago. Until his fiancée had their baby aborted while he was at the training academy, just before joining DHS. It damn near killed him. He had relationships, but never with a woman close enough to an operation to be identified or endangered."

Eve was so thankful she hadn't been looking at Dawg when he spoke of Brogan's fiancée's abortion that she nearly closed her eyes thankfully.

"I met Brogan just before he joined the academy," Dawg reflected as Eve hung on every word. "I think it was a few days after he left his fiancée. He was talking to his father as I walked up to the table." He shook his head regretfully, compassion filling his odd green eyes. "His fiancée had informed him within minutes of his arrival that she had aborted the baby. It damned near broke him. He looked his father right in the eye and told him he'd wanted that kid. That he'd have never turned his back on his child as his father had. Then he stood up and walked away from this big, tough FBI director as though he didn't have the power to yank his placement at DHS in a heartbeat." He rubbed his jaw before scratching at it thoughtfully. "I'd trust Brogan Campbell with my life, Eve. I know I never showed it, but he was undercover. Showing it would have endangered him, and though I trust him, there's not a whole lot I know about him. But I know he's not a man who trusts women, and he's not a man who ever gives all of himself except to his job. I guess I worried about that. Worried about you and your tender heart."

And he was right to worry, Eve thought as she swiped at another tear. Here she sat, her heart broken, wishing she knew how to deal with what Brogan had done, and the impact it had had on her heart.

"What would you do," she whispered, tears thick in her voice. "What would you do if it were you, and something happened?" She swallowed tightly, lifting her gaze, knowing he would know once she asked. "If something happened and there was a possibility your lover was pregnant after that happened to you?"

Another tear fell.

For a moment it was all she could do not to start sobbing, to beg him to fix it like he had every other problem she'd ever brought to him.

He watched her in confusion for only a second before understanding filled his gaze, darkened it, and shadowed it with pain.

"Ah, Eve, sweetheart," he whispered sorrowfully, that understanding filling his voice along with the pain. "What happened?"

Briefly, her voice breaking, she explained the condom breaking, then Brogan's admission that he hadn't intended to tell her. At least, not until it had been too late for her to do anything about it.

Dawg didn't appear to get angry, though he did tense, and for a second his eyes flashed with something dangerous.

Finally, he exhaled roughly as he rubbed his hand over his face.

"Do you know yet?"

She shook her head. "But that's not why it hurts, Dawg." Her breath caught as she continued to fight her tears. "What hurts . . . He knows me," she cried, her fists clenching, the pent up sobs escaping. "I know he does. Everyone thinks he's a traitor, but I knew better. All the nights he was sitting on the porch when I would come in from the bar, we'd talk." She sniffed. "For two and a half years, Dawg. We talked and we've laughed. And through those conversations I knew things about him, and he didn't have to say it." She swiped at more tears. "But something this important, as important as a child, and he thought I was that cold?"

Dawg's arms were suddenly around her, pulling her against his broad chest as she sobbed. As the grief tearing her heart in two escaped once again.

She knew things about him, she knew *him*. Why hadn't he known her?

She knew he loved his mother, but he resented her, even though he hadn't told her about the resentment. Resented her for dying and leaving him to a father who had no idea what to do with his bastard son. She knew he loved his sister and his baby brother, but he worried because his sister wouldn't let him protect her and his brother refused to try to protect himself. He loved the color green, but he hated the color blue just because it seemed to be everyone else's favorite. She'd known he loved children because whenever her mother had the kids at the house he always found time for them. She hated, hated with a passion, anyone who dared to so much as speak ill to a child. He loved dogs but didn't care much for cats.

He hadn't told her any of these things, but she knew.

She knew.

When the worst of the tears finally eased, she drew back and accepted the tissues he pulled from the box on the table next to the couch. Wiping them away and blowing her nose, Eve finally managed to pull the ragged threads of her control around her emotions enough to sit up and stop sobbing like a baby.

"What are you going to do?" he asked gently.

What was she supposed to do?

She shrugged, wiping at her tears again. "I'm really mad at you, too," she informed him, her voice hoarse from the tears she'd shed. "I'm not a baby, Dawg. You could have told me, and I would have stayed away from him."

"Would you have?" Gentle amusement filled his voice. "You knew him so well you didn't know he was working something?"

"Of course I did." Indignation filled the tears. "I knew he was working something, but I thought he was doing the surveillance."

"What surveillance?" Drawing back, Dawg stared at her in surprise as she wiped at her tears again.

"The surveillance on Judge Kiser." She sniffed again.

"Who has surveillance on Judge Kiser?" He frowned, obviously either unaware of the surveillance or trying to hide his knowledge of it.

"I don't know who does." She shook her head. "It's not like they introduce themselves, Dawg."

"How do you know about it then?" he demanded instead, frowning back at her.

Maybe he didn't know about it.

"I heard Jed outside the other night." She had to smile at the thought of it. "You can't convince these city boys how sound travels at night, can you? He was around the side of the house talking on his cell phone about the surveillance on Judge Kiser. Do you think it has anything to do with his connections to the Freedom League?"

"He's connected to the Freedom League?" Dawg was trying to hide his shock.

"Damn, Dawg, I thought you knew everything that was going on." She actually managed a laugh.

Dawg shook his head. "How's Kiser connected to the Freedom League?"

She actually sat back and stared at him in surprise. "You really don't know about this, do you?"

"I really didn't know about this," he agreed, disbelief echoing in his voice.

"Oh, well, maybe you'd better check into it." She smiled back at him, though it was short, and she knew it.

Turning her gaze to her lap once again, she watched as she twisted her fingers together.

"I wish I could fix this," she whispered, her tears finally no longer falling. "I wish I could go back and understand things better. I would fix it."

"How would you do that?" he asked softly.

"I would have stayed away from him," she insisted, looking up to meet the somber compassion in his gaze. "It was my fault, Dawg. It wasn't his."

The shake of his head was followed by his strong arms wrapping around her as he pulled her to his hard chest. "It wasn't your fault either, little sister. It wasn't your fault either."

Dawg stared across the living room, glaring at the wall, fighting to hold back the anger brewing inside him. He'd grown, he realized. Christa had actually managed to mature him a little bit, because he wasn't storming out to kill the little bastard. He was still sitting here, comforting his sister and considering the best way to handle the situation.

His best bet, though, was to kill the little bastard.

Or at least beat the shit out of him.

Unfortunately, he had a very bad feeling he was going to have to settle for a forcible discussion with Mr. Campbell.

A very forcible discussion.

SEVENTEEN

Entering the inn through the front entrance the next day, something she rarely did, Eve started toward the stairs that led to the main residence, and her mother's rooms.

"Eve, sweetie, did you need something?" Her mother stepped from the kitchen into the dining room and called out to her.

Stepping back, Eve turned and entered the dining room, moving to her mother.

"Are you busy, Momma?"

Of course, her mother was always busy. Mercedes Mackay wasn't a person who could tolerate sitting still for long periods of time. Unless she was asleep.

"Of course not, I was just making pies for dessert tomorrow. Come into the kitchen."

She almost laughed. Her mother didn't consider baking pies a chore?

Stepping into the kitchen, Eve moved to the counter in front of the wide center aisle in the middle of the kitchen floor and pulled a stool from beneath the attached counter.

Taking her seat, she watched as her mother rolled the pie dough carefully, Eve's mouth already watering for the taste of the flaky crust she knew would emerge once her mother was finished.

"Is everything okay, Eve?" Mercedes paused in her pie prep, her gaze intent on her daughter's face. "Are you okay, baby?"

"I'm fine." She nodded as she drew her hands from the counter and clasped them underneath it.

"No, you're not," her mother guessed. "If you were, you wouldn't be hiding your fists under the counter, and your eyes wouldn't look like bruised emeralds."

Eve blinked back the emotion threatening to fill the eyes that were already betraying her with the tears that never seemed far away.

"And now you're on the verge of tears." More than a little concerned now, Mercedes set the pie dough to the side, washed her hands quickly at the small sink in the counter before drying them and moving to where her daughter sat on the other side. Pulling herself to the bar stool beside Eve, she drew Eve's fists from beneath the counter. They were so tight her knuckles were white. Running her hand gently over them, Mercedes watched Eve silently for long moments.

When the words started pouring from Eve, she couldn't stop them. All the things she couldn't tell Dawg while they talked spilled out to her mother: the pain, that sense of being so fully connected to Brogan that no one else in the world existed, the sure and certain knowledge that he cared for her, cared for her deeply, and Eve's certainty that he would turn her away.

"It's like he was determined to push me away, even as he pulled me to him," she grieved, her heart so heavy in her chest that the physical ache was draining. "I don't know what to do, Momma," she whispered, staring back at her mother almost pleadingly. "I don't know how to just let him go. I don't know how to give up, because he already owns so much of me, I don't know whether my heart would survive just giving up."

Yet she didn't know what else to do. Brogan had been gone for over a week now, and though Jed and Eli were still in town, they were rarely in their suites either.

Mercedes listened, her heart breaking for her daughter and for Brogan.

He was a good man. She knew he was. Her Tim thought very highly of him, and Tim was an excellent judge of character. But just because he was a good man didn't make him a man who knew how to care for a precious heart given to him.

"Do you think you're pregnant, Eve?" Mercedes asked then.

"Well, now, Momma, I've never been pregnant, so I don't really know," Eve exclaimed in frustration. "How do you know?"

Mercedes's eyes darkened with concern, though there was a glimmer of excitement in the depths, Eve noticed. "You can feel it, Eve. From the first day, if you're still and just think of the child that could be growing inside you, you find you can just feel your child." Reaching out, she cupped Eve's cheek with her palm. "I knew the moment I conceived you," she whispered. "Chandler had left that morning, and there I sat in the house without him, terrified of being alone in a strange country, unable to understand the people's language or their ways, and I was so very frightened." The memory of those years haunted her mother, Eve knew.

"I was sitting there at the kitchen table watching the sun rise, spreading its warmth across the canyons and buttes, reaching out for the house. It slipped through the windows, edged over the floor, and I watched as it inched a trail across the kitchen, coming nearer each moment." She laughed. "One ray was very adventurous. It slipped over my bare foot, moved up my leg. . . ." Her mother touched her stomach as though remembering that moment. "The moment it reached me here"—moving her hands, she pressed her fingers to her abdomen, her face lighting in joy as though she had returned to that moment—"I felt you then," she whispered. "My first. There was this warmth, like the sun had sunk inside me to touch you. And I knew I would no longer be alone. My child would be with me, and she would fill my heart."

Eve marveled at the expression on her mother's face and the love that seemed to transform every inch of it.

"But, Momma," she whispered. "He raped you. Over and over again, in his attempt to force you to breed sons."

"But I didn't have sons, did I?" Mercedes reminded her with tender emphasis. "I had my beautiful, beautiful daughters, and through all these years they have sustained me."

"You could have gone to school, Momma," Eve protested. "A real school."

"I could have been returned to Guatemala, just as Chandler threatened to do, but I was not," her mother pointed out before clasping both her hands and staring into her daughter's eyes. "Love him if you must; release him if you must, because you cannot hold one who does not feel the death of all he is inside, without you. If he does not feel that way at the thought of losing you, then you do not need him, precious. You deserve far better. If you carry his child, then treasure it; give it all the love you will find exists inside you the day your baby is born. But"—holding Eve's hands tighter as she leaned closer, her momma sharpened her gaze, making it harder—"do not let him steal your soul, Eve. He can hold your heart and your woman's spirit, but if you let him steal your soul, then you and your babe will only suffer for the loss. Your sense of adventure, your independence, and your love of the world you've created for yourself are yours alone. No one can take this from you if you do not allow it."

Eve stared back at her mother in confusion. "What do you mean?" But she had a feeling she understood completely.

"Ah, Eve, you know what I mean," she whispered. "You are letting this man steal your soul and it should not be his to own, unless he gives his in return. As long as you have that part of you, you will always have the will to ensure that he never breaks you, or breaks the joy you find with your child."

Eve's lips trembled for a moment before she found herself suddenly dry-eyed, that core of strength that had always sustained her finally awakening again with a vengeance.

"I can live without him," she agreed.

Her mother's fingers trailed over her cheek as an approving smile shaped her lips and filled her golden brown eyes. "You will weep often," her mother assured her. "You will rage and you will cry and you will ask God why. But you will always find yourself again, and you will never sell your soul to a man who cannot love you. If he cannot love you with all his heart and all his spirit as well, then you are better off without him."

Eve nodded. Reaching out, she wrapped her arms around her mother and held on tight. "I love you, Momma," she whispered.

"And I love you, my Eve," her mother swore, hugging her just as fiercely. "And if you carry his child and he does not wish to be a part of your lives, then your sisters and I will surround you and that precious babe with all the love you could ever need. I promise you this."

Eve nodded against her mother's shoulder as a single tear escaped.

The last one, she knew. The last one for the child she had been until that final maturity had occurred in Brogan's arms. One last tear for what might not be, and what she may not ever be able to fix.

She could love him, and she did love him.

But she would never again lose herself for fear of his walking away.

Or for fear of his taking her heart with him.

Timothy stepped back from the kitchen doorway, turned, and slipped through the dining room, his hands shoved into his slacks as a frown pulled at his brow.

He'd heard it all. Dawg had told him most of it at the re-union, then called later that night to tell him the rest. Neither he nor Dawg had been certain how Eve would deal with it, though. Whether she was strong enough to truly love and understand a man such as Brogan.

She was too strong for him, Timothy decided.

Hell, Eve was too good for the likes of Brogan Campbell and his damaged heart.

He'd give the boy a chance, though. Mercedes would ask that of him; he knew her well enough to know that. And there was nothing he could deny his Mercedes.

———

Showered and lying back on her bed, naked and relaxed for the first time since leaving Brogan at the cabin, Eve realized how desperately she had missed him.

Most of it had been her fault, she admitted. She'd kept herself away from the house and away from him until she'd heard he'd left town. Even Dawg didn't know when he would return, and she was hesitant to ask Timothy.

Timothy was as protective over her and her sisters as she imagined he would have been over the daughter he had lost so long ago. Fortunately, she hadn't had to rouse his suspicions; nor had she had to tempt that protective side of him.

Lying in the bed now, drifting in and out of a peaceful dreamscape, she found her memories turning to the pleasure she'd found in Brogan's arms.

Those heated, completely destructive kisses. The way he touched her, as though he knew from one touch to the next exactly what she needed. The way he could make what should be painful, exquisitely pleasurable. A mix of pleasure and pain that she might be becoming addicted to.

As her body began to heat, to pulse with the memories, she found her hands straying to her body, stroking down her side, across her abdomen. One hand caressed her breasts—along the rounded curve, cupping one, her thumb sliding over the nipple as her breathing began to accelerate.

Pausing, her eyes opening on a frustrated groan, Eve moved from the bed and collected the dildo she'd bought for herself a few years before and had never used properly. After meeting Brogan, she had been determined that if he ever took her, then there would be no mistake that he was her first. That she had saved herself for him.

That veil of innocence was gone now. It had been given to the only man she knew would ever hold her heart as fully as Brogan held it.

The warmth beginning to rise in the tender tissue and delicate muscles of her pussy tormented her now. Her nipples and breasts ached, her body tingled for touch, and she was certain bringing herself to release would be better than nothing.

She had the memory of his touch, knew it as freshly as if he had just taken her the day before.

Lying back on the bed, Eve resumed touching, stroking. In her mind he was with her, drawing the breathless little moans from her lips and filling her with a hunger she couldn't control.

Her own touch wasn't nearly as heated and knowing. It wasn't as instinctively experienced. But it was enough. Enough to build the need and the pleasure until she was able to slip the vibrating dildo inside the snug channel with a desperate moan.

She ached for him.

She needed him.

But if she had to, she'd live without him. Now all she had to do was convince her body of that.

The compensation package the Mackays wanted wasn't easy to acquire. When it came right down to it, Brogan had to threaten Doogan with his father, and apprising the director of his actions, if he didn't get it.

Nearly three days after leaving for D.C., Brogan drove back into Somerset after midnight and headed straight to the inn.

He'd missed Eve.

Admitting it hadn't been easy. He'd lost two nights' sleep, jacked off more than he wanted to, and found he didn't get aroused in the slightest when he visited what had once been his favorite watering hole for drinks with his father.

He wasn't a one-night-stand sort of person, but that didn't mean he didn't get aroused when obvious interest was shown. Until now. Until all he could think about was Eve and the feeling he'd had as he came inside her. That feeling that he could sense part of her soul that he had no right knowing. Parts of her heart that he knew no other man had ever felt, had ever gotten close to.

Pulling into the parking area and cutting the Harley's motor, he breathed out a sigh of relief before slipping off his helmet and hanging it over the handlebars of the cycle. Looking toward the side of the house, he could see the faintest sliver of light beneath Eve's curtains, and his cock came to instant attention.

For the briefest, briefest moment, a sense of knowledge shot to awareness inside him and his entire body tightened.

Son of a bitch, he knew what was going on, but he was damned if he wanted to admit to it. Not yet, at any rate. There was no way in hell he could have such a connection to a woman. That he could feel her, that he could imagine exactly what she was doing and know to the depths of his soul that he was right.

Blowing out a hard breath, he moved to the porch, making his way quickly along the wraparound porch and moving past the door to his own suite, toward Eve's instead.

He didn't bother knocking.

Sliding the key he'd lifted from her room and had copied before he left, he quickly, quietly unlocked the patio door and stepped inside.

"Fuck me," he groaned roughly, his eyes widening, his breath stopping in his chest at the sight that met his eyes. "I swear to God, if you move, I'm going to die."

She didn't move.

Knees bent and lifted, her pretty delicate feet planted against the mattress, emerald eyes slitted and burning with lust, she slid the dildo free of her gripping little pussy until nothing but the head remained, then pushed it in slowly.

So fucking slowly he swore he held his breath waiting for it to stop. Her hips lifted, her breath catching as the toy delved deeper inside her until her lashes fluttered when she could take no more.

Closing the door carefully, locking it without taking his eyes from her, Brogan moved one hand to the buttons of his shirt and quickly released them.

Sitting in the chair next to the bed, he pulled his ankle boots from his feet, then stood and shrugged the shirt from his shoulders. He was breathing heavily as his hands went to the metal buttons of his jeans, released them, then quickly shed the jeans. Still watching her, fighting to remember how to breathe, he wrapped the fingers of one hand around his cock and watched her, mesmerized.

He stroked the hardened flesh from base to tip, a groan working from his chest as he watched the artificial dick pull free of her clenched inner muscles. It glistened with her juices as they clung to the latex form. The realistic design with its flared head and bulging veins was a poor substitute for what she wanted, though.

Desperate for her, his knees weak, Brogan moved to the bed, his jaw clenching as he watched her fuck herself with the dildo, watched the need burning in her eyes. Stepping to the side of the bed, he moved onto it carefully, kneeling on the mattress at her head as his gaze narrowed on the tube of lubrication next to her.

"Ah, baby," he whispered, watching as her tongue flicked over her lips. "Keep fucking yourself with that toy dick." Moving closer, he pressed his cock to her lips, watching in anticipation as they parted and her hot little tongue licked out to taste the head of his dick.

Her hand faltered, the dildo pausing in its strokes. Brogan slowly sank the head of his cock past her lips as her tongue rubbed against the sensitive underside and a breathy moan vibrated against his cock.

"Beautiful, beautiful Eve," he moaned, reaching for the lube as she wrapped her fingers around the shaft of his dick and began working her mouth and tongue over the head as though she were starved for the taste of him.

That was okay, though; he knew what to do for her. He knew how to make her feel damned good. He knew exactly what to do to ensure that, once she came to her senses, those senses would be so infused with him that she wouldn't have a chance at convincing herself to deny him.

"Ahh, sweet Eve," he crooned, pushing the dildo slowly into her accepting body. "Let's see what we can do to take care of you."

With the dildo lodged in her pussy, the bare, saturated folds parted and gripping it snugly, Brogan carefully coated his fingers with the gel from the tube he'd found at her side. Spreading her legs firmly, he reached beneath the toy and found the tight, clenched entrance to her rear.

Sensual, lush, his Eve gave all of herself to him. Rather than stilling or freezing in shock at his touch there again, she lifted her hips, her thighs spreading as she surrendered the brave sensuality and erotic depths of the woman she was.

Clenching his teeth, reining back the need to satisfy his

hunger like an animal desperate to fuck, he forced himself to be patient.

With one fingertip he began working the intimate little entrance open a little at a time. Using the lubricating gel as well as her juices as they wept from her pussy, Brogan prepared the entrance, then applied layer after layer of the cool gel as he worked his finger inside her.

The delicate bud of her clit swelled until it peeked above the folds around it. Her juices wept from her pussy, spilling along the folds, dampening her thighs and sliding slowly to the tight entrance of her ass as Brogan worked it open.

Her mouth worked on his cock, sucking and laving it; she drew on it with heated pulls of her lips as he felt her become lost to the hunger sweeping through her.

Little moans vibrated against the head of his dick, her desperation, her need to be fucked reflected in the deepening moans as he fucked his finger inside her ass.

As she began to take one finger easily, Brogan added another. Pressing inside her, he had to forcibly restrain himself, to do calculations in his head long enough to keep from giving in to the clawing, raking need to come—to end the erotic torture gripping his cock and balls.

Lifting himself until he was staring down at her, watching as he fucked her mouth with shallow strokes, Brogan knew there was no hell he could survive without her—without this.

He'd run out of time, though. If he didn't pull back, it was all going to be over for a while. If he was going to take her as he was dying to do, better to do it in the first round. He wouldn't last as long this first time, not after spending more than a week away from her, craving her.

Holding his breath at the sensual agony, he pulled back from her.

"What are you doing?" Moving to sit up before him, to capture his cock in her hands once again, Eve found herself flipped to her stomach instead as Brogan slid between her thighs, keeping her from closing them to hold the dildo inside her.

Pleasure streaked through her as he gripped the base of the fake cock and slid it back slowly before working it inside her once again. He repeated the move, sending forks of fiery sensation to attack the internal nerve endings and draw a ragged cry from her lips.

"Does it feel as good as I do?" he whispered behind her, his lips pressing against her spine, between her shoulder blades as she drew in a hard breath beneath him. "Tell me, baby, does this little dick feel as good as my nice thick one? Does it stretch your pussy as wide, make you as wild for the next thrust as I do?"

"No," she cried out breathlessly, her hips lifting, thighs spreading as she arched.

Fuck, yeah, that was what he wanted.

The lubricated anal entrance glistened with a mix of the slick gel and her juices as she lifted to him.

He slid the fingers of his free hand along the narrow cleft that separated her rear cheeks. Finding the clenched opening again, he watched, his dick clenching and throbbing as he pressed the tips of two fingers against the opening. Easing them slowly against the puckered, nerve-ridden entrance, he watched as the delicate muscles slowly parted, accepted the tips of his fingers; then he felt the inner muscles draw his fingers inside.

Eve was suspended on the edge of pure electric sensation and racing shocks of burning pleasure. The feel of his fingers easing inside her rear as the toy vibrated gently inside her pussy was filling her with such pleasure she felt tortured by it.

"Damn, Eve, how I love your body." He groaned behind her. "No matter what I do, it loves my touch. Loves every caress, every kiss, every penetration."

No, she loved it. Loved every caress, every kiss, every penetration.

"Do you know what I'm going to do to this hot little rear of yours?"

She shivered beneath him, anticipation sending a rush of adrenaline tearing through her and sensitizing her body further.

"I'm going to stretch your pretty rear nice and sweet; then, when you're taking three fingers instead of two, I'm going to leave that dick buzzing in your tight little pussy while I fuck this tight, hot little ass."

Quivering, heat burning through her flesh, she thought the words should have been vulgar. They should have never turned her on with the force that shot through her, nearly pushing her into orgasm from the excitement alone.

Pulling his fingers back from the gripping, responsive flesh, he laid another kiss between her shoulder blades before straightening behind her. When his fingers returned they were cool and slick with the lubrication. His fingers slid inside her again, stretching her slowly, patiently. Pulling back again, relubricating his fingers, he returned.

This time the wider, burning penetration assured her he was reaching his goal.

The thought of taking him there, of feeling his cock throb inside her rear, had her juices rushing from her, spilling along the dildo lodged inside her.

"Do you like that, baby?" he crooned behind her, leaning over her to allow his lips to press to her shoulder. "You're taking three fingers, sweetheart. You're so hot and tight around them. It's going to feel like sinking inside the tightest, hottest little flame. You're going to burn me alive, Eve."

If he didn't burn her alive first.

His fingers pulled back. He moved over her again, supporting his weight on an elbow next to her shoulder as his lips brushed against her ear.

"Are you ready, sweetheart?" he growled as the thick, flared crest of his cock pressed between the cheeks of her rear and found the tender anal entrance.

"Brogan." She was burning with excitement and a pleasure so heightened it was nearly agony. Eve's breath caught at the feel of the broad crest pressing against the tender entrance.

Blistering, hot, the nerve endings the thick flesh stimulated sang in ecstasy, creating a feeling of such intense pleasure, such burning pain, that she had no idea which should be uppermost.

"Bring your legs together," he said in a groan behind her, easing his legs from between hers until his knees bracketed her and she was suddenly gripping the fake cock vibrating inside her pussy as the additional pressure created a firestorm inside the delicate flesh.

It was the slow, searing impalement of her anus that was stripping her of any sense of reality, though. With each roll of his hips, each press of the thick cock head working its way inside her ass ravaged her self-control.

"Brogan." She gasped his name, certain she couldn't bear another touch, yet desperate to be touched everywhere.

Unclenching her fingers from the blankets at her sides, Eve

slid one hand beneath her, her fingers finding the achingly hard tips of her breasts and enclosing one between her thumb and forefinger.

"Oh, God, Brogan, please. Please . . ." The sharp flare of heat that pulsed from the nipple she rolled and tugged at with burning pressure struck her to her clit, to her womb.

The muscles of her anus clenched around the throbbing tip of his cock, making her hungry for more as the vibration in her pussy rippled through her clit with an intensity she had never felt before.

His free hand gripped her hip as his lips smoothed down her neck, over her shoulder. As his teeth gripped the base of her neck at the point where her shoulder met the sensitive column, the head of his cock slipped fully inside the clenching, quivering entrance and sent a shocking surge of pleasure through Eve so intense it bordered on agony.

A hoarse, throttled scream escaped her as her hips jerked, lifting, pressing closer, fire and ice streaking across her nerve endings as her senses slipped into chaos.

"You belong to me, Eve," he urged her softly, the deep, sexual tone of his voice sliding across her consciousness with an eroticism that pulled her deeper into the dark sensuality holding her captive.

There was no room for deceit, no place to hide or to deny what she knew was the truth.

"Tell me, Eve," he demanded, his tongue licking over the bite before his lips moved to her ear. "Tell me you're mine, Eve."

"Yours," she cried desperately, her anus clenching involuntarily as she fought to press closer, to drive his cock deeper.

At the same time, his hips eased forward, the added pressure suddenly driving the broad head past the snug ring of muscles that tightened in response to the pressure before the burning width cleared it. Ecstasy and agony poured through her senses. Fire and ice raked over nerve endings that seemed bared to his touch and screaming out at the overstimulation.

Her hips jerking, her back arching as she felt him drive in to the hilt, Eve cried out in tortured pleasure as her senses expanded in brutal awareness.

Sliding his hand between their bodies and finding the base of the dildo vibrating inside her pussy, Brogan found the controls. The gentle rasp became a furious, never-ending pulse of sensation that traveled through her vagina to the point where the nerve endings of her clit met the rarely touched flesh high within her pussy.

The stimulation rocked through her body as his hips moved behind her, driving his cock into the milking tissue of her rear.

Each stretching, burning stroke sent spikes of ever-increasing sensation tearing through her senses as she felt Brogan's hand gripping her wrist, pulling her fingers down her body as he drove his cock inside her, stretching her anew with each thrust.

"Touch yourself, baby," he growled behind her. "Let me feel you stroking that pretty clit, baby."

Mindless, she concentrated her senses fully on every fiery stroke into her rear as the dildo's hard vibration and the stimulation of her fingers against her clit sent rapid, driving pinpoints of sensation surging through her.

"Fuck, yes," he snarled behind her, straightening, both hands gripping her hips firmly as he began to move harder, faster behind her.

He dragged his cock fully from the gripping channel, only to return immediately, fucking her to the hilt as an agonizing ecstasy tore through her, raking her senses with burning force.

Each hard thrust pressed the dildo deeper inside her, as each retreat lessened the pressure. Harsh groans spilled from her lips as each rasp of the vibrator's tip against inner muscles connected directly to her clit had her begging—begging, pleading with the rapidly increasing pace of the strokes of his cock.

Eve couldn't breathe. She couldn't think. She wasn't going to survive.

"Fuck. Eve . . ." The growl of male ecstasy came as she felt herself unraveling.

Sensation. Agony. A pleasure that bordered on insanity.

Her orgasm tore through her, melting her senses as her pussy, the spasming muscles of her milking anus, the hard throb of her clit exploded in excruciating sensation. She was flung into rapture. Brutal waves of agonizing pleasure battered her senses as each nerve ending seemed to explode, sparking a conflagration inside her body that wiped her mind and sent her hurtling through chaos.

Fear could have dragged her back. The complete destruction of her senses could have been weakened by an inborn sense of survival that would have driven the sensual creature exploding in rapture back into the confines of her body.

But she wasn't alone.

Brogan flew beside her, his spirit wrapping around her, infusing her, holding her secure in a world of blinding, overwhelming ecstasy.

She was crying. She could feel it, sense her own tears as the exploding pleasure threw them higher, harder, and bound her closer to the man leading her through each chaotic storm of rapture that tore through her.

The feel of his release spurting against the naked nerve endings inside her anus was an added pulse of sensation, another explosion.

"Mine," he snarled, his lips at her cheek, the growl surging through her with another pulse of sensation. "Tell me, Eve. Tell me."

"Yours. Yours," she said in a sob. "Oh, God, Brogan. I love you. I love you . . ."

He owned her.

EIGHTEEN

Brogan awoke with Eve cradled in his arms, the warmth of her naked body invoking a response he was certain he wasn't quite ready for.

Hell, he wasn't ready to face the warmth he could feel moving through him. The warmth threatened to overtake him and claim parts of him he hadn't known existed until Eve. He felt drained, physically and emotionally, but his cock was assuring him it was more than ready to rumble.

He smiled against her hair at the thought. Her cheek was cradled against his heart, his arms holding her snugly to him, and for a few short minutes he actually contemplated going back to sleep. Until he felt her breathing pattern change, and he swore he felt her wake up.

There was an awareness that he could feel moving through

him, a gentleness, an initial confusion and then a feeling of contentment and satisfaction.

"I didn't expect you to be here when I woke," she muttered with a drowsy smile against his chest as the fingers of one hand curled against the mat of hair that covered his chest. "Do you know how good it feels, Brogan, to awaken with you?"

He knew, because he felt the same. He didn't just feel his own contentment, but he knew he was feeling hers as well. It had to be hers, because it was completely different from what he knew contentment felt like.

It was gentle; it was innocent. And Brogan knew he had no innocence left inside him. His innocence had been ripped out of him the day he learned his child had been deliberately destroyed before it could even begin to live. An innocent life barely formed because a condom had failed and had somehow acquired a tiny, tiny hole at the tip.

It had been so long ago, he should have forgotten it by now.

It had been years ago, and it still felt like yesterday.

"What?" she asked, watching him closely.

"What?" He shook his head, confused.

"That look on your face," she told him. "What were you thinking?"

He breathed out heavily. "I was engaged once."

"The fiancée who aborted your baby?" She nodded, her palm flattening against his chest comfortingly.

Pushing her hair back from her cheek, he watched as it fell about her face and over her shoulder.

"Like you, my father wasn't married to my mother," he told her softly, his fingers tangling in her hair as he felt a sense of comfort wrapping around him. "Like yours, my mother struggled—until I was five, when she was murdered by a drug-crazed teenager who had stolen a gun from home and came to the diner she worked at looking for a meal." He shook his head bitterly. "If he had asked her, she would have bought him a meal, but he asked the owner first. When the old bastard wouldn't feed him, he pulled the gun and shot Mom in the head. Then he turned back to the owner and asked again. He got the meal. He sat and ate it as Mom bled out on the floor and the customers in the diner rushed to save themselves."

"I'm so sorry, Brogan," she whispered, her compassion wrapping around him.

A bitter smile tugged at his lips as he let his hand cup her cheek for a moment, drawing in the gentleness that was so much a part of her.

"I want you to understand," he explained. "As I said, I was five. My father didn't know I existed. When Child Services showed up on his doorstep with me, he looked down, and I saw disgust curl his lip when he said, 'Hell, I paid her to abort the little bastard.'"

Her eyes widened in outraged pain.

"He took me in, though." He sighed. "Two weeks later I was in a military school four states away. I came back to Somerset during the holidays and for summers and stayed with my aunt until she died in a car crash when I was sixteen."

"What an abrupt change from a loving home to a cold, emotionless world," she whispered, her emerald eyes dark with distress, with banked anger at the thought of his father's cruelty.

And yes, it had been cruelty.

"I was eighteen and working with the FBI as an informant against a particular clique of students I was a part of when John David Bryce was assigned as the director of the bureau office I reported to." There was something about the fact that he was holding her, his hands stroking her shoulders, his fingertips relishing the feel of her soft flesh, that dimmed some of the fury he usually felt at those early memories.

"What happened?" she asked.

He snorted at the question. "I was the pride of my regional office because of the information I was reporting on a small, select group of students creating their own homeland militia group. I was pulling in information on their parents, political and military figures, their sharing of information and top-secret files. And when John David, or JD as I usually call him, came into the office he felt the need to announce the fact that I was his son. Pride and all that." He grunted in disgust. "Thirteen years of being ignored by the bastard and suddenly I was his son. When graduation came I dropped out of the program and went my own way for a while. That was when I met Candy."

The feel of her lips pressing against his shoulder soothed him, and he found he didn't want to get pissed. He didn't want that darkness to mar the peace he found with her.

"I missed you, Eve," he admitted as she lifted her head and stared up at him.

Regret filled him at the memory of the pain he had caused her the week before, the feeling of betrayal he knew she felt. Hell, he didn't blame her for feeling it.

"I missed you. More than you know, Brogan," she admitted as his lips lowered, taking a small, lingering kiss before pulling back.

The memory of last night swept over him again. The feel of her coming for him, destroying his senses with their combined pleasure and the heat that had built between them. Even clearer, though, was the memory of her crying out her love for him, and how he'd known in that instant that the emotion that swirled and drew them together was indeed love.

Yet he hadn't told her he loved her as well.

He'd tried. His lips had parted, the words lying ready on his tongue before instantly shrinking back in response.

As that memory tempted him, as the words waited, once again at the tip of his tongue, he found himself once again unable to utter them.

Why? What could be holding him back?

She stared up at him expectantly, waiting. She wasn't going to ask, and she wasn't going to beg for his love. He would give it willingly or she wasn't going to take it at all.

She wanted more than what he was giving her. It didn't take an extra or heightened sense of what she was thinking to figure that one out.

She was going to make him say the words, he thought, feeling his throat tighten at the thought of it. He hadn't said those words in a hell of a lot of years. More years than he often cared to remember. He didn't even know whether he was aware of how to say them now.

"I missed you a lot," he tried, brushing his lips against her brow as she continued to stare back at him.

A backbone of pure steel, Timothy had once accused her. As stubborn and determined as the mountains themselves.

And she was at that. But his block against the emotion that he had lived with for so damned long was just as stubborn.

He couldn't say it. He wanted to, but there was always the chance he could have the girl and protect his heart at the same time.

And that was important.

Eve stared back at him for long moments, feeling a hint of nerves, a bit of uncertainty, but also a great capacity to love that he was still holding inside him like a miser held on to his gold.

She wasn't satisfied with that now. She wanted the love that he was still holding inside his soul like a captive he refused to release.

She wanted all of him, not just the parts of him that he was willing to give her right now. She wanted the heart he was so protective of, the one she knew belonged to her, yet that he kept just out of reach.

She wasn't satisfied with just knowing he cared about her. She didn't want to just sense those emotions held trapped inside him. They weren't going to do her any good if they weren't allowed to be free.

She waited.

If she didn't get the words verbally, even though she could feel them as he stared back at her, then she wasn't going to accept any of it. She deserved much better. She deserved all of the man she loved, not just an awareness that he could love her if he let his emotions free.

She wasn't going to let it break her, though.

No matter how much it hurt, no matter how much she ached for him or how it would kill her to lose him, she wouldn't let it break her pride. There was no way to keep it from breaking her heart, but the rest of her emotions were salvageable.

Besides, if she was pregnant, her child would need a mother fully capable of caring for him. If he had to do without a father, then he at least needed more than just half a mother. Or a mother who couldn't forget that she had had to beg his father to love her.

He. She kept thinking of the baby as a he. Just as Christa,

Chaya, and Kelly had claimed they had done with their daughters, she had already assigned a sex to the child she might have conceived.

As she stared up at Brogan, he laid his forehead against hers and closed his eyes as though he meant to nap a bit more this morning.

It was apparent he wasn't going to say a damned thing.

This time she didn't have to fight the tears back, though her chest tightened with aching regret. There were no tears filling her eyes; there was only acceptance—an acceptance tinged with bitter regret.

"It's time for me to get up," she told him, pretending everything was fine. "I have things to do this morning."

Slowly, watching her carefully, he let her go.

Uncertainty flickered in his gaze, and despite having sensed it in him before, she still found that small bit of vulnerability endearing. Brogan wasn't a man who admitted to any sort of weakness, and he would see uncertainty in any area as a weakness.

"Will I see you this evening?" she asked as she moved to the closet and pulled out a light blue casual chiffon skirt that fell just below her thighs, along with a loose matching camisole top.

"Definitely," he answered, propping his hand on his palm as he watched her, his gray-blue eyes reflecting simmering lust. "I may even be able to get away from the job early. We could go out to dinner."

He was willing to take her out now? Why now? Because he was afraid she wouldn't wait until he was ready to stake his claim? Her dinner with Chatham—or Doogan, as Brogan had called him—hadn't pleased him in the slightest.

Brogan was ready to stake a public claim on her now, while he was always willing to walk away from the more private claim.

Her jaw tightened in anger as she turned away from him and moved back to the closet, where she pulled free a pair of flat, strappy leather sandals. She was not going to let him see how hurt she was, or how angry. If he didn't want to own her heart, then screw him; she had no problem at all trying to take it back from him.

"If I'm not back when you return, then I won't be much longer," she promised, fighting to keep her voice even, her tone casual.

The last thing she needed was for him to suspect her plans.

But if he thought she was going to hang around Pulaski County and watch him flit around like a buck in rut while all the women swarmed him, like they had since he'd arrived, then he was crazed. She'd be damned if she would have to deal with the smart-assed territorial women who seemed to think he was their own personal prize.

It wasn't going to happen.

"Where will you be?" Suspicion entered his gaze as well as his voice, though maybe he was finally figuring out that things weren't going to go all his way any longer.

"I had a job offer." She shrugged as though it didn't matter, while she gathered clean underclothes together before heading to the shower. "I'm going to meet with the company's owner today so he can explain the job."

The offer had come from another of John Walker's friends from Boston the day before. He had enough of those to go around, it seemed. At first she hadn't been interested, until she had talked to her mother the night before.

"Where is this job, Eve?"

Brogan could sense the ax getting ready to fall, and he could kick his own ass for letting it go this far.

Staring into his eyes moments ago, Eve had shown him more clearly than words what it would take to keep her, and he had ignored her.

Stubborn arrogance, his father called it, and now Brogan might very well pay for it.

"Where do you think?" She laughed as though he should know. As though the question were moot.

"My guess is, outside Kentucky," he stated.

Eve turned around slowly to face him, and the answer was in her eyes.

"Boston." She confirmed his guess. "It's a wonderful opportunity. I'll be managing several offices and client lists. My degree is in business administration, and there are just so few—"

"I love you, Eve. . . ."

She froze.

Shock registered on her face as she stared back at him as though she were certain she hadn't heard right.

"What did you say?"

Rising from the bed, he moved to her. Clasping her shoulders in his hands, he stared into the naked vulnerability of her gaze.

"I said I love you, Eve," he repeated. "I love you, heart and soul. I don't know why I've fought it. Even before we spent that first night together, I've known I loved you and that I couldn't bear to lose you. I sure as hell don't want you moving to Boston, where I'm afraid I would lose you forever."

Joy exploded in her gaze, flushed her cheeks. Brogan swore he could feel it now: an explosion of heat and happiness that filled her entire consciousness and then whipped into his.

Before he'd left for D.C., the Mackay cousins had detained him for a few hours. Somehow, Brogan had found himself trying to vocalize the confusing mix of emotions he always felt whenever he and Eve were in the same room. Dawg called it a mating. Natches called it a soul thing. Rowdy had laughed at all of them and told Brogan to prepare himself; it was this little thing called love.

Some couples—most couples—waited years and years before they developed the ability to read or to feel each other so well. Then there were those very few who touched each other so deeply, so perfectly that first time that the bond was almost immediate.

For the Mackay men and their wives it hadn't happened until each of their wives had conceived their first child. Each cousin swore it was the first time he felt his child kick. Connected as they were to their wives and, through their wives, to their children, that bond had kicked into place.

"You really love me?" she whispered as he came to her and framed her face gently. "You really love me, Brogan?"

"Past forever, Eve," he promised to her. "How could you doubt it? You've felt it, the same as I have, since we spent that night together. I felt your heart touch mine, and I know mine touched yours. What else could it be but love?"

"It's love," she whispered, that explosion of happiness radiating from her soul to warm his own as she threw her arms around his neck and hung on tight. "Oh, God, Brogan, it's love."

A part of him had been dark for so many years, even before Candy. The deliberate destruction of his child had only cemented the bitterness that had raged in him for so long.

The moment he met Eve, he'd felt light touch that darkness. Each time she touched him with her smile he had become even more vulnerable to her. He'd become locked firmly beneath her spell.

"Have patience with me?" he whispered as he buried his face against her neck again, holding her close to his heart.

"Always," she swore, and he was warmed by her heart touching his.

"It may take me a while." Closing his eyes, he prayed—prayed he could keep the evil of his world from touching her. "I promise to get the hang of it soon." He lifted his head from her neck; then his lips lowered, touched hers, and he belonged.

"I love you, Eve," he vowed.

And her smile completed his dreams, filled his life with light, and once again Brogan knew hope.

"And I love you, Brogan Campbell. Forever and always. I love you."

NINETEEN

There was something about Eve, Brogan decided, that just made it impossible to maintain distance.

She'd declined the job offer before they had shared a shower, then cussed him out when she realized she was too sore to take him again. She'd decided instead to make the trip to the store for the groceries her mother needed, kissed him with enough heat to damned near blow his tiny mind, then drove off.

Shaking his head at her particular brand of revenge, Brogan mounted the Harley, listened to the smooth throb of the motor, then pulled out of the inn's gravel parking lot and headed toward the Mackay Marina.

He'd accomplished what they wanted; now he wondered what those three intended to do with, basically, a license to kill with impunity.

It would have been damned concerning if he didn't know the Mackays as well as he did.

Fortunately, he did know them that well, and he knew they weren't stupid men. They wouldn't risk the agreement, especially considering the compensatory package was for the single purpose of ensuring that nothing risked their ability to protect their family, friends, and the county itself from the undercurrents of treason and homeland terrorism, and the people who had been attempting to use the sheltering mountains as a cover for their activities.

The same thing he intended his own agreement for. He wasn't a stupid man either. While ensuring the Mackays' protection, he'd taken steps to ensure his own, as well as that of any family he might have. How much more dedicated could a loving husband and father be?

He intended to find out.

Pulling into the marina's nearly full parking lot, Brogan wasn't in the least surprised to see the three men leaning against Natches's black-on-black Mercedes Roadster, waiting for him.

They didn't look too damned happy with him either. Especially Dawg. Brogan was guessing Eve had gone to her brother for advice while he was gone. Not that he could blame her. It wasn't as though Brogan had been there for her, or had given her reason to believe he would return.

Pulling the Harley in behind the expensive little Roadster, he inhaled for strength. For a man who prided himself on never asking anyone for a damned thing personally, he was about to ask the Mackays for a hell of a favor.

Stepping from the bike, he moved the slight distance to the three men and stared back at them without so much as a hint of the nervousness he could feel in his gut. His nerves were on edge, a sense of foreboding that made no sense filling his gut.

As he stepped to them, the three men watched him with narrow-eyed suspicion.

"Dawg, Natches, Rowdy." He nodded in an attempt at politeness. "Before we take care of business, I need to ask a favor."

Dawg's gaze sparked with anger as the other two watched him with cool suspicion.

"Seen Eve since you got back?" Dawg actually showed his teeth.

Brogan turned his gaze to Rowdy, usually the tolerant one of the group. There would be no hope there.

"Dawg, could you stop . . ." *being an ass*, he wanted to say.

"Have you stopped breaking her heart? Because once was too damned many times to hold my sister while she cried over your worthless ass."

"I still say, get the papers we need, then tie his feet to cement blocks and dump him in the middle of the lake," Natches grunted.

Brogan forcibly controlled his grin as he turned back to Dawg. As he started to speak, the door to the marina offices opened and Ray Mackay stood in the doorway. Dawg might be Eve's brother, but Ray was the acknowledged patriarch of the clan.

"Brogan, son, is Dawg giving you problems?" Ray shot Dawg a warning look.

"Sir, I've been trying to ask Dawg to accept my request to marry his sister Eve, but he doesn't seem too inclined to let me get the words out."

Even Ray appeared completely shocked by the request.

"You're joking," Dawg said, the look in his eyes nearly dazed as he stared back at Brogan.

"And you're trying to piss me off," Brogan decided. "Now, while I'm away from her, I'd like to go to the bank and take my grandmother's ring out of the safe-deposit box I have there. But it will do no damned good if you refuse the request."

"Why?" Dawg was still staring at Brogan as though uncertain whether he should believe him.

Brogan shoved his hands into the back pockets of his jeans to keep them away from Dawg's throat.

It would be simpler, easier to explain what he wanted, further, he decided.

"My grandmother left me her engagement ring and her and my grandfather's wedding bands," he gritted out in irritation. "But I can give them to my fiancée only if a male relative gives permission for her to marry me."

Dawg frowned. "She won't like wearing a ring your first fiancée wore."

Yeah, Dawg was just trying to piss him off; that was all it could be.

"Candy never wore my grandmother's ring," he snapped. "No other woman has even seen it since my grandmother's death. Candy had no male relatives to ask, so I couldn't have done it even if she had known about it."

"There are ways around that." Natches grinned. "You could still have given it to her."

"Dammit, I didn't want to give it to her," Brogan snapped furiously before turning back to Dawg. "Yes or no, dammit. And if you say no, I'll show her the rings and tell her you're the reason she can't have them."

Dawg's eyes widened in mocking innocence. "I never said such a thing as no, Brogan."

"You didn't say yes, either."

Dawg grinned. "Hell, I didn't. Did I?"

Brogan took a step toward him, intent on cracking the other man's jaw on his fist.

"How bad do you want that compensatory package, Dawg?" he asked instead.

"Pretty damned bad." Dawg's eyes narrowed thoughtfully.

"I'll take that as a yes then. . . ."

"Well, now, I don't know about that. . . ."

"Hell, you have my permission to marry her," Ray snapped, glaring at Dawg. "You want to see her cry again, moron?" he asked with more playful affection than true anger.

"I was going to give him permission," Dawg growled as he propped his hands on his hips and stared at his uncle with a fierce frown. "There was no damned sense in making it easy on him."

Brogan snorted at the smirk that curled Dawg's lips then as Brogan glared back at him.

As Brogan opened his lips to say something particularly insulting, Dawg's expression suddenly creased into one of concern a second before a blaring horn had the rest of them turning quickly. The two-year-old bright blue BMW barreled toward them quickly.

"Samantha," Brogan shouted her name, sprinting toward the vehicle as it suddenly slammed into another parked car. Racing to the driver's side, his heart in his throat, he jerked the door open, only just barely catching his baby sister as she toppled from the vehicle.

Mackays were cursing as Brogan caught her in his arms, the sight of her blood matting her hair from a jagged gash in her scalp, a deep puncture to her shoulder, and a slice across the side of her neck that only narrowly missed her jugular. Glimpsed, but not ignored by Brogan was the sight of her partner, Kraig, in the passenger seat staring unseeingly into the window, half his face blown away.

Brogan felt his insides freeze to jagged chips of ice inside his soul as he heard Dawg ordering an ambulance to the marina.

"Brogan," Samantha sobbed weakly, her normally tanned skin paper white. "They have her; he betrayed me, Brogan. He betrayed both of us."

"Who, Samantha, who do they have? Who betrayed you?"

"Kraig," she sobbed weakly as he tore the bottom of his shirt before folding it to apply pressure to the wound at her neck, where she was losing more blood than she could afford. "I think I killed Kraig, Brogan." She stared up at him, her gaze feverish and dazed. "I killed him, but he let them take her, I'm so sorry."

"Who?" he wheezed, but he knew. He knew who had been taken even before she whispered the information. Samantha stared up at him miserably.

"Eve, I'm so sorry, Brogan, I tried to stop them but they took Eve," she sobbed. "She was going into the grocery store when we pulled in. Judge Kiser's big white truck pulled up and his foreman jumped out and grabbed her. I tried to get out of the car and save her, but then Kraig pulled a knife on me. He sliced me pretty good until I could get a shot off. My phone got damaged in the fight—thank God you told me you were meeting Dawg here," she whispered hoarsely as Brogan stared down at her and felt a darkness unlike anything he had ever known before fill his soul.

Brogan could hear Ray, Dawg, Rowdy, and Natches as they contacted Alex Jansen, John Walker, and Sheriff Zeke Mayes, and ordered them to the marina.

"Forgive me, Brogan," Samantha cried weakly. "Please forgive me."

"It's not your fault, Samantha, I promise, I don't blame

you," he managed to say through the awful buzzing that filled his mind.

"Samantha. Samantha, sweetie." Dawg knelt beside them as he tore his own shirt from his back, folded it, and pressed it to her head wound. "Did Kraig say anything?"

"He said you and Brogan would know why." She stared back at Brogan painfully. "He said I would be dead, but you would know why."

"No, Samantha." He held her to him, cradling her against his chest as Dawg fought to stem the flow of blood from her wounds. "You've never failed me, sweetheart." Brogan stared at Dawg, feeling nothing inside him, not even desperation.

Dawg blew out a hard breath. "I should have known—she told me DHS was watching Judge Kiser's home and suspected him of being part of the Freedom League with Dayle Mackay, before Dayle's death. I should have checked into it immediately."

"When did she tell you this?" Brogan narrowed his eyes on Dawg. "DHS has not had Judge Kiser under surveillance."

Dawg frowned back at him. "Eve overheard Jed talking about watching Kiser's house. She told me about it the other day at the family reunion."

The ambulance screamed into the marina followed by Zeke, Alex, and John Walker's vehicles. Immediately the EMTs surrounded Samantha and the dead Kraig still in the car.

"Find her, Brogan," Samantha cried as the EMTs lifted her carefully to a gurney. "They're going to kill her."

Agony threatened the ice that had his emotions in deep freeze, saving his sanity. As Brogan rose to his feet, Donny and Sandi pushed through the crowd surrounding them, and went straight to Dawg and pulled his attention to them as Donny hurriedly whispered something quickly in Dawg's ear.

"Brogan, the office," Dawg ordered, staring around at the crowd. They moved quickly to the marina office, closing the door behind them as Dawg turned to Donny as Brogan glared at them. Donny shocked him, though, Donny and Sandi. They flashed their badges and identifications declaring them FBI Special Agents Clarke. Hell, they were married.

"We know where she's at," Sandi said in a coolly authoritative tone.

Brogan glared at Donny. "What the fuck is going on here?"

"Sorry, Brogan," Donny sighed. "We had to hold our cover even with you. Though it was damned hard to hold the part the night you visited."

"Where is she?" he rasped again, his fists clenching furiously.

"Kiser's not involved with this," Sandi said quickly. "His foreman is another story. He was one of Chandler Mackay's partners. He believes Brogan has the coordinates of the stolen gold. He's holding Eve for the gold."

"Where is she?" he rasped again, his fists clenching furiously.

"You're not going in alone," Donny stated firmly, coolly. Before Brogan could stop himself he had a handful of the agent's shirt as he hauled him nearly off his feet, dragging him nose-to-nose with him.

"I will kill you," he stated with an icy calm. "Where is she?"

"They stole the *Nauti Buoy*." Donny grimaced. "It's currently anchored in the middle of the left fork of Lake Cumberland. Kiser's foreman, Kai Maynard, is a former Special Forces and one of his cohorts is a formerly dishonorably discharged Ranger named Joel Keller."

Brogan turned to a fuming Rowdy, the owner of the *Nauti Buoy*. "How do I get to that boat and how do I get on it?"

"Getting on it is easy," Rowdy answered. "Getting to her is another thing, according to where they're holding her."

"According to our information she is on the first level, tied to one of the bunk beds on the right, in the hall," Donny stated.

"Where are you getting your information?" Brogan snarled.

"Poppa Bear's with them," Donny admitted. "He's been part of Kai's group for several years. Before that he was with Chandler Mackay. But he's always been a federal agent and informant." He gave Dawg and Brogan a hard look. "We don't have much time. Now do we get onto that fucking houseboat?"

Brogan's gaze sharpened on the other man. "Kai has more than just Eve," he guessed in a dangerous voice. "What does he have that the FBI is after?"

Donny's lips tightened as Sandi whispered something to him. His gaze shifted to Brogan furiously as he gave a tight nod. Sandi stepped back. "One of the files Kai Maynard stole had a list of agent code names assigned to several subversive Homeland Security groups. If he gets away with that file, a lot of agents are going to die."

"He's definitely a dead man," Brogan declared as he turned to Dawg. "You ready to go?"

Dawg nodded, his smile savage. "Let's go."

TWENTY

Eve sat on the bunk, her arms stretched above her and secured to the bottom of the metal bunk frame with a pair of handcuffs. Her fingers bit into the metal slats above her as she held onto them in an attempt to keep the pressure of the cuffs from tightening around her wrists each time her arms got tired and slipped. Not that holding them up by her fingertips tucked beneath the slats was really helping a lot.

"Here you go, cutie pie." Poppa Bear gripped her shoulder and pulled her forward to tuck another pillow behind her without asking if that would make her more comfortable.

She glared at him, taking in the Santa look of the full head of gray hair and the well-trimmed beard and mustache of the same color.

"Why are you doing this?" she whispered, staring up into the dark brown eyes that held a twinkle of a smile.

"Because it makes me happy," he laughed jovially.

He may look like that jolly little elf, but she couldn't remember a single story where Santa took hostages or where he threatened to kill them. Unless that was fun and games in his off hours, she thought half hysterically.

This was just wonderful. She was definitely living on a much shorter time line than she had ever imagined and here she was worrying about Santa.

"Too bad we lost Kraig," Kai grumbled as Poppa Bear moved back to his seat just inside the hall where he could keep an eye on her. "He'd make a hell of a scapegoat."

"Once we get the gold we'll just take care of both of them." Poppa Bear shrugged as he looked back at Eve, grinned and winked merrily. "Don't worry, sweetie, I'll make sure it don't hurt."

She sneered back at him.

Yeah, that was a comforting thought. It just wouldn't hurt.

Kai laughed at the other man's comment as Eve glimpsed him prowling about the other side of the kitchen.

"How long do you think it should take?" Kai asked. "I have to call them soon. I don't want anyone getting any ideas if they figure out we have the boat and where we are."

"It's all depending on where that gold is." Poppa Bear shrugged. "It will take them a while to load it, though. Chandler never got it all transported after he stole it. Though, I'd say Dawg can get it all in one haul in that heavy-duty delivery truck he has for the store if he can get it to wherever his daddy hid it."

"Too bad it wasn't hidden in the house." Kai grimaced.

"I spent three nights searching that house after Chandler died." Poppa Bear sighed. "If it was there, it was hid so damned good that even my electronics couldn't find the shit."

What gold?

God, she hated this. If she ever got out of it alive and Brogan kept so much as one damned secret from her then she was going to end up shooting him.

Besides the fact she was way too damned nosy and hated, absolutely hated, not knowing what was going on, she had also not been prepared for Kai Maynard. Perhaps if she had known what was going on, she would have been prepared.

"If we could have gotten rid of Brogan's sister, then none of us would have been identified," Kai snapped, his anger obviously brewing. "Son of a bitch, Bear, this is ridiculous. How the hell did he manage to fuck up?"

"We warned him," Poppa Bear seemed to be reminding him. "Samantha Bryce ain't no man's dummy. And her instincts are out of this world. She was already gettin' suspicious of him and he wouldn't hear it."

Kai muttered something that caused Poppa Bear to chuckle in amusement. "Just 'cause she's a lesbian don't make her no dummy, Kai."

"Fine, she's no dummy," Kai snapped, his tone hard and angry. "Kraig wasn't stupid either. So how did she manage it?"

"I told you Kraig was underestimating her," Poppa Bear retorted, obviously becoming irritated. "I even told Kraig and he wouldn't listen to me."

"Stupid bastard," Kai cursed again. "I should have called one of the men in from Illinois. They wouldn't have put up with her shit."

"Yeah, us Southern boys just seem to have trouble believin' our womenfolk are as smart as we are." Poppa guffawed. "It ends up gettin' most of us hurt. Boys like Kraig end up gettin' killed."

Poppa Bear looked back at her, winked again, this time with-

out the smile, but with a warning look instead before turning
back to Kai.

"Give 'em a call, Kai," Poppa Bear told him patiently. "Make
the call to Ray, he has a cooler head. Those boys just blow up
and lose their senses when they get pissed."

"Now don't it just break my heart that they're gonna get
pissed," Kai sneered. "See if you can find that location scrambler
for me."

"Hell, I told you to keep it with you, Kai," Poppa Bear
growled in irritation. "Hang on."

Straightening from his chair Poppa Bear moved down the hall
to the back bedroom. Watching him, Eve saw him going through
the blankets on the bed before turning into the bathroom. Empty-
handed, he moved back into the bedroom, started going through
some bags then moments later gave a muffled "Aha."

Stepping back into the hall, he paused.

Pushing a small metal key quickly into her hand, he whispered so low she barely heard him. "Wait for the sign. Unlock.
Go over back into water. Hear me?"

She nodded quickly.

Rising, he took a quick step away from her as she felt the cool
light weight of the key in her curled fingers.

"I got our location scrambler," Poppa Bear announced as he
moved back into the kitchen. "Is there anything else you need,
young'un?"

Kai laughed fondly as he stepped to the other man and took
the device.

"Two hours," Kai remarked. "That should be plenty of time
for them to get everyone together."

"Definitely," Poppa Bear agreed. "Make sure old Dawg has
plenty of help loadin' all that purty gold."

Eve watched as Kai plugged his phone into it then quickly made his call.

Location scrambler?

She knew it was possible to track cell phones, but strangely enough no one had taken her cell phone from her bag, nor had they turned it off. It was lying at the bottom of the bunk bed, and she prayed it was providing a beacon to the houseboat.

As she watched, Kai moved past Poppa Bear toward her as the phone rang.

"Hello," Grandpa Ray answered the phone carefully.

"Ray Mackay?" Kai asked.

"It is."

"Your niece Eve wants to say hello," he spoke into the speaker phone. "Here she is."

"Grandpa? I'm fine," she told him, avoiding Kai's cruel, hazel eyes. "Tell Brogan not to worry."

Kai pulled the phone back.

"Ray, if you ever want to see Eve alive again, then listen up. And tell your boys they better follow my directions exactly." He chuckled then. "And tell Brogan to worry. 'Cause if they don't hurry, then I'm going to have a little personal party with Ms. Mackay here. I'll show her how a real man fucks."

He smiled down at Eve in leering lust before turning and pacing back to the front of the boat before he began conveying his "orders" to Ray.

As Kai spoke, Poppa Bear moved back to the hall, turned, and mouthed "Now."

Eve moved. Carefully turning the key in her fingers she inserted it into the lock and turned it carefully.

The cuffs clicked open.

Glancing up the hall again to see Poppa Bear's wide form

blocking Kai's sight down the hall, she quickly slid from the bunk before slipping into the back room and moving nervously to the sliding glass door at the back.

Sliding it open just enough to slip onto the narrow deck, she edged over to the ladder that led into the water and quickly began descending.

The water was still chilly.

Summer hadn't gotten as hot as it normally did by now, but even then, the deeper waters took longer to warm.

Not quite icy but definitely uncomfortable, the water washed over her ankles, her knees as she glanced up quickly, all too aware of the two men Kai had directed onto the top deck of the houseboat.

Thankfully, the overhang from the second floor and deck roof provided just enough protection that they wouldn't see her easing into the water, but after she got into the cold lake, there would be no swimming for shore.

The water lapped over her waist, causing a shiver to wash up her spine as she ran out of ladder and finished lowering herself by holding onto the ladder's rungs with her hands.

She was at the last rung, thinking desperately, trying to figure out how to hide when a hard hand suddenly capped over her mouth.

She froze.

"Hello, baby," Brogan whispered at her ear. "Ready to go hide with me?"

Relief rushed through her with tidal wave force, sucking the strength from her knees and making her damned glad she didn't need them right now.

As he helped her, she turned in his arms, feeling the wetsuit he wore and seeing the oxygen tank on his back, the rebreather on his face.

"We're going under the boat," he explained quickly. "On three take a deep breath. One. Two. Three."

They went under as a sudden shout exploded from inside the houseboat.

Holding on to Brogan she was surprised when he ducked straight under the houseboat then resurfaced beneath it in the cavity created between the two floaters the boat was built on.

Brogan wasn't alone.

As they resurfaced Dawg was suddenly pushing a diving tank over her arms as Brogan held her up, his hands gripping her waist.

Natches and Rowdy were behind him, Chaya behind them.

"Remember how to use this?" Dawg asked quickly as a regulator was attached and Natches ducked under the water.

She nodded quickly.

A second later fins were being pushed on her feet as Brogan quickly fitted the weight belt around her waist.

"Go with Chaya. Once they can't find you they'll start the motor and we'll all be in trouble if you're not out of here," Dawg growled.

"Brogan . . ."

"Don't get him killed, Eve," Dawg snapped. "Go with Chaya now." He pushed the regulator between her lips.

"Love you, Eve. Always," Brogan whispered at her ear before Dawg pushed her beneath the surface and Chaya grabbed her hand, pulling her out of the way.

It was like a war zone under the water, she thought in amazement as Chaya continued to drag her out of the way.

Brogan, Dawg, Rowdy, Natches, and Chaya weren't the only ones beneath the cool surface.

Deep enough beneath the boat for safety and to ensure they weren't seen, two underwater propelled, sled-like vehicles waiting with two frogmen outfitted with military rebreathers such as the ones Brogan and the Mackays were wearing.

Of course, Eve hadn't been that lucky. She couldn't see, couldn't hear anything going on. All she could do was hold on to Chaya as the other woman directed her while unclipping an underwater propulsion device from her waist belt and activating it.

Immediately they were drawn through the water as Eve saw the first lines of water being split from bullets firing into the depths. And all she could do was worry and pray.

Two minutes flat, Brogan thought in disgust as he surveyed the interior of the *Nauti Buoy*. Kai was dead, and unfortunately Poppa Bear had been wounded. The bullet he'd taken in the leg would put him out of commission for a while.

The three men that had been on the upper deck had been taken out in twenty seconds flat with only a few wild shots getting off.

Two were only badly wounded; one was dead.

Staring down at Kai's body he felt the irritation rising inside him.

"Fuckers say they don't know anything," Dawg announced as he came from the makeshift interrogation room the upper bedroom had been turned into. "Timothy's having a boat dispatched, it should be here in about five minutes to haul their asses to the nearest Homeland Security holding cell."

"Bye-bye, bad guys," Brogan muttered.

"Or something," Dawg snapped, turning back to him, his hands propping on his hips as he stared at the bloody mess that had been made of Kai. "Hell, the girls are going to make us clean up this mess, you know?"

Brogan shrugged. "Have fun."

Dawg laughed. An amused, evil laugh that had Brogan staring back at him askance. "What?"

"Oh, you'll get to have fun with us, ole boy, you just watch. Chaya will have taken Eve straight to Kelly, Christa, Janey, and Rogue, and she'll be given the full lowdown on how things work. And trust me, those girls stick together like glue against us."

"But Eve's future husband isn't an asshole." Brogan grinned confidently. "So have fun without me."

Dawg chuckled at the declaration. "You know, Brogan, it's going to be fun watching you learn the ropes. Lots and lots of fun."

The look on his face wasn't one of amusement, though. Brogan couldn't help the trepidation that slowly rose inside him at the pure anticipation that filled Dawg's, Rowdy's, and Natches's gaze.

And he really hoped they were wrong.

EPILOGUE

She hoped.

She prayed.

She paced the marina office even though she could hear everything coming through the radio Chaya manned and knew they were okay. She hadn't really believed it until Brogan had walked through the door.

He caught her as she threw herself at him.

"I don't clean blood out of houseboats," he suddenly hissed at her ear. "You hear me, Eve? It's not happening."

"Just take me home." She buried her head in his shoulder and held on tight, praying he didn't catch the smirk at her lips. "Just take me home."

He didn't exactly take her home. They stepped into one of the Lake Patrol's boats and once she was strapped in, felt the speed of the craft as its nose lifted and flew over the water.

Before long, it was turning up a long tributary, working its way through a series of twists and turns, sandbars and fallen trees that turned out to be automated blocks easily opened when using the right electronic device.

It didn't take long to reach the cabin retreat Brogan had taken her to before. And much, much less time for him to carry her to the bedroom.

She'd showered and changed clothes at the marina, while he'd showered and changed on the *Nauti Buoy* with the others.

He paid little attention to the pretty skirt and blouse she wore, though he did give her an appreciative look when he glimpsed the lacy white bra and panties. Two seconds before he all but tore them off her.

His own clothes were disposed of just as quickly and when he tossed the last sock aside he hooked her around the waist and dragged her immediately to the extrawide bed, pulling her beneath him.

His lips came down on her as his hands caressed down her arms, her hips, one sliding between her thighs and finding her already wet and wild for him.

"I can't wait," he growled, moving over her.

The wives had warned her to expect this. She'd been in danger, and his male instincts would go crazy until he had her again, marked her in some alpha male way, and assured himself she was alive and all his.

Then he would be normal again, she was promised.

Spreading her thighs with his knees, his fingers gripping the base of his cock, he pressed the engorged head against the slick folds of her pussy and began pressing inside.

Immediately, curling heat and that pleasure-pain ecstasy began to overtake her.

Lifting her knees to clasp his hips as her own arched into the penetration, Eve felt the sudden remnants of despair and grief, love and pain, joy and pleasure.

His emotions.

His fears and his pleasure.

They moved into her, over her, mixing with her own as her pussy slowly stretched around his cock, working open to accept the width of him.

Each thrust pushed him deeper, stretched her internal muscles, and caressed oversensitive nerve endings and delicate tissue. Each time his cock plunged inside her, pushing in till the hilt of his erection met the clenched entrance before he was moving again.

Pulling back, thrusting inside her with increasingly quick thrusts, burying inside her again and again as the pleasure rose, slamming through her senses again and again.

Coming over her, his lips covering hers as he fucked her desperately, his hips twisting, thrusting, stroking her internally with such heated pleasure Eve felt herself rapidly teetering on the edge of bliss.

"I love you," he groaned against her lips.

Her lashes lifted, her eyes immediately meeting his.

She was being dragged into a chaotic whirlwind of pure sensation.

Pushed from the edge, ecstasy surging through her as she began to unravel beneath him, her release exploding through her with rapid pulses as he thrust deep inside her, stilled, and the throbbing heat of his release began spurting inside her and mixing with hers.

They cried out, meeting, merging, and with a sense of shock, Eve felt his soul open to hers and felt them entwining in such rapture she lost herself to him.

But, he lost himself to her as well.

Holding tight inside her, his body trembling, rapture lashing him as he felt his lover, his other half, heart and soul, Brogan knew he'd never be lost again.

There would always be a port in a storm. There would always be a partner to share the joy, as well as the grief with.

There would always be Eve and Brogan.

"I love you. . . ."

They whispered the words as one.